Lava Love

A Dating Story

Scott Parry

Contents

Dedication

A shout out to my older brother, who went on most of these crazy dates and shared his humorous perspective with me.

Chapter One

Roger looked out through the upper-level window of his sister's three-story house overlooking the Fraser River in Citadel Heights. It was a large and spacious house she had bought ten years before Roger moved in with his two girls, Brooke, and Rose. After his wife, Michelle, had her fatal car accident two years earlier, Roger was a broken man and had allowed himself to accept the help of others. In this circumstance, he was asked by Anne, his sister, to move into her house to get his feet set squarely on the ground again. Roger had been fighting the overwhelming sense of depression for some time and the rest of his family encouraged him to move his daughters into Anne's house with her own two daughters, Hope and Joy. Surprisingly, all of the girls were remarkably close in age and even closer in their lives. Joy was the eldest of the girls at nine years, Hope, her sister, was seven, Roger's oldest, Rose, was eight, and Brooke, his youngest, was six years old. Obviously, the girls had known each other since they were born, and because of the family connection, they had been through many adventures and sleepovers together. Like peas in a pod, as they say.

Spring was in the air that warm day and temperatures were finally starting to rise. The air was still too cold for a T-shirt, but perfect for a light sweater or hoodie. Roger continued to stare out the window and take in the mesmerizing view and breathe in the fresh spring scents in the air, but he was half looking at the computer screen glowing in front of him. Through continuous encouragement from his brother, sister, and the entire family, they had all urged him to check out the on-line dating sites just to see what it was like. Actually, they were hoping for him to create an online profile so that other women would be able to connect with him. Roger had not been on a date since Michelle had passed two years earlier, but it did seem high time, at least to the whole family, that Roger should venture out to try and meet someone new. No one was trying to rush Roger into anything he didn't want, but he had changed so uncharacteristically over the last two years. He went from being the life of the party to NO PARTY in record setting time. This was, of course, understandable after he lost his wife, but they all gave him a little push any time they could to get him back out into the world. His new comfort zone was hiding in his house and simply going to and from work every day without ever stopping to smell the roses. Roger was only thirty-five years old and still very handsome. He had a rugged look about him, but he had no body hair except under-arms and down-under and had lost most of his hair off the top of his head. Most people never took notice because he was six foot three inches tall and had a well-built body. He did not look like a professional bodybuilder, but it was clear to see that Roger had worked out with weights most of his life and supported a look that would be attractive to most women. He was two hundred and forty pounds with a ridiculously low percentage of body fat and was still quite athletic when he took part in sporting activities.

He had ventured onto an online dating site and was reading over the profile sheet provided to him to fill in the blanks for potential matches. The thing he told himself from the beginning, was to have integrity. No BULL CRAP. "Just be you," he thought to himself as he perused the extensive list of questions to figure out his perfect match. There were so many questions that seemed completely irrelevant to him; however, he was going to answer them all truthfully so he could possibly meet his perfect match on the first date. Well, at least what he thought was going to be his perfect match.

1. Are you looking for a long-term relationship?

2. Are you looking for a long-term sexual relationship?

3. Are you looking for a sexual relationship?

4. Etc.

5. Etc.

The questions kept coming at him. All these aspects of a relationship that he had not thought about in over a decade. Even forms like this one he would usually ask Michelle to come and fill it out for him. (Well, not actually fill out an online dating form - he had never done that before.) He followed the old-time rule and read all of the questions first before he went back to the beginning and started to fill in the blanks. So many questions and so many that he wasn't really ready to answer. Not even for himself. "Hey bro, where are you hiding?" his brother Mitch yelled from the front door of the house.

"I'm up here in my office Mitch." He responded.

"I'll be right up. Beer?" Mitch called out.

"No. I'm good." Roger replied.

"BEER?" Mitch asked again, knowing the Canadian Beer Rule. (If someone asks you if you want a beer and you say no, the rule is, you simply ask the question one more time - with vigor. Hence, all Canadian men will say yes to the beer on that second ask, just cuz).

"Yeah. Sounds good." Roger said.

Mitch headed to the outside fridge where their sister Anne kept a healthy supply of beer, and other adult drinks on a regular basis. He grabbed a couple and headed upstairs to the room that Roger was staying in as both an office and a bedroom. It was a large room with a walk-in closet, ensuite bathroom and massive floor-to-ceiling windows that let the light stream in when the blinds were open. Mitch stuck his head in the door and said, "Hey dude. Whatcha working on?" Mitch stepped in and tossed the can of beer to Roger, who deftly caught it without even looking in the direction of the flying object. "Fsst" hissed the beer can tab as it peeled back. Roger gulped down some of the golden liquid and exhaled the standard, "Ahhhhhh" sound that one would expect. Meanwhile Mitch had already drank half the can on his first sip. "Why the hell do they make beer cans so small. I love those big ole cans they have in Australia for the Foster's Beer. You know the type I mean bro? The big-boy beer, not these wimpy little Canadian beers." Mitch remarked.

"No matter how big the beers are, you always remark on their size. It would be easier for you if you just drank beer out of a pitcher like at the pub." Roger snickered.

"I'll have you know I've really trimmed back on my beer consumption. I've drawn a line in the sand bro, and I refuse to drink any more than one full keg per week. That's it. I have my standards and I'm sticking to it." Mitch laughed.

"Perfect. The next time you come over do you mind bringing a replacement keg with you to replace all the beer you'll go through today?" Roger said.

"Absolutely. I'll bring two so we'll have a backup. So…what are you working on up here, being so clandestine. Working on a new project for your company?" Mitch asked.

"No, not really. Something a little more personal. I'm filling out the profile sheet for an online dating site. I'm sure you've heard of these before?" he said.

"Well glory to God you're going to try to get back to living your life. Who are you and what did you do with my big brother?" Mitch asked.

"Seriously Mitch. I've been thinking about it for a while now and I can't deny I'd like to be with a woman again, if you know what I mean?" he mused.

"I know exactly what you mean Roger. I'm still impressed that you've made it two full years without anything…at all. So, which dating site piqued your interest?" he said.

"The one I started reading through is Lava Love. This site says it is geared more towards meeting women for long-term relationships rather than just hookups for sex." He explained.

Mitch had heard enough, and he was making his way across the room to take over the helm at the computer. Mitch was much like his older brother in looks and physical presence, but Mitch had an edgier look about him and he still sported a full head of hair. Both brothers were big men, and both were superlative athletes. Whatever sport they tried; they would be proficient at it. Not quite ready to join the ranks of the professionals, but good enough that you would notice them on the field. Mitch sat down in a five-castor base style office chair, bumped Roger out of the way and commandeered the keyboard tray. "Alright then. Let's just have a little look-see as to what you've been screwing up so far, which I'm thinking, is pretty much everything you've done." Mitch said in a highly sarcastic way.

"Look, I'm trying to read over these questions and answer them as real as possible, so hopefully I'll be matched with a woman that has something in common with me. I don't have time to play games with potential matches, I need to find a woman that I like, but most importantly, that my two girls like. You know what I mean bro. I can't turn this into a revolving door of women. I want to find the woman that the computer tells me they match up to my personality and presto! The perfect girl will send me her contact info, go on a few dates, meet my kids, fall in love, and of course, live happily ever after. Or at least something like that. You dig?" He said.

"Holy Kamaole bro. I felt like you just did a scene from "Invasion of the Body Snatchers," because everything you said was total crap. You've had someone give you some bad advice but not to worry dude. Your baby brother is here, and he only knows the truth and the truth shall set you free, or something like that. Let me review the answers you've been entering into those little questions." Mitch said.

"What the hell makes you an expert Mitch? You've been with the same girl since you were in high school. Actually, have you ever dated anybody other than Chanel in your life? I'm only curious about what made you the go-to expert on this subject. One girlfriend for life. Yeah, you're the one I should be putting all of my faith in at this point of my life." Roger added.

"Have I ever steered you in the wrong direction before? Come on bro. You know you can trust me. Now move aside so I can see your web of lies that you've created for some unsuspecting Vancouver women." He chuckled.

Mitch began poring over Roger's personal online profile, laughing the entire time. "This is all crazy. It's almost like you were telling the REAL truth to all of the questions." Mitch said.

"I am telling the truth. I want to meet a woman that knows something about me. Some shred of the truth can be added to find my perfect match." Roger replied.

"Sorry dude. You're not going to meet any women ever with the answers you have put on here. Going fishing? You and I have been fishing on a lake, on a river, on the ocean, and what have we never seen?" Mitch asked.

"A hundred-pound Coho salmon?" Roger joked.

"No, a woman! Never. Not once. Sure, we've seen them on TV fishing all day in their bikini swimsuits and gutting and cleaning fish but how many have you actually seen in real life? That's right bro, none. You wanna know why? Because apparently, most women DO NOT like going fishing all day on a lake, on a river, or on the ocean. So, that is why we tell harmless lies to each other, so we can get the ball rolling. Like they always say, the truth will set you free. It might, but for sure it will keep you single. Now, let's just start at question one and work our way through this, shall we?" Mitch said. He drank the remainder of his can and stated, "Well before we can start, I think it's time for a cold beer. I'll be right back."

He rose from his chair and disappeared from the room. Moments later he came back with the beer, sat back down, and continued their information quest. Line-by-line and question-by-question Mitch kept shaking his head and removing and changing everything that Roger had already filled in. Mitch was determined to do a really respectable job to help Roger find a new girlfriend to share their life with him and his two girls. Always the statistic taker, Roger had polled a lot of people over the last year about the online dating success ratio and the results were clear. It was definitely hit and miss. Some people he knew had met their significant others online, yet other friends would tell their stories of woe and all of the online dating pitfalls. One thing was for sure, he wouldn't find anything out by playing it safe and staying at home. "Are you going to mention your kids in the profile?" Mitch asked.

"Absolutely. I want whoever I meet to know that I have two girls because, if we hit it off, I don't want Rose and Brooke to be a shocking surprise." Roger said.

"Sounds good to me. Full disclosure up front." He replied.

After a couple hours, the two of them had completed Roger's online profile and they were getting ready to hit the send button. Roger stared at the screen as if he were waiting to get approval from somebody, but who? He was a single dad now. The love of his life was gone, and he knew that he must move along and face the reality that he was a single dad and besides, soon his two young daughters could really use the guidance of a woman. Especially farther into the future where he knew the limits of his masculine skills would be challenged to the ultimate degree day after day. He just had to hit the send button and get it all started.

"I think I'm going to wait a couple of days before I send this Mitch. I want to read it over one more time and make sure it sounds perfect, you know what I mean?" Roger said.

"Sorry Rog. I kind of lost you for a second there because I don't speak or understand total chicken shit." Mitch mocked. "You can read this over twenty more times, but it's not going to bring Michelle back. Nothing is. You just have to get on with your life, not just for you but for the sake of all of you. You're a cool dude and a great dad. You have to get back on that horse, hombre, and get to it." Mitch leaned over and hit enter on the keyboard tray. "Pitter patter, let's get at er."

Little did Roger realize that Mitch had not actually sent the revised profile into the dating site. His brother felt that it needed to be tweaked one more time in order to generate some attention to his dating resume. Mitch simply was going to wait until he had a few minutes alone to make the final corrections/changes that would garner Roger the most interest possible.

"Oh well, I guess I won't review the profile carefully before I send it." Roger said. As the two men sat in the upstairs office, they could hear the shuffle and bustle of people arriving on the main floor of the house. It was their parents, Maxine, and Clyde, coming back from an outing with Roger's two girls, Rose, and Brooke. Bringing up the rear was Anne and her two daughters, Hope and Joy, filled with excitement and laughter. The four girls got along like sisters and did everything together that they could. Since Roger moved into Anne's house on a full-time basis, the kids loved every moment of it and every little thing became an event like having the "Beatles" come to town. The girls were all having the best time and it was a blessing for Roger to always be trying to keep his girls busy and not stop thinking about their deceased mother.

It was over two years ago that the accident took place. It was a day like any other and Roger's family was converging in the kitchen one by one and taking their spots at the breakfast bar to see what Michelle had concocted for them that day. Dinosaur shaped pancakes and maple syrup, a child's breakfast dream. Maxine and Clyde arrived shortly after Roger and the girls were already assembled in the kitchen. Michelle quickly got a coffee with real cream for Maxine. It always had to be real cream.

The group ate their fill and Roger headed for work and the two girls ran upstairs to change for school. "Sweetheart, Clyde, and I can take the girls to school if you want. We are going to drive right past Seaview Elementary on our way to town." Maxine said.

"No, it's okay Mom, I will drop them, and I have some errands to attend to, so thank you but I'm good today. Thank you for offering." Michelle said.

Once everyone had left Michelle scurried her girls into the minivan and took off for school. Minutes later Michelle eased her van into the kiss-and-go line up at the school and was in and out in under a minute. She turned her van right rather than left that day, like a voice in her head told her to go in this new direction. No big deal, this was still her neighbourhood, and she knew all the streets for miles around. That day when she drove through the middle of the small town only a mile or so from home Michelle slowed her van to a complete stop and waited for the light to change to green. That day, as she pressed down on the accelerator pedal, she could not have known that a full dump truck with its heavy trailer was heading towards the intersection at 40 kph. Its brakes were locked up, trying with all the truck's might to come to a grinding stop. This was not going to happen. The mighty machine continued its path and drove right over top of Michelle and her minivan. Flattened. In that instant, there was nothing left of Michelle or her minivan except pictures and memories. She was gone.

When Roger heard the news, it was devastating. The love of his life had been snatched right out of his hands at such an early age. How was he going to carry on alone and raise Rose and Brooke? Roger's life changed forever that day, but so did everyone else that was close to him. So, they did what families do best and that is, to stick together. Anne, Mitch, Maxine and Clyde, and Michelle's parents Gus and Betty, all united that day at the hospital and there was never another disagreement with any of the family again. They all rallied around Roger and his girls to help give them the best life they could live. Everyone co-operated like a football team on their way to a Superbowl victory. All for one, and one for all. For the children, especially Roger's girls, it was remarkable to never hear a discouraging word exchanged whenever they were around. A cohesive team trying to smooth over a tragedy that couldn't be undone.

Roger and Mitch made their way down to the main floor to catch up on all of the commotion going on with the return of most of the family. "Hey Mom, hey Dad, how you guys doing?" Roger asked, as he swept across the room using big wide steps to scoop up Rose and Brooke in his arms and pretend, he was going to eat them both for his dinner. This was a favorite of his girls, but it was also now the favorite of Anne's two girls so instantly all of the adults in the room had become big, horrible monsters thumping their feet down heavily on the floor and roaring all kinds of roars and chasing the four little girls until they simply could not laugh anymore. Then Anne piped up and said, "It's time for a snack for the girls, but not too much because we are going to eat dinner soon. Mom, Dad, do you guys want to stay for dinner with us?"

"No sweetie, we are going out with the Mercers tonight. We're going to go out on their boat this evening for a harbour tour. Should be absolutely lovely." Maxine said.

"Okay then. Mitch, are you staying for dinner?" Anne bellowed out.

"No, I'm heading home sis." Mitch said.

Mitch realized that with all of this commotion going on in the kitchen it was the perfect time to head upstairs and revisit Roger's dating profile. He slid the five-castor base chair up to the keyboard tray and Mitch worked his magic. He changed things like, the truth, and switched it with, all lies. Mitch was genuinely concerned about his older brother because he still saw Roger as vulnerable and naïve. He didn't want some savvy computer dating expert to come along and break his heart and especially not get involved with Roger's girls until the entire family had approved of them. Just a few more embellishments and…send.

It was now official. Roger was now a member of the world-wide-web electronic dating system, just not as himself.

"That ought to do it." Mitch said as he rolled back the chair and headed back downstairs to the kitchen.

Maxine and Clyde got their things together and headed for the door. Mitch rinsed his empty beer can, put it into the recycling bin and stood at the door with his mom and dad, ready to leave. The family came around the corner into the entrance hall for a typical family hug fest goodbye. The children just loved it and PS, so did the adults. Maxine and Clyde headed off for their boating excursion and Mitch headed home to see his wife and two boys, William, and James.

What made this all funny was, Mitch had been with his high school sweetheart since eighth grade, which meant one thing, he had no idea what he was doing to aid and assist Roger because the last date he had he was thirteen years old, and a virgin. Suddenly, the realization slapped Mitch square in the face – he chuckled to himself thinking about the fact that he had no clue how to lure in an internet beauty. He had no clue how to lure any woman, at any time. Just the kind of person you want advice from on your internet dating search.

Roger had been tossed into the deep end of the dating pool and would either sink, or swim.

Chapter Two

It didn't take long before Roger got his first responses from available matches in the Vancouver online dating scene. At first, he found himself feeling a little embarrassed to open the screens and review the information. It almost felt like someone was watching him out there in cyber land. One by one he opened all of the invites and began to carefully read through all of the posted data trying to find the new perfect girlfriend using technology as his wingman. He was pleasantly impressed to see how much the women were ready to reveal to a total stranger, but he also understood that this is the new way to communicate with potential dates. Put yourself out there and see what comes back. What did he think? He would just go online, meet some new woman, and the two of them would hit it off right off the bat, get married, buy a cabin by a lake in Penticton, and live happily ever after. Is that just a theory, but a wishful one?

After spending time with each woman's profile, he thought he would pick someone with lots of commonality with himself so his inaugural date would be fairly safe and not too much pressure to chat all day long and gaze into each other's eyes. Roger wasn't really sure that he would be able to gaze into anybody's eyes with the same love, respect, and intention that he had shared with his wife. Even as he thought about this alone in his own private space, he still felt himself blushing and having to turn off the profile picture that was staring back at him on the screen. It seemed funny to him because sitting at home alone he still was feeling edgy and unsure about moving ahead with the first step, the return email. He got that nervous feeling in the pit of his stomach, and he had to rally up the courage to set out to meet new people or, possibly, be rejected by new people. Either way, this was the new way to the promised land. He thought for a minute, conjured up what he thought would be the perfect first response, and hit send. There it was. Done. He was now in the arena of the "Lonely Hearts Club" looking for Mrs. Right. He knew she was out there.

Later that evening he received his first response.

"Hi there. My name is Tina, and I am a Virgo. I am athletic and up for anything physical you want to do. You name the sport, I'm competent at most of them. Swimming, biking, tennis, volleyball, downhill skiing, just pick the sport and I will meet you with the proper gear and attire." Tina's message read. "Looking forward to seeing what your poison is."

Roger was impressed. Tina seemed so confident. Any sport. Just pick. Roger pondered this for a while and came up with a brilliant game plan. A little spring skiing at a fabulous local ski hill called Grouse Mountain. Minutes from the city with fantastic vistas of the city, lower mainland, and the Georgia Strait. It would be an ideal situation because they could ski down the runs and chat a bit on the chair lift on the way back up the slopes. It would be a lovely opportunity to get to know each other a little better as the day went on. And who knows, if they had an enjoyable day, they could go into one of the restaurants and possibly share a meal together. The day seemed well prepared and ready to get the first date jitters out of Roger's mind.

They decided to meet in the Grouse Mountain parking lot at 9:00 am. She had told Roger she would be easy to spot because of her bright yellow Bogner Ski Suit with black helmet and matching high gloss black ski boots. Roger exited his vehicle and walked around to the back of the pickup and lowered the rear tailgate and collected his required ski equipment. He looked over at Tina as she walked towards him, and he was pleasantly surprised to see that she was a real stunning beauty with a curvy figure and a huge friendly smile. "Are you Roger?" She half yelled across the parking lot. He smiled back and acknowledged her greeting.

"Hi there Tina. So nice to meet you in person. I am Roger Miller." He extended his hand in her direction as he approached her to shake hand, but she decided to modernize it with a fist bump.

"Nice to meet you too Roger. Have you ever skied here before?" She asked.

"Oh yeah, at least twenty times." He answered. In the past, Roger, Anne, and Mitch had all had season's passes to the mountain, so they had enjoyed the wide variety of runs available at least one hundred times but he was sure not to sound like he was bragging in any way.

The two of them collected all of the necessary gear together and headed to the pay booth to buy their required day passes to the gondola and the chair lifts. Roger pulled out his credit card and said to the ticket booth attendant, "Two day passes please," and surrendered his card.

"What the hell are you doing?" Tina snapped at him. "I have my own money, you know. I did make it to this point of my life without having to live off the avails of a man." She turned to the ticket agent and said, "We need two passes on separate bills please. I don't want you thinking that I somehow owe you something at the end of the day if you know what I mean." Roger was taken aback. He was not used to independent women paying their own way after spending the last few years of his life covering the costs of his wife and children.

"How presumptuous of me Tina. I am very used to paying the bill, but it is a mistake I will not make again. I promise." He said.

She looked over at Roger, gave a little smile, and said, "You're forgiven."

Tina appeared to be exceptionally confident with her ski gear. She quickly bundled everything together and headed for the tram to ride up 3,000 vertical feet to the chalet. They climbed inside the tram, which was full of passengers from front to back, standing shoulder to shoulder as they began their accent. The tram only takes about ten minutes to arrive at the chalet and from there people go to ski the runs that are suited to their abilities. Along the ride up Roger had a chance to make some small talk with Tina to try to get to know her a bit better, however, with the tram at its passenger capacity, it was hard to think straight with someone's ski pole wedged in his back and the sweet aroma of day-after booze breath emanating from another person. Yuck. Roger just wanted to get to the top and exit the tram into the cool fresh air.

Roger looked out the windows and was still in awe of the view. It was amazing. He looked at Tina and realized her face didn't look quite right. She seemed like something was wrong. "Tina, are you doing, okay?" He reached out and tapped her on the shoulder to get her attention.

She turned to look up at Roger and said, "I am feeling a little queasy suddenly. Never had this sensation before. I will splash some icy water on my face when we get to the chalet to bring me round. I'll be fine."

No sooner than she finished that sentence she reached out wildly and grabbed a hold of one of the hanging straps for passengers to keep their balance while going up or down the tram ride to keep herself upright. Moments later the tram arrived at the top of the mountain and the double doors slid into an open position allowing all of the patrons to exit. Roger could see that Tina was having a tough time standing and an even harder time walking. He slipped in close to her and put his arm around her waist to help but realized that he had now taken the full weight of her body. She was on the verge of passing out. Roger could see some accessible areas with benches nearby and he aimed for their salvation. As he got Tina to the bench her eyes rolled over, and she went limp just as he was placing her onto the bench. He at once laid her down flat on her back on the bench and checked her pulse. Her heart was beating at one million beats per minute so she must be okay. He knelt beside her and hovered over her until she slowly came back to consciousness. Roger held her hand and waited to see what was going to happen. He wasn't prepared for tragedy on the first date, but he was St. John's Ambulance trained and certified, so he knew how to stay calm and rational in a panic situation. Tina's eyes started to open, and she began to look around at her surroundings and had a look of, "Where the hell am I and who is this dude holding my hand." Tina then hauled off and slapped Roger across the face. Roger understood right away that she was disorientated and continued to hold onto her even though it appeared she didn't want that to happen. Roger just kept calmly telling her, "Everything is okay Tina. You are okay. You are with friends, it's all good."

Her facial colour began to change back to its original shade and Roger could see that she was coming out of the funk she had fallen into. Tina turned head to face Roger still kneeling beside her and said, "Who the fuck are you?"

"I'm Roger. Your Lava Love date. Do you not remember?" he asked.

She continued to be quite still, but Roger could see her vitals were all returning to normal. "Oh my God. I feel so embarrassed. This has never happened to me before. How did I get to this bench?" Tina asked.

"I had to carry you. I am sorry about that because I know already that you wish to be totally independent, but I had no choice. I had to get you off the gondola before it headed back down the mountain to collect more skiers." Roger answered.

"Oh, my goodness. Can you please help me to sit up? I am starting to feel normal again." Tina said. Roger slipped his hand around the back of Tina's neck and slowly aided her to an up-right position.

"No rush Tina. Let's just take our time and make sure you are 100% before we go anywhere." Roger said.

"I need to use the washroom. Is there one around here close by?" She asked.

"Yes Tina. There are some inside the main chalet. Let me help you get there. I can wait out here until you're ready." Roger said.

The two of them made their way to the main chalet doors where Tina entered and went to the washroom. Meanwhile Roger quickly returned to collect all of their ski equipment still scattered around the bench they were using for triage. Roger found an Adirondack chair facing the view and placed the ski gear nearby and leaned back and enjoyed one the best vistas in Vancouver.

About an hour later Tina crept up behind him and placed her hands over his eye and said, "Guess who?" Roger was completely taken off guard because while he was waiting for Tina's return, he had fallen fast asleep in the sun. Although they were up high on a mountain the temperature in the sun that day was about 10 degrees Celsius.

Shocked by the cold hands on his face he was awake in an instant. "Well, hello there. I hope you are feeling better. You had me worried. I am so happy to see you up and about." Roger said.

"I know, right. That was totally weird. That has never happened to me before, but I asked one of the ski patrol people inside and they told me it could be altitude sickness. It throws off your equilibrium and makes people feel sick but apparently it doesn't seem to last exceedingly long so, are you ready to hit the slopes?" Tina said.

"Are you sure Tina? We can just relax here for a while and head back down the mountain and try this on another day if you want." Roger replied.

"No, I'm good. Let's grab our gear and head off to the chair lifts." She said.

With total efficiency, Tina had all of her gear on within seconds and was prepared to head over to the base of "The Peak Chair" for their first run. The Peak Chair just happened to be one of the steepest and hardest runs on the mountain, so Roger was mystified when Tina insisted that they go down this run first. Tina was very competent when skiing over to the base of the chair lift and then the two of them got into the line of skiers to wait their turn. Minutes later they were next in line to jump into the seats and climb to the top of the Peak run. No sooner had they taken their seats and started their ascent to the top, Tina started to look a little green again only this time she was not in a big, closed in gondola, she was sitting outside on a chair lift with a metal bar across one's lap for protection. Before Roger could get out, "Hey Tina, are doing alright?" She was out cold. She started slipping off the seat and had lost her ability to hold onto her ski poles so down to the snow below they fell. She slumped over the safety bar, but Roger was suddenly trying to stop Tina from falling off the chair completely. She went as limp as cooked pasta and Roger began struggling to keep her in the chair. He was freaking out and realized he needed to get a better grip on her, or this would end in disaster. Roger let both of his poles fall to snow below and used both hands to secure her. He yelled out to the couple on the chair in front of theirs and pleaded for their help when they got to the top of the chair ride when Tina was to slide down the small mound that takes you to the plethora of ski runs. They acknowledged Roger's situation and had agreed to help get Tina safely off the chair lift. Roger could see the snow mound approaching and one of the two people from the chair ahead was waiting to help ease the burden. Three, two, one and contact. Roger hoisted Tina with all of his strength into an upright position and the two met up with their new Savior and skied off the snow mound and out of harm's way. "Thank you. I really needed that." Roger said to the helpful stranger.

"No worries, dude. Hope everything works out." He replied and skied off down the mountain.

Roger stood around the corner of the snow mound that was as busy as a Costco checkout on a Saturday. "What the hell am I going to do with this woman to get her off this hill" He thought to himself. She was lying on the snow still completely out. Her vitals were still strong but clearly her body was not liking the altitude that day and Roger knew that he needed to get her back down the hill to the parking lot…or hospital. Within a few more minutes, the ski patrol showed up and began their flurry of questions and procedures. Needless to say, Roger couldn't answer a single question because he had only met her hours before. He didn't even remember her last name from the dating site. "Who is the emergency contact?" One of the ski patrol asked.

"I don't have a clue guys. This is our first date. First time to meet, period." Roger said.

The ski patrol strapped Tina onto a board with skis and had a snow machine hook up to the basket and began the slow and careful descent to the chalet. With all of their years of experience, they had Tina in the chalet within thirty minutes bringing her body temperature back to normal. "Are you the husband?" A voice from beside Roger asked.

"No. We just met today in the parking lot. This is our first date." Roger said.

"Well, this is going to be a unique experience for you today. We need you to go in the ambulance with her to the hospital until we can contact a family member or a guardian." The on-site doctor explained.

"If you need me to, I can, but I do not know her or any of her friends or family. How can that be of any help to you?" Roger said.

"Look, at this time we need to get her off this mountain and back to sea level ASAP. When she comes to, the only face she will be able to recognize is you. Once we have her stabilized in the hospital, you can go about your business. Till then, Tina needs you, Roger." The doctor said.

Roger went down in the tram with Tina and the ski patrol team and then transferred into the ambulance that was waiting at the parking lot. Sirens blaring, they zipped through the city and quickly arrived at the hospital. Once inside, the doctor on duty asked questions about their day and how it led to this. Roger co-operated fully and waited for Tina's mother and father to arrive at which time Roger had to tell the exact same story over again for the fourth time. Her parents were incredibly grateful for all of his help and asked if he wanted to peek in on her and see how she was doing. Roger entered the dark and quiet room and made his way to the edge of Tina's bed. "How's it going Tina?" he asked in a whisper.

Her eyes suddenly opened, and she began scanning the room until her eyes met Roger's and then, whap. Tina had slapped Roger across the face for the second time that day. She was scared and hadn't fully recovered as of yet, but Roger was glad to see she was coming around. He stood up and said absolutely nothing and left the hospital. He thought to himself, "Could this date get any weirder?"

A few days later Roger was delighted to see a note from Tina.

"Thank you for your help on the mountain. I have never had anything like that happen to me before, so I was truly not prepared for it, but you were genuinely nice making sure I was looked after. The only other thing I would like is for you to pay for my equipment that you lost that day. Eyewitnesses said they saw you throwing my ski poles off the chair lift as well as my helmet, gloves, skis. I went back to the store where I bought all the gear originally and it came to approximately $3,500.00 dollars. However, because you were so nice to me and my parents, I am willing to take $3,000.00 dollars so that I can replace what you lost. Please e-transfer me the money this week so I can book my trip to Maui with my parents and my new boyfriend for some recovery time." Tina's email read.

Roger was delighted to have had the chance to get that first date out of the way. After a shitstorm like that he assumed it would be clear sailing from here on…so he thought.

***

Roger knew that dating new people was a process and would mean some good and some bad would-be part of it. He decided to allow himself to forget the first, and awfully expensive, date and push on to find someone to spend time with and hopefully one day meet his daughters and see where that would lead him. He found a woman named Fern. He had actually never met a girl named Fern so for some reason it intrigued him. Her profile was nice, and she seemed to be a very decent person, who was also immensely popular with people, Roger had assumed, because of the inordinate number of friends she had on Facebook, which was over one thousand. Roger giggled a bit because he had only about fifty friends on Facebook, but then he also was not active on any social media channels looking to find people. For a long time now, he had been a husband and a dad. That's it. They had agreed to meet at the Totem Poles in Stanley Park and go for a walk around the Seawall, a popular place to visit in the city of Vancouver. It was a large park with a beautiful seaside walking path all the way around the park about 10 kms long, which is always a pleasant day. It also lends itself well to getting the opportunity to chat with people at a leisurely pace. Roger saw this as the perfect way to get to know Fern instead of what happened on his first dating experience.

He arrived early at the Totem parking lot and secured a spot and waited in his pickup truck to see if he could spot Fern from the photos she had posted on her profile. They were meeting at 1:00 pm and it was a sunny and warm day, so Roger leaned back in his seat and felt good. The cloud of his wife's tragic death was slowly lifting.

He was so comfortable he started to doze off a bit while he waited. The fresh smell of the ocean and the trees was spectacular. Vancouver at its best. He was listening to Tony Bennet's "The Good Life" and his ears were assaulted by some techno gibberish coming from the parking lot. He opened his eyes and looked around. "Holy cow," he thought to himself, it was almost 2:00 pm and she still wasn't here. Maybe she decided to do something else that day. He looked at the little yellow convertible VW Bug with the top down and the techno music blaring and tried to get a visual of the driver. The driver stood up while standing on the front seat of the car and he could see that they were scanning with squinty eyes the entire car park looking for someone. "This must be her." Roger thought to himself. She began to yell out into the parking lot to no one in particular, "Roger? Where are you, Roger? Are you here Roger?"

He felt rather embarrassed to leap from his truck and announce himself but what was he to do? She was there and he made plans to go for a walk so Roger opened the truck door, stood on the side rail, waved his arm, and said, "Fern. It's me, Roger. Over here." As he continued to wave as friendly a wave as someone can do.

Her friendly smile and return wave showed him that she wasn't unhappy to be there, so he felt there could be the potential for an enjoyable day. Fern was wearing a white semi-transparent sundress and had donned a fashionable sun hat for the walk with sparkling new white sneakers. She looked terrific but Roger did notice she had put on some weight around her midsection. It didn't really matter however because she was a stunner. As they began their saunter, they headed across the paved road to the dedicated walking path, and they continued to make their way around the seawall. She was in her mid-twenties and had already graduated from UBC in criminology. She had not found work in her chosen field but, from what he could figure out, he wasn't clear if she had ever worked a day in her life. She regaled Roger with story after story of this party here and that rave there, and he kept thinking somebody who parties this much has probably never worked a day in their life. He wanted to ask direct questions, but he still wanted to play it cool and not turn this date into 20 Questions.

After a few hours, the two arrived back at the parking lot and they stood and talked for a few extra minutes. Roger had actually enjoyed listening to Fern but had also realized that Fern had yet to ask him a single question. Nothing. Not one.

"Do you want to go grab a quick bite? Not a full dinner, but a snack?" Fern asked him.

"Sure. That sounds great. What were you thinking?" Roger replied.

"I don't come downtown Vancouver very often so I'm really not sure what's around here." She observed.

"I've got the perfect place," Roger said. "Just follow me. A few minutes' drive from here is a hotel called The Bayshore Inn. It is quite nice with a few different bars and restaurants to choose from. How does that sound?" Roger asked her.

"That sounds awesome." She answered gleefully.

The two of them got into their vehicles and made the ten-minute trek over to the Bayshore and parked their cars. They made their way to the front doors and walked in the glorious entryway of the hotel. On the wall there was a sign with the different available venues. Roger asked Fern to pick whatever she liked. Fern selected the H Tasting Bar and the two of them strolled to the restaurant. They met with the hostess and were whisked away to a table looking out over the water and at all of the boats in the marina in front of the hotel. Fern picked up a menu and quickly scanned through the information.

"Holy shit. This place is mega expensive. I really can't afford to be here." She commented.

"Not to worry Fern. I have it covered." Roger replied.

"So, what are you, some kind of rich guy?" She enquired.

"Not at all. I have my own company and it does quite well so yes, I can afford to go out once in a while and have some fun." He said.

"Okay. If you say so." She agreed.

The waiter arrived at the table and asked if anyone would care for a cocktail with the lunch. Roger looked over at Fern and asked her if she was going to have anything. "I am starving so could I get the rib-eye steak, medium rare, and the shrimp cocktail to start? How about you Roger? Are you going to eat?" She asked.

"I will have a Bud and a burger. All the fixings. Fries on the side." Roger answered.

"Miss, do you wish to have anything to drink?" The waiter asked.

"No. Just water for now please." Fern said.

The two exchanged pleasantries while they ate their fill and laughed frequently. Roger was beginning to enjoy this young woman's company, which really surprised him. He never seemed to like anybody.

The waiter returned to the table and asked, "Sir, would you care for another beer?"

"Yes please. How about you Fern? Are you sure I can't interest you with a drink?" Roger said.

"Well, I'm tempted but I really shouldn't drink when I'm pregnant." Fern said.

Roger sat in his chair and wasn't sure if his ears were operating at full capacity anymore. "I'm sorry Fern, it sounded like you said you are pregnant."

"I am. I just found out a couple days ago so now I need to stay away from booze, I guess." Fern said.

Roger was flabbergasted. He was at a loss for words, so he asked her, "So do you know who the father is?"

"Well Connie and I were at a Rave a while back and we have narrowed it down to three potential guys. There was so much sex going on that night and I had taken "Ecstasy," so I am not 100% positive which guy it was, but Connie and I are pretty sure that it is one of those three that I mentioned." Fern said.

"It could be one of the three, but you're not sure?" Roger quizzed.

"Yeah, it was a crazy weekend, but I know that sooner or later we'll figure all this out." She surmised.

"And you have continued to go on dates with people? You do know that in a fleeting period of time most people will be able to figure out that you are pregnant, right?" He said.

"Sure, I know that, but I will give it up for adoption, so I am just trying to keep my options open to see what else is out there for afterwards." Fern said.

"Well, that does make really good sense, Fern. Options open. Incredibly good plan." He said.

Before either of them could speak another word Roger piped up and said, "Waiter, check please."

The two walked back to the parking lot and said their goodbyes. Fern actually leaned into Roger, kissed him on the mouth, and said, "I like you. You're a keeper." She winked at Roger, climbed back into her car, turned on her techno music and drove away.

"Oh yes. She's a keeper all right. The keeper of batshit crazy!" Roger thought to himself as he made his way to his truck. Man, this online dating is a blast.

Chapter Three

"Hey bro, how is the dating world treating you so far?" Mitch asked.

"So far bro it's been a bit of a gong show. Had a couple of dates but I don't think a long-term girlfriend will come out of it. Both women were attractive, but certainly not what I'm looking for at this time. It's only been two dates, so I haven't given up hope just yet." Roger replied.

"So, are you and your girls still going over to Tofino next week? It should be a bright, sunny weekend, according to the local weather forecast. Are you going to stay at the Wickaninnish Inn like before or are you concerned about too many memories of being there with Michelle?" Mitch asked.

"No, I think I will be good. Besides, I'll have the girls, and mom and dad want to come along for the trip. They haven't been over there in a number of years so I know they'll take the girls out and keep them super busy so I can wallow in self pity in my room." Roger said with a chuckle.

"I sure wish we were coming with you guys, but Chanel and I have that big install going on in Oregon over the next couple of weeks at the hotel we have been working on, so we are jealous, but we are also glad to be putting this project to bed. Work first, right bro?" Mitch said.

"You know it. Make the money, then have the fun. Okay dude, I will call you when I get back. Speak to you then." Roger said.

"Later bro." He answered.

Roger hung up the phone and went back to pre-organizing the girls' stuff for going to the island. He knew that the easiest thing to do was bring everything they owned and then that way he wouldn't be surprised by any requests for a special toy, outfit, swimsuit, or just the right shoes. He was a veteran at taking the girls for outings and that meant bringing everything to keep them happy and occupied. He also knew that his mother would pack everything that the girls had stored over at his parent's house, so he felt fairly safe, but you never know what new thing could capture their attention and send them both into a "Daddy we just gotta have it," routine. Nevertheless, he was looking forward to a bit of time on the beach watching the Pacific waves roll in for a few days. It was still something that Roger had always found that really relaxed his soul and allowed him to gain clarity.

***

Roger found himself reading through some of the responses on his dating account and decided to try something simple. Meet a girl at a coffee shop and just try to talk and enjoy some coffee. What could be simpler, so he thought. He sent a text to Rhonda who surprisingly wrote on her note to him, "Let's just meet and have coffee," which sounded perfect. They picked a time and place for the following day.

Roger arrived early, like always, and ordered up an espresso and a Danish and went to sit down inside the café and wait for Rhonda to arrive. He found a seat by the front windows which was going to be a strategic position so he could see if he recognized from her profile picture when she came in. People came and went over the next thirty minutes or so until he looked out the window and saw a woman who looked like she could be Rhonda sitting at an outside table at the café. He went outside and approached the stranger and said, "Hello there. You wouldn't happen to be Rhonda, would you? I am Mitch, the guy you're meeting." Roger said.

"No. I am just here alone trying to take in some sunshine and coffee." She replied.

"I'm so sorry to have bothered you. I hope your day goes well." He said. As he turned to walk away the woman burst out laughing and said, "No, I'm kidding with you. I am Rhonda. I just wanted to sit and watch you for a bit and see if you were here to meet me or here to ogle all the pretty girls coming and going today. It's kind of like a test. Does he want to meet me or every available girl in

Vancouver? So, yes, it is me, Rhonda. Why don't you go in and grab your coffee and come sit out here?" Rhonda said.

"Fantastic. I'll just be a second." He replied. Roger rapidly entered the café and returned with his coffee and untouched Danish. He extended his hand towards her to shake as a greeting and she obliged. She was an attractive woman with a feature Roger noticed instantly. She had large well shaped lips with newly applied bright red lipstick, which really made them pop. Roger giggled to himself and thought, "It looks like she received a bee sting that made them puff up, because they were so full in their appearance." He sat down and they began to chat. She was well spoken, articulate, and smart. Roger was taken aback to meet a woman that knew car repairs to sports teams with a prediction for next year's Super Bowl Winner. He had never met a person like this before and he was impressed. As the time went on, she asked Roger about his uneaten Danish that was just sitting on the plate just looking so tasty.

"Are you going to eat that?" She asked.

"I had planned to get around to it, but I was so concerned about getting food all over my teeth while I am trying to talk and eat at the same time, I have just been admiring it from afar. Do you wish to have it?" He queried.

"No no no. I couldn't. Well…maybe just a bite." She replied.

Rhonda slid his plate a little closer to her side of the table and viewed the Danish. Her hand reached out and she hoisted the treat and took a bite. "Oh, my goodness, that's so good. You have to try it, Roger. You are going to love it." she said excitedly.

They continued to talk smoothly and pleasantly to each other over the next hour. Little bite by little bite Rhonda finally got the Danish down to one last mouthful and said, "Please Roger. You must try this pastry. It's just to die for. So yummy."

She held the last gooey, sticky, offering between her thumb and forefinger and lunged it at Roger's mouth. He was surprised by this action, but he used the old rule his grandmother had always taught him, "If a woman is trying to put food directly into your mouth it makes them feel really good when you just open up and eat it. No questions asked." Roger leaned towards her and tried to remove the pastry with his lips and tongue but found himself having to literally lick Rhonda's finger to get the object from her hand into his mouth. He started to blush at this action and tried not to let on that he was embarrassed at having licked a stranger's fingertips but what else could he do? To cover up his feelings he said, "Wow. That Danish really is the bee's knees."

"Well at least I won't have to go into the loo to wash my hands seeing that you have done a superlative job of cleaning my fingers. Both hands." She held her hands in a friendly gesture and turned them front to back to indicate all of the food debris was eliminated. The two of them burst out laughing at this silly turn of events, but it did help to alleviate some of the tension Roger was feeling. It was nice that these two strangers were getting along and having something Roger hadn't been having lately and that was fun with an adult of the opposite sex. This was turning out to be a grand day.

Moments later a giant bee came swirling around the table, like bees do, and did a couple of flybys on its way to who knows where when it did a second pass and landed on Rhonda's arm. Roger quickly noticed it and made her aware of its presence but no sooner that he began to say, "Rhonda. There's a bee on your…" He said, but too late. The little rapscallion had already done the damage and stung Rhonda on her upper arm in a split second. "Holy shit. Are you okay with bee stings?" He asked.

"No! Oh my god, oh my god." She responded.

"I will call 911. Do you have an epi-pen with you?" Roger asked.

"No…" And she reached for her own throat.

"Rhonda, everything is going to be okay. 911 is on the phone with me currently. They have a unit on its way to us." Roger announced to the other patrons of the café, "Does anybody have an epi-pen with them? My friend has just been stung and is about to go into shock?"

"I have mine," the waitress offered and scooted off into the back room to recover it and bring it back. Within seconds she had returned with the needed instrument and administered the drug. It was like watching a TV commercial by the way the waitress handled herself and administering the medicine. The drug began to work immediately, and Rhonda's breathing sounded better, and her skin colour was coming back to normal. Not long after she was sitting in the chair in a comfortable way and talking when the paramedics arrived to check her over thoroughly. As they approached, the two paramedics got to their job and checked all of Rhonda's vitals and remained at the scene for a long while as Rhonda's condition improved rapidly. Once the situation was stabilized, one of the paramedics said to Roger, "Hey Grouse Mountain, this is the second time we've seen you this week. I hope your friend Tina is doing better." They stood up, collected their gear, and asked Rhonda one last time if her condition was okay. Once they had her confirmation, they were on their way.

Roger continued to try and comfort Rhonda after the paramedics were gone and things began to settle down in this quiet, little street café. Once Roger was convinced that Rhonda had returned back to feeling herself again, he was hoping that they could continue on the track they were on when Rhonda asked him, "So, you have seen those guys twice this week?"

"Yeah. I went to Grouse to do a little skiing and this woman got altitude sickness and passed out on the chair lift, and I kept her from falling from the chair as we ascended the mountain. When I got to the top, I had some people help me get her off the chair and ski patrol came to bring her down off the top of Peak chair lift. It was a crazy experience. When we got to the parking lot the paramedics arrived, those guys as he waved his hands in the air to indicate the men that had been there earlier, and they made me stay with her until she got to the hospital. It was my first ride ever in an ambulance. So, like I said earlier, a really epic experience." Roger explained.

"And who is Tina?" she asked.

"She was the lady that got altitude sickness." He answered.

"So why did they make you get into the ambulance with some random woman at Grouse Mountain day skiing?" Her look was angry and accusatory.

"That is an excellent question. The truth is I was on my first ever date with her, Tina, and somehow it became a very intense day for me." Roger answered.

"Intense day for you?" She shouted back at him. "How do you think she felt about it?"

"Well, I can assure you that she is doing better than fine because Tina and her new boyfriend are going to Maui with her parents next week so I'm thinking she is over it." He said.

"And how is it that you know all of this? Planned trips. Her condition. No, I would have to say that you don't know Tina at all." She sat staring back at Roger, but he could already see that she was the judge and jury and the decision had been made. Roger Miller is a player. She reached over and picked up a Grande size container of ice water, paused a second for dramatic effect and then splashed all of its contents onto Roger's surprised face.

She grabbed her purse and stood up in a military way and said, "Well I want to thank you for wasting my entire day with all of the tales that you spun. I also want to thank you for saving my life and making sure I wasn't left for dead at the local café. And I would also ask that you never call me again, Player." She swiveled as deftly as a Latin dancer and strode away; and never looked back.

Roger giggled to himself as Rhonda sauntered off and wondered, were those lips real, Botox, or bee sting?

***

Roger and his girls caught an early morning BC Ferry from Horseshoe Bay terminal to Nanaimo and would continue to drive across the island to Tofino. As they pulled into their designated lane,

Grandma and Grandpa were there to meet them with sunny smiles and positive vibes and, of course, a box of Tim Horton's Timbits. Nothing fancy, just the forty-piece box to get his children completely wired. Rose and Brook begged, "Daddy, can we please go and sit in grampa's van?" Rose asked.

"Look both ways before you walk anywhere around here." Roger said.

"We'll keep an eye on them. Don't worry." Maxine replied.

"I was talking to you and dad. This is a nut house. Please, watch out." He cautioned.

The girls gleefully skipped over to grampa's big ole Ford Econoline full-on shaggin wagon. Not really, but it did have carpet on the walls and mood lights on the ceiling. It was legitimately all factory-made and installed. The girls loved the four captain's chairs and the little detachable table with an inlaid chess board pattern. It also had a small TV, the kind you see a channel on every once in a while, but of course it could play Disney videos and the girls could sing along and spin in their chairs. And of course, Grandpa and Grandma were very generous to all the grandkids over the years. Clyde, although all of his work friends and associates referred to him as Bill, had a successful career as a Life Insurance salesperson for one of the major firms and worked his way up the ladder almost to the top. He was VP of Sales Canada and a number one producer.

He won countless awards for sales achievements and was asked to remain with the company even after his retirement however, once the grandchildren started arriving, Clyde decided to retire and work full-time trying to spend as much time as he could with all of the kids. His success now offered him the freedom he desired and was happy to work in the field that he did, but he was ready to think about important things like birthday parties and hopefully, one day, weddings. His efforts netted him a lovely antique Chris-Craft boat, a huge cabin on a lake in Penticton, BC, and the family home that Clyde and Maxine had built with their own two hands in the city, and a second house in downtown Victoria. The Victoria house was Clyde's sister's house, but she left it to him in her will when she passed years before. Clyde also couldn't part with her Green 1965 Ford Mustang in mint condition with almost no miles on the odometer because his sister, Vera, lived three miles to and from work at the BC Parliament Building. He and Maxine were set. They could finally focus on their interests now.

Just before the ferry boarded, Grandma reappeared with the girls, so they were with their dad when they got onto the ferry. "We'll see you on board the boat." Grandma smiled and waved eagerly.

Once they boarded, Roger and the girls sprinted up the stairs to get to the restaurant and eat some ice cream with Grandma and

Grandpa. It was a ritual already at this youthful age of their lives, and they loved it.

They arrived at Departure Bay one hour and thirty minutes later and began their drive to Tofino. It takes about four hours to make the trek at a safe and comfortable speed from Nanaimo to Tofino, so they chose to drive right through the city and straight onto the highway. It was a beautiful drive with extraordinarily little traffic and nature soothing your senses. The sun peeked through the trees as they drove through some of the dense forest canopy that Vancouver Island had to offer, and the sunlight strobed in the children's eyes as they twisted across the island.

They got to the Wickaninnish Inn in the late afternoon and Grandma and Grandpa were close behind. They all met in the two-bedroom suite they had reserved and had a quick sit-down rest and a cocktail. The ocean views were stunning and when you are there, you never want to look away. Each new wave that finds its way to the rocky shore explodes and cascades over and over again. Breathtaking.

The next morning, they all fetched their pails and shovels and made their way to one of the many beaches on the west coast of Vancouver Island. The waves on Long Beach that day were not huge and scary like they can be on a stormy day. The girls were determined to find sand dollars on the beach so they could take them home and paint and decorate them with Grandma at her arts and crafts table she had for all of the girls. Mitch had two boys, so they were seldom interested in tea parties and seashell painting with the four young women of the family. They did other things with their grandpa, mostly.

Rose and Brooke worked hard all day with Grandma and Grandpa combing up and down the beach hunting for their beloved sand dollars. Roger stayed back in the distance that day and reminisced about days gone by with his first love Michelle. He couldn't stop himself from coming to the Wickaninnish Inn because of all the memories for him at this seaside resort. He and Michelle had their honeymoon at the same resort years before and, like so many women wanting to know the exact day the child was conceived, she knew it was that special week at that Inn when she became a mother. As he walked along behind the group, he could feel the tears trying hard to find a way out but held firm. He had to be tough and move on, he kept telling himself. Right or wrong he had to keep going. Like his dad always said, "Change is constant." Roger pulled himself together as Brooke came running back to find out why daddy was taking so long.

"Daddy, you got to move it, move it…" Brooke said.

"Sorry sweety, daddy was in a time warp." He replied.

By the time they returned to the resort, the girls were hungry. The girls had a bath together with the aid of Grandma and decided to eat in the room that evening. Maxine placed the order with room service, then hung up the house phone. "It will be here in about forty minutes. In the meantime, I will help the girls get ready."

"Awesome Mom. Thanks for looking after that." Roger said.

Roger looked down on the floor of the porch to see three full buckets of sand dollars. Treasures to last a lifetime. Roger and Clyde stood out on the veranda and had a beer while they waited for room service.

"You okay with all of this son? This is the place where you and Michelle spent your honeymoon. Just want to check in with you and make sure you are getting the support you may need emotionally while you are here." Clyde said.

"It's okay Dad, I swear. Having you and mom and the girls be so happy and enjoying this amazing place is all a son could wish for. It would be totally cool if Mitch and Anne and their families all came here for a real family vacation." He said.

"Well, if we all came here and stayed for a week, I think we could afford to buy a place up here for the same money. All kidding aside son, when you need us, your mother and I are there for you, always. Except the Mustang, we are there for you without the Mustang."

"Thanks Dad. It always warms my heart to know I've always been number two." Roger quipped.

"No son, number three. Maxine still gets to ride shotgun no matter what, okay son." He reached out and grabbed his shoulder and gave Roger a little shake and said, "That's just the way it always has to be." Then he winked at his son instantly as the front door sounded and he said, "Maxine, could you please answer the door? It's time to eat."

Chapter Four

After a refreshing break from the city with his kids, Roger was hyper focused on work. He wanted to work non-stop to keep his mind clear from the lure of the dating app. He went about his daily routine, like he always had, but now he found himself wanting to have a little peek at his profile and see if he had any new visitors. There were usually a few women that had contacted him but some of them he ruled out quickly, for one reason or another. If they were too young, he felt that he could not impose the obligation of a man with two young children and he really believed that they would not be interested. If the attached photos of a woman were the least bit provocative, he would pass by them with the fear that he was not prepared to try and satisfy the sexual urges of a beautiful young woman when he was still struggling with himself to imagine seeing another woman naked let alone the possibility of a sexual encounter. He knew all too well that he was not the most romantic person alive, and he was slightly nervous even thinking about being intimate with a woman again. He continued to realize that things are different now and that he needed to start getting his head around this new age of online dating and that meant he had to keep at it to be successful.

He scrolled through the faces and the names, and one caught his eye. Her name was Heather. Roger smiled, remembering that Mitch had gone to interior design school with a woman named Heather and she was hilarious. Seldom do you find a girl that does funny voices, fake accents, and is 100% willing to give anything, within reason, a college try. What you might call a real keener! Mitch had several get- togethers over the years, at his house, while he was attending college where Roger would be present and get the opportunity to sit back and watch the younger generation just be silly, which he knew he could count on. Heather's profile mentioned that she was an avid sailor and loved to be out on boats as much as she could, the profile went. Roger thought to himself, "Maybe we could go boating and see how that goes? If she has some skills, then we could plan an overnight trip at some point on Dad's sweet Chris-Craft." A smile came to his lips just visualizing the image.

Clyde had bought and completely restored a 36'-0" 1965 Chris-Craft Constellation several years ago when his kids were young, and it gave them all a never-ending project, but mostly a fantastic excuse to have his children around with a purpose. Clyde had rented an area in a large open gravel parking lot where he erected a cover large enough to encompass the entire craft to keep it dry and allow the repairs and renovations to continue year-round. It was as they say, "A labour of love," to complete the task which took about five years. When they had finally finished and removed the canopy covering the boat for all those years and hours spent restoring that boat, it was worth every hour. It was magnificent. It was so well preserved; it was tough to tell the craft was over three decades old. The entire family was as pleased as punch and Maxine even made sure that there was a christening to mark the event of re-launching the fully restored craft. Or, as Clyde would frequently say, the money pit. When that smooth fiberglass over wood hull slid back into the ocean, it was a match made in heaven. The twin V8's hummed when it started but once out onto open water, the twins could roar like they were meant to when they were first manufactured. The "Idle Times" was a wonderfully rebuilt boat that Clyde had forever dreamt of owning and now it was his to use and…to share.

Roger sent off a message to Heather to see if she would be up for a casual visit at a mutually friendly location to see how things went from there. Later that evening, Heather replied with a yes and a happy face emoji, so he was delighted that it was a positive thing. Roger was hoping he could find a woman with a common interest like boating. Like his dad would say, "There are a lot of people who like boating, but there aren't a lot of people who can afford boating." Just to fill up the massive fuel tanks on the vessel was hundreds of dollars, so when taking people out for day trips or overnighters, one needed to select their passengers carefully. Any part for a boat will always be three times the price of a car or truck part. It is just the way it works in the elite world of yachting.

Heather had agreed to meet Roger at the Vancouver Yacht club where he still maintained his Junior Membership status from when

Clyde kept his boat at the downtown Stanley Park location years before. With his junior membership he could attend all of their events year-round, but Junior members did not have to own a boat, yet. The idea was to get young boating enthusiasts involved with the club at a youthful age; bring them into the fold once they had become seasoned boaters, and possibly entrepreneurs, who would buy their own vessel and moor it at this exclusive marina. It was a beautiful facility and in an ideal location because within minutes of powering up in the Inner harbour you pass under the Lions Gate Bridge and would be into the Georgia Straight, which was a massive body of water and less than twenty miles from the

Gulf Islands where there were countless marinas and quiet bays to moor one's craft for the day or evening. Every time Roger would attend any function at the Yacht Club he felt like a big shot. His father's thirty-six foot was a far cry from some of the brutes that were moored there but the staff paid no favourites to anybody, unless you were a generous tipper and then things went smoothly. He parked across the street in the Members Only parking lot and made his way over to the entrance. He decided to sit on one of the multitude of benches throughout the park and wait for Heather to arrive. As normal, Roger was there thirty minutes early, but he strongly believed that he would rather be waiting in the parking lot or inside of some meeting destination than be stuck in traffic and show up late. It just wasn't his style, especially on dates.

An alarmingly attractive woman stood before him and said, "Hello there. Are you Steve?"

Oh well. Looks like a guy named Steve was going to sit across a table from this captivating woman for the evening. He turned his head to face her directly and said, "No, sorry I'm not."

"Oh, too bad. What's your name?" She enquired.

Roger rose to his feet to be polite and replied, "I am Roger Miller. I'm waiting here for a blind date if you can imagine."

"Imagine which one? That your potential date is blind or that you're sitting here waiting?" She giggled as she replied.

"I don't think she is blind from her profile, but that might work to my favour." He said.

"How so?" She asked.

"That way she wouldn't have to look at me all night and she could be under the illusion that she was at a restaurant with a tall and handsome man." Roger raised his eyebrows up and down in an amusing way.

She laughed out loud. "Is that your dating MO? Date blind girls so you can stay incognito?"

"It's actually two-fold. If they seem to like me, I can tell the waiter to tell her when I go to the loo how undeniably handsome I am. If things don't go well, I can pay the bill over at the counter and sneak out without her ever knowing where I got off to." he said, chuckling in his response.

"More of a stealthy date. Always leave them wanting more." She quipped.

"Yeah, something like that. How about you? What brings you down to the park this evening?" He asked.

"Me? I am waiting for a date also. I can't say for sure if he is blind yet because I too, like you, have not met him." She said smiling.

"So, there's still a chance?" Roger asked in a funny, curious voice.

She nodded in agreement and went, "Mmm hmm." She started to giggle again and the two of them continued chatting comfortably on the bench awaiting the arrival of each others' dates until Roger looked at his watch and shrieked, "Holy crap. I think I've been stood up!"

"Oh, that's terrible." She said.

"I better give her a call and make sure she is okay." Roger said.

"I've got a hunch she is okay Roger. My name is Heather. I'm your date." She paused and said, "I was totally freaking out about meeting you and going on a date. When I saw you and saw how handsome you were, then we started talking and I found out how funny and nice you were, I couldn't find the spot to come clean and confess my identity. I hope you can understand." She explained.

"When you said you were looking for Steve, I swear to you I said to myself that Steve is one lucky "son of gun" to be on your arm tonight." Roger barely completed the sentence as he restrained his emotions to stop himself from crying. Heather could sense his mood and knew that he was vulnerable, so she reached her arms around his neck and pulled him in for a long romantic kiss. She pressed back gently and stared directly into his eyes and said, "Could I interest you in some dinner? I'm a little bit cold and would love a drink. The grown-up kind." She suggested.

"Grand idea." He extended his elbow in a pleasant way and waited to see if she would receive it. She did. "This is going wonderfully so far," he thought to himself. The two strolled down the path to the front doors of the yacht club and entered. Being taken to their seats immediately was a welcome bonus. They shared an intimate table for two at the Marina's vast windows located on three sides of the space. It was open, lofty, and felt nautical in its decoration and skilled use of interior design. It was a marvelous time. He had so much in common with this woman, it was quite remarkable, or she was an amazing storyteller; time would tell.

When the check arrived at the table, Heather was comfortable with Roger covering the dinner bill. The two of them headed back to the parking lot and had a quick and Innocent kiss and they were both on their way.

"What just happened?" Roger said to himself, "Is she into me, or was that just a friendly gesture?" As Roger headed home that evening, he started to get the notion…Mrs. Miller?

The next agenda item for Roger was…asking his dad to borrow the boat for an upcoming weekend. Nothing like a romantic journey and a midnight swim. That is, if you're allowed.

***

Roger pulled his truck out of his parents' driveway and headed down the road after dropping off Rose and Brooke for a sleepover with Grandma and Grandpa. The girls were still at an age when they were only interested in the simple things in life, which took much of the challenge out of having them around. Making pancakes with Clyde and Maxine were on the top of the list of fun and amazing things to do and Roger was always grateful to his parents for their undying support. He had a great family, and he was thankful.

He arrived at the Reed Point Marina in Port Moody where Clyde moored the "Idle Times" to get it ship-shape for a couple nights over in the Gulf Islands. Roger had already mentally planned out his route and his first night's destination. He would head westward across the Georgia Straight to Degnen Bay on the east side of Gabriola Island, which has a cozy little bay where the water stays as smooth as glass, most of the time, because it is so protected from the open ocean. There is a government dock there but typically Roger would remain on the boat, drop an anchor, and use the generator for electricity, if needed, rather than trying to get a slip at the dock and plug into shore power. It was a beautiful area surrounded by a wide variety of flora and fauna and the fresh smell of ocean air.

He climbed into the wheelhouse, checked the controls, and started the twin engines to give them time to warm up before he took the craft over to the gas dock at the marina so he could fill his tanks and empty his pockets. Every time someone from the family used the boat, they followed the ritual of making sure that Clyde's tanks were always full to the top and ready for heading out on the water. Roger would also grab some chips, pop, and candy, for no particular reason except for habit, for when he had his girls with him because three minutes from shore, they would need to use the bathroom and would want a snack…of chips, pop, and candy. He stealthily piloted the boat to the fuel dock and filled the tanks to the brim. He checked the oil and then took on as much fresh water as the tanks could hold, paid the attendant, and took the boat back to his usual slip. He changed the sheets on the beds and gave everything a wipe down and freshen up so all would be ready for his romantic rendezvous with Heather. He was still thrilled to have met someone with common interests, just so he didn't have to start from scratch with them every time he went on a date. This was going to be a nice retreat for him, and hopefully, for Heather also. Everything was ship-shape and ready to go. He turned off the light and closed and locked the main door behind him.

That Friday he made sure that he was at the marina ready to meet up with Heather as soon as she arrived. He had already picked up a weekend parking pass for her car to stay in the marina's guest area. When Heather arrived, she called Roger on his cell phone and he skipped his way down the long finger slips to the main dock and made his way up the gangplank to the controlled main gate, which was locked at all times so there was no entry without a member or a dock key. He made his way over to her car and collected her bags. "Two bags full?" He thought to himself. A lot for two nights but he wasn't going to get all twisted about it. The two made the long trek down the dock to the "Idle Times" and climbed aboard. Heather was taken aback by the condition of the beautifully appointed interior and the immaculate state of this vintage vessel. She began to walk about inside with a non-stop series of oohs and awes, which absolutely stroked Roger's ego knowing how much of the work had been completed by himself and his family. Heather made her way down the short set of steps to the lower stateroom area and fell in love. "Oh, my goodness, we get to stay here this weekend. Colour me extremely impressed." She was grinning from ear to ear. "This boat is just magnificent. So, let's get those engines started and get out on the water."

"Aye Captain." He responded. Roger headed back up to the wheelhouse and fired up the engines to warm them up before they headed out on their weekend excursion. Five minutes later the boat was ready for travel. "I checked the tide charts, and we are in luck because the tide is ebbing, so we'll have little hull resistance on our way through the first and second narrows. Thank goodness for small miracles."

"Yeah. Thank goodness," Heather sheepishly concurred. Was now the time to tell him the truth? No, it can wait, she decided.

"Okay Heather. I'll drop the stern and ketch lines if you don't mind removing the bow line?" Roger said.

"Sounds good." She headed to the bow of the boat and looked down at several ropes going to different things and saw the rope that went over the edge of the boat and thought that this must be the culprit. She quickly untied the line and allowed the line to slide through her hands and fall into the water below. "Okay! She bellowed. We're ready to go." She exclaimed. Roger had no idea that she had just let the bow line fall into the water, which meant they would need a replacement bow line later on when they went to tie up at a dock.

"Pull up the starboard bumpers if you don't mind Heather. Appreciate it." Roger yelled to her over the roar of the motors now under power.

Heather made her way to the edge of the boat to seek out these bumpers he mentioned. Where the hell are they? She looked all over and could not locate these bumpers. Maybe Roger had looked after it already. She headed towards the bow and said, "I can't find them. Did you bring them up?"

Roger poked his head out of the sliding starboard wheelhouse door and looked over the edge. The two bumpers were still dangling from their deck hooks and splashing in the ocean as they continued to increase their speed. He walked back to the opening at the top of the indoor staircase and said, "Hey Heather. I thought you were going to raise those two starboard bumpers. Everything okay or are you too nervous to walk the deck edges as we are moving?" He asked.

"You got me. I am too nervous to be out there while we are moving. I'm sorry. I wish I were braver but I'm just a chicken." She replied.

Roger popped out onto the starboard side deck and quickly pulled up and stored the two bumpers. While he was doing this Heather watched him intently to see where on the boat was this starboard thing about which he was talking. It seemed to Heather that the right side of the boat was starboard. "Well, you learn something new everyday." She smiled and felt a sense of accomplishment with this radical discovery.

The ship finally powered its way through the turbulent water below the bridge deck of the Lion's Gate and they headed into the Georgia Straight. Roger glanced at his watch to determine the current time and how long until they would arrive at Degnen Bay. He smiled because they were moving rapidly and would get to their destination while it was still light outside, which made things easier to position the boat and moor by anchor. Roger set his heading and then raised the RPMs of the engines to get the craft to plane and smooth out the ride. Once they were up to a comfortable cruising speed, he aimed his bow for the Silva Bay lighthouse and sat back in his cushy pilot's chair. He took in a deep breath of sea air and finally felt like it was time to relax a little. "Hey Heather, why don't you come up to the wheelhouse and take the helm for a few minutes while I create a couple of libations for the two of us?" He said.

Heather came to the bottom of the staircase leading up to the wheelhouse and said, "It's okay Roger. I would be happy to make us some drinks. Where do you keep everything?" She queried.

"Seriously, just come up and steer. Nothing to it, just aim for that lighthouse that is flashing white light off in the distance. I brought along a couple of unique types of drinks that I would love for you to try." He said.

"Well, okay. Just aim the boat at the lighthouse. Got it." She said.

He held out his hand in order to assist Heather up the short set of stairs to the wheelhouse deck. He could sense that Heather seemed nervous about something. "Is everything alright Heather? You seem filled with trepidation. This is supposed to be fun and relaxing, not filled with pressure." He took one step back from the steering wheel and made an open gesture for Heather to come and manage the helm, but it seemed clear that she wasn't having any part of it. Roger was quite surprised considering the amount of time she had spent on the water with her own parents. Roger was actually a little anxious about having someone of her skill level, in all types of boats and conditions, watch him so up close and personal, but he was always ready to be educated by superior skills. "No worries, Heather, I can grab us something simple to drink now and we can make some fancy ones later. Do you want a beer or a cooler of some kind? I've got a seriously stocked fridge." He said.

"You're busy. Let me be useful and go get us a beverage. I'll be right back." She said. In no time at all she returned with two cold beers. "I hope you're okay with a cold Bud?" She said.

"Music to my ears." Roger smiled and eagerly took the beer. "Thank you." He tipped the can towards her and nodded.

She saw the controls to the wall mounted built-in sound system and said, "May I?" As she pointed to the stereo.

"I can't wait to hear your musical tastes. Everybody's likes are all so different." He said.

Heather ran through all of the stations until she came across a seventies rock station and said, "How bout this?"

Fog Hat – "Everybody wants you."

"Perfect." Roger smiled gleefully and bobbed his head in time to the music. Great start to a great weekend.

Two hours later Roger was dropping the RPMs to slow down the boat to enter into Degnen Bay. It was light outside so mooring would be quite easy. They crept around the jagged reach of some rock formations and headed into the middle of the bay where thirty other boats were anchored and enjoying their own piece of heaven. Right about here should be good. "Hey Heather, do you think we will have enough room to swing fully if we drop anchor here?" He said.

She looked at him with wild bewilderment as if she were hearing English for the first time. "Well, what do you think?" She waited for a response and added, "Looks A-One el capitano." She jokingly answered.

"Fantastic. Could please go up to the bow and toss in the anchor? I'll hold our position." Roger requested.

"Sounds great." She carefully edged her way around the narrow front edge of the boat where it meets the superstructure and found the anchor laying on the front deck of the boat. She bent down and took hold of the weighty metal object and picked it up with all of her strength and looked back at Roger who was watching from the wheelhouse and inched her way to the boat rail and heaved with everything she had and off it went into the air. Unfortunately, there was no rope tied to this anchor, as of yet, and sploosh, it was gone, forever. "Okay Roger. Anchors away." She shouted back to the bridge.

Roger was in a state of shock. How could this experienced power boat and sailor not realize that she hadn't tied a rope to the anchor as of yet? Did she NOT know what the hell she was doing on his boat? On any boat? Heather dropped to her knees on the bow of the ship and began to sob uncontrollably. He threw the engines into idle and came out onto the front deck and knelt beside her. "Hey Heather, why all the waterworks? It's just an anchor. I can replace it easily. Please do not allow something so silly to spoil your good mood. This happens all the time." He said apologetically.

"Roger, you are such a nice man. I feel like an idiot. I am dreadfully sorry about this. I promise I will pay back every dime I owe you for that anchor." Heather said as the tears began to slow.

"No sweat. But now that we no longer have an anchor we need to move over to the dock and see if we can arrange for a slip to moor overnight." He said. "Come back inside and we will get to another location."

The two of them returned to the wheelhouse interior and Roger swung the boat around quickly to get to the dock before a grouping of arriving boats came into the bay. When they pulled alongside the dock, Roger was scared to ask her if she could give any assistance because curiously, she appeared to be so fragile. Roger was highly adept at putting this thirty-six feet right against any dock anywhere. Adeptly he leapt from the boat onto the dock and Heather jumped simultaneously and aided in securing the lines. He made his way up to the wharf attendant to make sure he could stay and to pay for the overnight moorage fee. Once he completed that task, he stepped lively back to the boat to make sure Heather was okay. Heather was still noticeably upset but Roger couldn't really figure out why. It was a bloody anchor not the crown jewels.

"Maybe we should stay in the Inn tonight rather than the boat. They have bigger rooms and amazing showers. I think that would be nice and will give you a chance to clean up and relax for a bit. What do think of that idea Heather?" He asked her.

"I would love that." She smiled at Roger with tear streaks still coming down her cheeks.

"I'll head up to the Inn and arrange the rooms and be right back." He said.

"Rooms?" She said, "We can stay in one room Roger. I'm not saying that we have to have intercourse, but I would be willing to share the room. See if they have a room with two queen beds. That would work perfectly."

"I am pleased that you feel safe enough with me to share a chamber overnight. Maybe I should warn you now about my morning bathroom routine." he said, chuckling. "It can be quite treacherous."

"I have a dad, you know. It's nothing I haven't seen, I mean, smelt before." She laughed openly.

"Great. I'll go arrange the room and come back for the bags." He said.

"No problem. You head up to the Inn and I'll be right behind you. I'll close the doors and portholes." She replied.

"Fantastic. Could you double check the ketch line before you leave? Just cinch it one last time so we'll have a boat still here at the dock in the morning." He said as he jumped off the boat with his bag.

Roger got to the Inn and booked a room with two queen beds, as requested, and headed for the second floor. Once he arrived in the room, he immediately whipped over to the glass sliding door and opened it fully. The air was fresh and cool. He looked down the main slip and could see just the top of his dad's boat tied safely to the dock. Now he could finally try to relax. Minutes later there was a quiet tap on the door and Heather entered. To Roger's amazement Heather had changed her apparel to a form fitting dress and had let her hair drop down. In a word, stunning. He had no idea how gorgeous she was capable of looking, but he was pleased with the result. He hadn't had an opportunity to really observe her because they hadn't been together for any length of time. Her makeup was skillfully applied, and her clothes fit her splendidly. Before she could catch him ogling her, he said, "May I take you to dinner?"

"The best offer I've had all day. Shall we?" She stuck her elbow out and towards Roger the way he had on their first date and wiggled it at him.

He leaped to feet and took her elbow and walked toward the door. She stopped him for a second, looked into his eyes, leaned into him, and kissed him gently on his cheek. "Now you're ready to go." She said.

Like the first date, he enjoyed her company. He was still feeling so much guilt because he was out with a beautiful woman and his first wife was buried under the ground. He felt like he didn't deserve to be happy anymore, but his mother continued to reinforce to him that he was allowed to be happy again. Maybe fall in love again. These are all normal, healthy feelings.

After dinner, they strolled around the grounds for a bit to work off some of the meal and then mutually decided to head back to the room. When they arrived, the two of them agreed that intercourse was wanted but still too soon into the friendship. They had agreed to give it a little time. Roger was eager for sex but was also wanting to be careful and not dive into anything too quickly. They both laid on their beds and talked for a couple more hours about everything. They were becoming friends.

***

When Roger awoke in the morning Heather was already up, dressed, and drinking a coffee that she had secretly acquired without Roger knowing. He rolled over to face in her direction and smiled.

"Good morning sleepy head. I wasn't sure if you were ever going to wake up." She said.

"It's the sea air I tell you. It makes me feel crazy tired, luckily, it passes in a couple days. How did you sleep? Fantastic I hope." He said.

"Well, sort of. I have something that I have to tell you and I have to get it out or I will surely lose my mind." She sat up straight and gained her poise and said, "I know absolutely nothing about boats. Nothing. Port side, starboard side, nothing. When we met at the Vancouver Yacht Club, I figured that everyone that goes in there must be a boat fanatic or why else would they pay the ridiculous prices for everything there. I've never been on a sailboat, power boat, and really only a couple of small lake boats. It's just not me. Good God does that feel good to get that off my chest. I couldn't go another minute having you think I'm a nautical type of person. Well surprise. I'm not."

Roger started to laugh out loud. He didn't want Heather to think he was making fun of her, but he said, "I was wondering why you picked up the anchor and tossed it overboard without a line on it. I should have picked up on it then. Or even the ship's bumpers on the starboard side you never pulled in. It all makes perfect sense to me now." He continued to chuckle as he arose from the bed and walked over to Heather. "You never have to make up silly stuff like that for me. I'll take you just the way you are." As Roger was leaning down to kiss the top of Heather's head in a friendly manner he looked out at the marina and couldn't help but see that his father's Chris-Craft was not tied to the end of the dock where he had left it the evening before. It was missing. "Holy shit!" He exclaimed. "The boat."

At lighting speed Roger was dressed and heading out the door on the flat run until he got down to the end of the dock where the "Idle Times" was once resting alongside the dock. It was gone. Never in Roger's life had he known anyone that had a boat stolen from a marina. His eyes gazed down to the wharf cleats, and he noticed that all three of his lines were still attached to the cleats, but they all went over the edge into the water. "Who would have untied his lines during the night. Who could possibly be this much of a monster?" Seconds later Heather arrived at the dock where Roger was standing. "What happened Roger?" She asked.

Roger's world was spinning. He thought he might be sick. His gag reflux made him heave out loud a couple of times. His father's pride and joy, where could it be? "You checked the ropes before you came up to the room last night, right?" Roger asked.

"Yes. I had to loosen all three of them because the boat was really crushing your big round balloon bumpers hanging over the edge. I was sure they were going to pop if I hadn't eased up the rope on them." Heather explained.

As Roger stood at the edge of the dock mystified, a flash of bright light caught his eye. A half a mile away he could see something. He strained his eyes and realized that it was the "Idle Times" floating free and heading out of the small, secluded bay with the tide, and into the BC Ferries main line. He needed to act fast. He ran down the dock looking for any small boat that he could grab quickly and headed out the bay entrance. Finally, he came across a ten-foot aluminum boat with a 10HP Honda outboard motor. Two pulls and it was running. No time to explain anything to the owner, he had to move now. The water was smooth as glass and Roger aimed his bow for the bay opening that the moving tide had drifted the "Idle Times" out of and into the mainstream shipping routes. Roger held the throttle open full and stayed low to generate the most speed he could but then he heard a sound that was more frightening than the roar of a tyrannosaurus rex, the long clean blast of a mega BC Ferry horn to let ALL boats know, get the hell out of the way. He continued to keep his pace but was not close enough to see his dad's boat floating freely on the water. The blast again from the horn, only this time it was longer than he had ever heard before. A clear message to all to get out of the way. He was closing in on the small bay entrance opening when he came around the bend and could see the "Idle Times" off in the distance. He could also see the front bow of a 450-foot-long behemoth barreling down on the lonely little craft. Roger refused to give up hope and kept the throttle open full as he closed the gap between his father's boat and the massive front wake of the menacing beast. He suddenly came to grips with reality and he knew he was not going to be able to get to the "Idle Times" before the Queen of Saanich completely consumed her prey. Roger cut the power on the outboard motor and slowed to a halt as the ferry closed in on its victim.

Snap. Crunch. Crackle. Kaboom. The "Idle Times" was merely debris in the Pacific Ocean. A memory. The mighty diesel continued to destroy every inch of the boat and left her in their wake. The only survivor was the large Canadian flag that Clyde proudly flew off the top flagpole. Now it was floating on the surface of the water. Instinctively, Roger knew he had to evacuate the area quickly because the ship's wake was bearing down on him, and he could be sunk in a split second with no life jacket or safety equipment. He turned the small craft and hit the gas. Minutes later he returned to the dock to where Heather was standing with the owner of the dingy who wanted an explanation as to why Roger thought he could just help himself to his possessions. Roger pulled slowly up to the dock and tossed the bow line to the owner who was now realizing that Roger seemed to be missing his entire boat.

"Where's your ship son?" The old sea dog asked Roger.

"Davy Jones locker." He replied.

"So how am I supposed to get home from the middle of nowhere?" Heather asked Roger.

Roger was speechless. He was truly in a state of shock. He hadn't seen anything like that since a James Bond Movie. All those years, hours, money, it was now floating debris on the ocean's surface soon to find its way to the bottom, where Roger's heart was.

"Oh, my goodness," Heather piped up. "I left my Louis Vuitton purse on that boat and now it's gone forever. You owe me a new purse, mister. I saved for over a year to get one and you just sent it to a watery grave. Well, I hope you're happy?" Heather turned and walked back towards the Inn and all the people that had now gathered around asking questions and wondering what had happened.

A bystander on the wharf turned to some of the questioning crowd and said, "Seems to me that someone had no idea how to tie off boat lines, and the bloody thing got swept away."

Roger stood at the end of the dock that day for a couple more hours trying to decide if he should take his own life or go tell his dad what happened and let him take his life. Either way, Roger was in a whole heap of trouble.

Finally, after a spell Roger started thinking, "I wonder where I can get a replacement…PURSE?"

Chapter Five

After Roger conjured up the courage to tell father about the "Idle Times"' untimely demise, he took it well. Not really. Not at all well. Clyde was heartbroken when he heard the story of the boat and its bittersweet end. He thought back to all of the hours that they had spent together working on the boat and he began to smile like he had just been told a hilarious joke. It really didn't bother Clyde. He and Maxine had bought the boat years before as a project for the family to have something to work on together with a common goal. The boat had fulfilled its duty to Clyde and Maxine; finding a project that really had brought so much happiness to the family, for so many years. Maxine tried her hardest to be sad about the loss of the family yacht, but she also had renewed the insurance on the boat a couple of years before and, because it was now a collector's item, it was worth far more than they had ever invested in it. Even though the insurance premiums were exceedingly high every month, Maxine kept the maximum amount of coverage they could get just in case something horrible like this accident ever occurred. And guess what? It did.

Maxine continued to show remorse in front of Clyde, but deep down inside she was thinking to herself, "good riddance. Be gone, you floating money pit." Her wish was answered when she found out the boat had been pulverized into tiny little pieces and there was absolutely NO chance of salvage. Maxine clung onto Clyde's arm like a forgotten soul that had lost a valued family member, but really, she was simply fine. She couldn't wait to get the $500,000 cheque for the insurance payout and for the "Idle Times" to merely become part of the family's history.

Heather, however, would remain in infamy among the family members for all eternity. The Miller's could take a lot of crap, but nobody should ever lie about being a sailor. EVER!

***

Roger was well aware of his father's mantra, "If at first you don't succeed - try, try again." This is literally how Roger, Anne, and Mitch lived their lives. They all wished for the best on every endeavour, but the odds are that you may face some setbacks in life, and the dating game was no exception. Roger knew it would take a lot of dates to find the ideal woman. He had no intention of giving up so early in the pursuit. She was out there, and he was going to continue searching…for a little while longer.

Roger set a place and time with Amber. She was in film school at UBC in her fourth year and Roger was fascinated with the television and film industry, so he felt that it would be fun just to get a chance to speak with somebody who was aiming to make their living behind a camera. They met out at the "Dikes" in Maple Ridge, where there were long, elevated roads going for miles in every direction. People enjoyed walking and riding bicycles along them for hours at a time. This was ideal for family outings because all of the roads were quite wide and, best of all flat, so when someone wishes just to stroll aimlessly along, it was a wonderful place to stroll at your own pace. They met at one of the large parking lots available at the beginning of one of the many series of trails and grabbed their backpacks and water canteens and headed off for a few hours. Roger couldn't help noticing that Amber had a very sturdy set of legs on her. She looked like one of the models on the cover of Muscle and Fitness Magazine as she moved down the path with her leg muscles rippling with each step. She was quite beautiful with kinky, long reddish hair down her back and lots of freckles smattered all over her smiling face and impressive teeth. The Crest White Strips ads had nothing on Amber. As they pushed on that day, she relayed countless stories of things from the film industry and kept Roger intrigued for the entire walk, right to the end of the path at the old rock quarry. They sat down on some of the cut stones and had a bit of lunch and relaxation. It was peaceful and calming. They heard some rustling in the low brush across the dike and from out of nowhere a large black bear ambled out of the low bramble bushes lining the side of the water on either side. He eased into the water and in a few strokes, he arrived on the other side of the dike. Their side of the dike. At first it seemed to be only interested in chasing bees and rubbing its head on the ground, covered in dandelions, but then the bear saw Amber and Roger. They forever tell you to not run from a bear, but it is bloody hard to sit still and pretend that an 800 lb predator is your friend and means you no harm. Roger looked at Amber and said, "Let's start heading back towards the cars, shall we?" The two tripped the light fantastic and headed back to the parking lot, not running but with serious intent, meaning almost running. The two clipped along down this moat surrounded pathway that offered no escape at all. On both sides of the path were frighteningly large and prickly bramble bushes and at the bottom on either side were the dike waterways that allow fresh water to moisten all the grounds in the area. Eureka, Roger could see two bicyclists coming towards them so they knew that the bear would see them coming his way and would skedaddle back to the quarry, hopefully. The bikes rang their bells loudly as they passed Amber and Roger and called out, "Passing on your left," until they saw the black bear who was in pursuit and slowly closing the gap they had created. The two cyclists stopped at once, picked their bikes up, turned them back to face the other direction, and rode off at a frantic pace. Gling-gling their bells went, as they rode by the pair and began to increase their speed. It was like watching Lance Armstrong on those hills in the Tour de France; they just kept pulling away faster and faster. Roger and Amber looked back and could see the bear was still idling along but the two were both aware that the bear could close the gap between them in seconds. Roger felt a bit embarrassed thinking that he was good and scared of this major forest predator that was closing in on the two of them. "Amber, we need to pick up our pace without running. Do you feel comfortable with that?" Roger asked.

She looked over her shoulder to gauge the bear's distance and then looked back at Roger. "It's gaining on us Roger. Why can't it just bugger off and leave us be?" She said.

As they were speaking, the road swerved and had a long stretch of open gravel that leads back to the parking lot and other people. Safety in numbers they always say. The two were now taking full, long strides along the open road to try and create some distance between them and the bear, but it was not working. The bear shifted gears from a slow canter to a bit of a hop-along sort of movement but with this change of tactic he continued to close the gap. Now it was getting scary. Old Smokey the Bear seemed to have something in his snoot for lunch that day and it seemed like it was human. Male, female, he wasn't fussy. He was clearly tired of berries and dirty dike water. Yup, he had a whole new menu in mind.

Amber looked again and knew the bear was fifty feet away. Way too close for her liking. She said to Roger very calmly, "Roger, are you a jogger or runner of any sort?"

"No. Not at all. Why do you ask?" Roger queried.

"You know that story about getting away from something, and the most important thing isn't being the fastest. You just need to be faster than the slowest person. Right." She said, now with panic in her eyes.

"Sure Amber. I've heard of that." He said.

"Great. I'm sorry Roger, but this is where I leave you. We can chat once we get back to the car, but for now, I want to put some distance between me and the bear and I can see you being all cool and casual with it, but it is freaking me the hell out, so I gotta make tracks." Amber explained. She looked one more time at the bear, she turned and began to run. Flat-out full speed. Within moments she was fleeing the scene, leaving Roger in a state of shock. He had not had this happen to him before, so it was being processed under; "New Experiences." As Amber's muscular legs flexed off down the levy, he slowly glanced over his shoulder to get in his own head his GPS system on the bear. It was sitting right beside him. He tried to hold his breath at first but then realized, "Don't hold your breath." Roger slipped his hand into his backpack and found the package he was looking for instantly, the bag of beef jerky. He had about four or five strips. He pulled one portion out and barely dropped it two feet from where he was standing. Smokies' nostrils flared open trying to test the air to see if this offering was sufficient or if he should just eat the bigger portion. Smokey started moving the beef strip around with his nose and began to nosh on it. Smokey gave Roger a look like, "Yummy. I love teriyaki flavour." Once Smokey was halfway through the first nugget, Roger carefully tossed a second strip about two feet further away and stood still and silent. Smokey took the bait. He turned his girth towards the newly dropped meat chunk and began to enjoy the second slice. Now was his chance. Roger tossed one more meat slice another few feet away from the second piece and he started walking ever so slowly towards salvation. His car, with its big steel doors and a false sense of security. Step by step Roger remained calm and moved slowly away from Smokey. Before long, he was back to having a one-hundred-foot gap between him and the bear, then began to breathe normally again. That was as close as he ever wanted to be with a bear. He was far enough away now that Roger raised his pace to a medium jog back to his pickup truck. Roger popped open the door and climbed inside. He grabbed the large armrest and pulled the door tightly shut before he sat back in the seat and tried to not piss his pants. He scanned the parking lot for Amber to see if she was going to stick around. He got his answer within a second on his cell phone.

New Message: It read – "We are just heading in different directions right now. You seem like a really nice man, but I'm looking for someone different."

"Two different directions right now. I'll say. She's heading in the opposite direction of the bear that decided not to eat me today. Thank goodness I brought along that clandestine beef jerky today even though she was vegan. Well, she never stuck around long enough to make any comment about it." He said to himself.

***

Roger was no quitter. He knew he would have to kiss a lot of frogs before he found his princess. He had such a lighthearted nature that these little dating hiccups would not deter his resolve. He knew there were lots of amazing people out there and it was going to take time to connect with the right one. A firm believer that nothing in your love life is easy. You can only get out what you put in, or something like that. Roger wasn't giving up without a fight, so-to-speak.

He had made a connection with a woman named Pamela. She lived in North Vancouver, on the other side of the Burrard Inlet. Thank goodness there was a convenient transportation mode called the "Sea Bus" that ran every thirty minutes from morning till night at the foot of Granville Street. It whisked passengers across in approximately twelve minutes per ride to the other side of the inlet to the "Lonsdale Quay" on the North Vancouver side. At the foot of Lonsdale Avenue, it was always bustling with its boutiques, restaurants, window shoppers, and tourists. The Terminal on the

Vancouver side was far less populated because of the way the Sea Bus entrance was designed originally to rapidly move riders up and down the ramp and onto the Sea Bus wharf/platform for easy access for the loading of passengers. One needs to merely purchase a ticket, walk down to the loading area, wait for the boat to pull up to the dock and clamber aboard. This of course means that there are always two Sea Buses on the move simultaneously throughout the day. Because of this staggered schedule, it can be tricky to meet people on the Sea Bus because you can never be sure which boat your connecting party will be on until you board the ship or go back up to street level and find your friends outside of the Terminal.

Roger and Pamela agreed to meet at a local Starbucks at 6:00 pm by the Sea Bus Station. Could not be any easier. Walk in, scope out/find Pamela, get a hot beverage, and sit down and chat. Easy breezy. Roger arrived a few minutes early, as usual, and ordered a coffee to wrap his hands around while he waited for Pam. He sat right beside the front doors to be sure not to miss her in the surge of riders that frequent this location. Roger was gazing at the city in all of its wonder and then it hit him, "What if she is in the Starbucks on the North Vancouver side?" He thought to himself.

He checked the text message from Pam a second time, but he was correct in his assumption. They had not clearly determined at which side of the inlet they were meeting. He began to panic a touch in his chair and wondered if he had buggered this date up before it had even started. He reread the note and he felt confident that they were to meet on the Vancouver side of the water. Stay calm and just give it a few more minutes. Like before he was now looking at his phone clock every thirty seconds. "I've got it?" He thought. I am going to call her and find out for certain. Nothing to chance if they spoke on the phone, face to face…kind of.

"Hello there, you have reached Pamela's personal voicemail, please leave your name, number, and a short message and I'll get back to you." Pamela's voicemail replied. Now Roger was beginning to panic even more. Where is she? Am I in the right spot? No big deal. Roger would just walk downstairs and catch the next Sea Bus to the Lonsdale side and see if Pam were in that Starbucks. Buzz, buzz, Roger's cell phone notified him of an incoming call. He answered swiftly but no one was there. He somehow dropped the call. While he was looking at his phone cover, he could see that he had missed three calls from Pamela. A bit of frustration was setting in, but Roger was going to persevere through this and make this date work. He gulped down his last couple of ounces of coffee and bolted outside to the ramp to the Sea Bus terminal where he would board and get to the Lonsdale side, twelve minutes later. The doors opened and he hurriedly found a vacant seat and began his twelve-minute sentence. Less than one minute later Roger's phone buzzed again with more information.

"Hello…hello…can you hear me now?" He asked. The line was quiet. In no time the Sea Bus doors slid open, and he darted off to find the Lonsdale Quay Starbucks location and find Pamela. He searched the coffee shop thoroughly and could not find her. He went over to the lavatories but both of them had their doors opened. "Where the heck could she be?" He thought to himself. As Roger stood outside the door his phone rang again. It was Pam. "Hello there. I am at the Starbucks at the Lonsdale Quay. How about you?" Roger queried.

"Oops. I am at the Starbucks on the other side. Give me a minute…buzz, squeak, dead." She tried to explain as her phone lost its signal.

"So, was she coming or staying?" He thought. He dialed Pam's number to see if he could reach her and finalize the arrangements but no luck, her answering machine said she was away from the phone and to leave a message. "Pamela, its' Roger, I am going to get back on the ferry and come back to the Vancouver side and meet you at that Starbucks." He expressed himself in an exasperated manner.

He bolted down the gangway back to the ferry terminal and waited for the doors to slide open and allow him to re-board the ship and meet up with Pamela and get the night moving ahead in a positive direction.

He sat in one of the many empty chairs on that particular run and saw his phone screen light up again. It was Pam. Roger answered in an almost panicked breathy way, "Hello there, I'm here."

"You're where?" Pamela said.

"I'm on the boat heading for the Vancouver side right now. Where are you?" He asked.

"I'm standing beside the starboard exit doors watching the other ferry cross the inlet and we will be passing each other in…just…a few…seconds." She said. "I'm waving at you right now from the other ferry, can you see me?" She said.

"Yes. I see you," and Roger was waving madly at Pamela on the other boat. "Should I get off and come back over to your side to meet up?" He asked.

"I don't think so Roger. I think we will remain two ships passing in the night." She replied and hung up the phone.

***

Roger was devastated. He could not believe his fate with all of the dates he had attempted thus far. He decided to stop for a beverage at the Steamworks' Brewery on the edge of Gastown on Water Street. Besides, he had come all the way to downtown Vancouver, the least he could do was to enjoy it for a few minutes.

He entered the room that blasted him with the din of loud talking and very loud music. It was perfect. It had been forever since he was in a happening downtown venue with lots of different characters to check out, from afar. The room had a service bar that had to be forty feet long, with chairs placed in front with a comfortable low bar rail to put one's feet on. Roger went right down to the end of the wooden behemoth bar to stay out of the way of some of the people that were already there in their own groups having fun. He slid the stool up to the edge of the bar and rested an elbow and started watching the multitude of TVs strategically placed around the room, showing a myriad of sports for all different sporting tastes. He saw one of the TV's was tuned in to an NFL Football game, which would be simply perfect for Roger. He would watch any NFL matchup no matter who is playing. He genuinely enjoyed football. As time moved on, he was quietly taking in the sites and sounds when a young woman, covered in tattoos, came over and sat beside Roger. She had a very beatnik style about her, and she had ten earrings per ear and who knows how many more piercings that he couldn't see. "It could be a new game. See if you could guess how many tats and piercings a person had and then make them strip down to their birthday suit and have some judges do an official count. Some people have so many they probably have forgotten what the real number is anymore." Roger thought to himself.

"Are you here with someone?" A voice said to him.

"No. I'm here by myself just watching the game." Roger replied.

"Who's playing?" She asked.

"Packers and Cowboys. Are you a football fan?" He said.

"I went to a Canucks game once. It was extremely fast but extraordinarily boring." She said. "What's your name?" She asked.

"Roger. Nice to meet you." He extended his hand to shake hers, but she had moved on.

"Colleen. I work here but I just finished my shift, so I was going to have a drink and people watch for a while. You wanna join me?" She said.

"Colleen, it sounds like the perfect blend of fun and alcohol." He said. As the two talked and got to know each other a bit better, Roger could see that Colleen was in her mid-twenties and highly excitable. She ordered two beers and insisted that Roger try the BEST BEER EVER! He had never heard this kind of talk before…hahaha.

The barkeep returned to their corner of the bar and placed the two large beers down. Before Roger could take a sip Colleen decided to tell him all about the beer, the brewery, the hops, and so on, so before she had finished her novelette, Roger picked up the beer and had a long healthy swig. "It is quite good." Roger announced.

"Oh my god." She exclaimed, "We should have a chugging contest."

Roger was taken aback by this idea. Plus, he couldn't imagine that this little waif of a woman was going to down a 20 oz. beer in record time. This he would have to see to believe. "Sure. Let's see who can drink a 20 oz. beer the fastest." He replied.

The two of them stood side by side at the bar with their glasses of beer positioned for quick consumption when Colleen said, "Go!"

Just as Roger had anticipated, he drank his beer in a few seconds and placed it back up upon the bar, however, Colleen slowly laboured her way through the cold beverage until she was down to a few drops in the bottom of the glass and banged her glass down in a champion style, only to see that Roger was done and waiting on her to finish. She seemed like this had never happened to her before this day, which of course is crazy, because there are so many competent beer guzzlers out there, he assumed she must have come across one of them at some point in her life.

"Again." she demanded.

In the blink of an eye, two beers arrived at the bar and were placed in front of each participant. Colleen wrapped her small hand around the glass and gave Roger the stink eye, the one that says, "I'm going to kick your sorry ass dude and send you home to mother."

With her hand placed in position on the glass she gave the green light, "Go!"

Roger drank this beer alarmingly fast just to show Colleen what her competition was capable of in a beer swilling contest. She stood holding onto the bar with one hand and drinking with all her might with the other hand and she was finally able to empty the contents of the beer glass. She wavered, took a breath, and got back her legs and turned to Roger. "Not bad, not bad at all…" she was unable to complete her sentence. Her body had decided to place the contents of her stomach elsewhere which, unfortunately for Roger, was a full-on frontal, high velocity beer puke directly into Roger's face. He was soaked from top to bottom. He picked up some napkins, wiped his face dry and said, "What a pleasure meeting you this evening Colleen. We should make plans to do this again sometime." He said.

Roger reached into his pocket and pulled out his wallet. The bill for his and Colleen's beers was about forty bucks, so he threw the bartender a $100.00 and said, "Keep the change." Then Roger left the premises smelling as fresh as a Granville Island Pale Ale. As Roger drove home that night in his wet shirt he made a decision, no more drinking contests with strangers, ever.

Mitch sat in one of the guest chairs in front of Roger's desk, facing him with a grin from ear to ear. He was getting brought up-to-speed on Roger's quest for romance, but he could not help but laugh out loud when he heard of all the interesting events that had taken place since Roger had joined a dating site. Each date was accompanied by a tall tale that had Mitch thinking that all of this could be bullshit but he knew his brother and he never lied to him. "So, seven dates, seven disasters. Sound about, right?" Mitch questioned.

"Yeah. That sounds pretty accurate. But I know this is just a fluke. There's no way these dating companies could stay in business if nobody ever finds any romance or even love once in a while. The odds tell us that sooner or later you will meet a Winner." He said.

"Or maybe a stalker. A serial killer. An escaped mental patient?" Mitch roared with laughter. "Don't worry big brother. These sites have worked for thousands of people all over the world, so they are going to work for you. Like everything, you just gotta give it more time."

"More dates. Increase my odds of success." Roger quipped.

"Exactly. More dates. So, what's next on the dating agenda? Dad still has a lot of toys that you haven't destroyed, as of yet." Mitch said.

"Not to worry Mitch. Just give me a little more time." He responded sarcastically.

"So, what's next for you?" He asked.

"I'm going to take a potential match to the Tulip Festival in La Connor, Washington State later this week. If nothing else, the tulips are absolutely fabulous to see in person. You and Chanel want to come for the spectacle?"

"Do you mean the tulips or the spectacle in the front seat of your pickup truck? Trust me bro, this is a tough decision." He snickered. "However, I think we will leave you to get to know the new Mrs. Miller all by yourself, but thanks for the offer. By the way, are you thirsty? I've got a beer right in this area here with your name on it." He said rubbing his belly with his hand.

"Fine. Have it your way." Roger kidded back.

***

The following weekend Roger prepared himself for the quick jaunt over the US border and the drive south down Hwy I-5 to La Connor, where they host the annual Tulip Festival. The toughest part of the day trip is waiting in line at the US/Canada border crossing. Every weekend, without fail, every person from Vancouver feels like it is their duty to drive into the USA and buy something. Milk, bread, cheese, booze, the pilgrimage never ends. The great news is that there are some fantastic deals to be had. The unwelcome news is that the lineups at the border crossings are very full and exceptionally slow. This is never a major surprise to Vancouverites because it has happened every weekend year-round for the past 40 years. If they add more service lanes to speed things up, more people will show up and slow things down. The good news is, you have all the time in the world to get to know someone better with all that idling time and nothing better to do than talk. It has always worked well for Roger in the past when he had someone that he needed to have a heart to heart with trying to find the time and place to get that quality time together. Well, look no further. There is nothing like a sweet four hour wait to allow you to really open up and spill your heart and soul, especially if it's a stranger that you are trying to get to know. This captive audience routine had been working beautifully for years now and Roger wasn't about to change things up. He was looking forward to taking this woman to the Tulip Festival mainly because he enjoyed the beauty and colour that nature put on display each year. Roger was never disappointed with the trek.

Roger stopped at the Cloverdale Fairgrounds on his drive to the Canada /US border to collect his date, Carmen Sanchez. She decided to leave her car at the Fairgrounds and would pick it up on her return trip through Surrey later that night. Roger had received a message from Carmen suggesting an excursion of some kind and the dates happened to coincide perfectly, so when Roger made the tulip suggestion, Carmen was all for it. Roger could not help himself so he did a little research on this woman and all he could really think about was how unbelievably attractive she was. This woman could walk onto a swimsuit photo shoot anywhere in the world with any set of super models and not be out of place. She was a real stunner. He had been taught all of his life to not objectify women for their looks, but this was putting that to THE TEST! Her voice was smooth and easy like listening to a Sade album and when she explained the weather or how to peel a potato, it seemed so incredibly interesting. Roger continued to smile and drive his truck down the road knowing that sooner or later he had to stop and then he would be able to pay his full attention to her. She donned a soft flowing dress down to the knees and the bustier was tight and very form fitting. Her body was impeccable, and she clearly worked out regularly. Her hair was raven black, full down to her lower back, with an easy wave from top to bottom. Her eyebrows were full and well formed with a perfect nose and delectable cheekbones. She also somehow knew one of Roger's Achilles heels; she wore bright red, vibrant high-gloss lipstick. Roger loved a woman with red lips.

They talked continuously for the entire ride to the border crossing. They waited their turn to pull up and address the Border Guard. All of the usual questions looked over the passports, where are you going, and they were off. Roger did sideways glance at Carmen after the border crossing because her forehead was starting to bead sweat, which is rare for most women, but he did not know her well enough to recognize any of her personal nuances.

When they arrived at one of the large tulip farms, they leaped from the truck and began to walk up and down the rows upon rows of distinct types and colours of tulips. It never failed to mesmerize Roger and he could see that Carmen was also enjoying the afternoon. Beautiful things are just that, beautiful. They were strolling about the grounds for a couple hours when Roger started to get hungry. The two had already eaten some Churros from a food truck but Roger wanted something more substantial like a steak. "Carmen, are you feeling the least bit hungry?" He asked her.

"I could definitely see myself eating some lunch. What do you have in mind Roger?" She responded.

"Just up the Interstate there is a large casino with a full Top Shelf restaurant attached to the building. I've been before and it was quite lovely." He added.

"That sounds wonderful Roger. I am feeling a little peckish." Carmen said.

The two made their way to the eatery and got seated inside. The place was a grand space that the owners had clearly spent millions of dollars on to create an atmosphere of wealth and opulence. The place was beautiful, and the food and service were up-to-par with the rest of the facility. They talked on during their meal and Roger really felt at ease with this new potential relationship. Carmen was very smart and, as the time slipped by and she had a couple of libations, the truth serum was beginning to work. Her travels around the world were extensive, like nobody he had ever met before. Soon, Roger was trying to pick the most obscure places on planet earth to see if she had been there, and she had. He never knew anyone with a travel list this extensive. He started to wonder how this young woman would have had time to travel to all the spots they had discussed over their lunch date. Literally impossible. Roger was suspicious but he wasn't going to get into an interrogation with her about her past travels, but it was so extensive that he figured she was full of crap. She told him a story of some place in South America, but the details of the story were like listening to your own mom or dad relay an old tale from the past to you. He knew that at this point in the newly found friendship, it really wasn't that important. He knew that as time went by, if they continued to see each other, so many details would come out and he would have the answers that he thought he was looking for. Roger made sure to check with Carmen that it was okay to pay the lunch bill and she concurred with one of her bright smiles. Her teeth were so straight and white you couldn't take your eyes off of her while she was looking in your direction. Roger actually felt himself blush because he was staring at his date but looked away quickly so as not to get caught ogling. As he looked around the restaurant it seemed like everybody was staring at Carmen all of the time.

They headed outside and started to make their way back to the car. In a flash, two young men appeared beside Roger's pickup truck and stood between the truck and the small Honda Civic parked beside them. The gap was tight and unnecessary so Roger said, "Hey gents, could we get some room to breathe please?"

"No worries brother, we just want your money, now." One of them said.

"Okay guys, we do not want any trouble." Roger said. He began reaching for his wallet in his back pocket when out of the corner of his eye he saw a quick movement and one of the men went down to the ground. Roger took a step back in shock and saw that Carmen had a short black metal rod and she spun herself around in this tiny little space between two automobiles and kicked the other would-be assailant square on his jaw with enough force behind it that two of his teeth became dislodged and flew through the air as he slumped over and hit the ground. In under ten seconds these two would-be attackers were now in need of serious medical attention. "Holy shit Carmen," Roger exclaimed, "How the fuck did you do that?"

"We should go…quickly. Security will be by shortly to assist these two with their injuries. I am sure of it because they are using an exceedingly high grade of security cameras in this parking lot, so I'm not kidding…let's go." Carmen said.

They stepped over the two unconscious men laying on the ground, got in the truck and headed out of the busy parking lot. Roger was still stunned that, of all the people milling around, no one saw what had just happened with Roger's new Kung-Fu girlfriend. It was like watching one of the championship women fighters in MMA perform. Quick, efficient, and lethal. Roger was not used to walking away from a scene like this, however, he had actually never been in a scene like this. He pressed down on the gas pedal and made his way to the parking lot exit and crossed over the overpass that led the two of them back onto the interstate that headed back to the Canadian border. For several minutes they did not speak. Roger had no idea what to say. He really had never seen a woman disarm and injure two men with such stealth and accuracy. It was frightening and at the time it was exhilarating. He pulled his truck off the interstate into a roadside Rest Stop and pulled into one of the empty parking stalls and shut off the motor.

"What the hell was that, Carmen? I did not want to get robbed or get into a fight with those guys but how the hell did you learn to fight like that? You had them both down and out in ten seconds. I've never seen anything like that except for in a James Bond movie." He mumbled.

"Roger, I can explain. My previous job gave me self defense training in case any of the women that I worked with were in any trouble so they thought it would be useful for all of us to know how to defend ourselves. That's all. I swear to you that was the first time I ever used the training in a practical use, and it was highly effective. I feel like I was a great student because it got us out of potential trouble fast." She said.

"You do realize that when we arrive at the border crossing my license plates will have been tagged and the troopers and border guards will all be on the alert for us. My question is, how do we explain this? Why didn't we remain at the scene until the police had arrived, will be one of their first questions. What are we going to tell them?" He said.

"Hmm. This is an incredibly good question. I'll need a minute to collect my thoughts on this." Carmen answered. She looked over at the building in the parking lot that housed the lavatories and said, "Give me one minute to freshen up and I will explain everything. I'll be right back." She said. She opened the passenger door and leaned over inside the truck and gave Roger a passionate kiss on the lips, she leaned back and looked at him again like they had just met, leaned forward one more time for another kiss and she leaped off her seat and trotted off to the woman's washroom without looking back.

Forty minutes passed and Roger was getting worried. Where had this woman gone? He walked over to the woman's washroom and asked another lady to please go in and check and see if his date was still using the facilities. The helpful bystander went into the bathroom, returned in a flash and assured Roger that the bathroom was empty. WTF.

"What to do? What to do?" Roger thought to himself. To hell with it. He was going to go back to the Canadian Border and tell them exactly what had happened. He eased his truck through the lineup of cars until he pulled up to the open service window and the Border Guard said, "Need to see your passport please. Do you have anything to declare?"

. Roger leaned his head out of his open window and said, "You are never going to believe what I have to tell you."

The Border Guard listened for a couple of minutes of the story and then signaled for Roger to pull his truck around and go inside and see one of the officers there.

Roger explained his story from the beginning and the guard took notes while shaking his head the entire time as if to say, you are so full of shit dude. He excused himself and came back into the office with a supervisor in tow and then they asked Roger all the same questions again. Within minutes they had CCTV footage downloaded and on the small screen in the office they were occupying. Even as Roger saw her take down the two assailants on camera he couldn't believe the stealth, accuracy, and power she delivered on these two unsuspecting robbers. Neither could the Border guards.

Not long after, another gentleman in a black suit came into the room and closed the door. He began to explain to Roger that the woman that he thought he was on a date with was NOT Carmen Sanchez but actually Maria Gonzalez who has been wanted for many years now. Although she looks noticeably young and beautiful, she is actually fifty-two years old and has four children in their late teens and early twenties. Roger couldn't fathom that Carmen was that old, yet that attractive. The next few hours were damage control and Roger tried to be as helpful as he could. He even told them where she had parked her car that morning at the Cloverdale Fairgrounds. He was scared for himself and didn't want any trouble so he gave up anything that he thought could be useful to the Border Patrol and police. Hector Lopez, the man in the black suit, did tell Roger something before they let him head back into

Canada which was, Maria Gonzalez had never allowed one of her new 'friends' to live. All of her previous relationships had ended in tragedy, so Hector was amazed Roger was still alive. "She must have actually liked you, hombre. Consider yourself one lucky son of a gun." He said.

Roger left the Border Patrol building and headed northbound back into Canada. After he drove for a couple miles, he started thinking, "Maybe online is a little too dangerous for me." He was about to pull onto the highway when he saw a person thumbing for a ride. It was Maria Gonzalez and he just kept driving.

Chapter Six

After a couple weeks hiatus from dating and making sure that he was not being followed by Maria, he felt like he could swim around in the shallow end of the dating pool again. He opened his laptop and scanned through the newest group of potential partners when he came across a woman that caught his eye, Nikita. She was a twenty-nine-year-old born in Russia and had immigrated to Canada at the age of twenty, so she was well versed on North American ways and attitudes. He was particularly apprehensive because so far in his dating career he had only spoken to a couple of women for short periods of time and never really had the chance to get to know any of the women he dated at all. He knew his luck had to change. Onward and upward.

Roger and Nikita had decided to meet up and go for a bicycle ride. She had planned out an overly aggressive 80 to 100 km ride that they could start at her building in Vancouver's West End, which was made up of high rise after high rise in one of the highest densities of population in Canada. They would start there and then go over the Lions Gate bridge and ride all the way down to the second narrows, then ride over the Iron Worker's Memorial bridge back into Vancouver's east side. From there, the plan was to ride the side streets back to Nikita's place and stop for the day. It sounded like a demanding ride, but Roger absolutely loved bike riding and was usually up for anything biking related. Thinking ahead, Roger knew the chance of him finding parking for his truck around her residence was pitiful at best, so he was going to leave the truck at a city park a few miles away and then ride his bike to meet her at her apartment. He was quite excited because he loved riding but especially loved riding in the downtown core where they would be for most of the day. When he got to the building, he pulled up to the buzzer pad and looked for Petrov. He pressed the buzzer down and awaited the response. In a heavy foreign accent she answered, "Come." The door latch disengaged, and Roger stepped inside. It was one of the old original west end buildings that needed to be completely renovated or torn down. The building had that old people smell emanating from the lobby and aromas of every different culture in the city was oozing down the hallways. Borsch, or maybe it's perogies. Roger started to wish he had a bigger breakfast, but he wanted to be careful and not to fill himself up and then not feel energetic in his bicycle saddle. He got to the door, and it was ajar. He pushed it in slightly and said, "Hello there. Anybody home?"

"Of course I'm home. You just spoke to me on the intercom." Nikita said.

"Yes, I know. It's just a figure of speech." He replied.

"This is stupid this figure of speech. Don't do that today with me." She barked.

"Copy that. Are you ready to go?" Roger asked politely.

"Of course. That's why you came over. So, I should be ready for the event, yes?" She replied.

"Great. Well, let's get moving along, shall we?" He added.

Nikita was about six feet tall and approximately 77 kg, so she was well built. It appeared that she had lots of leg muscles from previous rides, so Roger was hoping that she could handle herself on a bicycle. Her hair was dyed platinum blonde with chestnut brown roots spread evenly all over her head and her hair coming down to just past her neck. She sported thick muscular arms and had small "A" cup breasts that were shoved into a stretchy tank top made of spandex that matched the shorts. She donned a lightweight riding coat and grabbed her riding helmet and her sporty sunglasses from the hall closet as they were making their way out the door. As she strode down the hallway, pushing her bike with one hand, Roger could see she was quite robust through the buttock area which was another indicator that Nikita might just be a real bike rider. They exited the tiny elevator and headed for the front door and emerged onto the street. The two spoke for a minute while they tied up their riding shoes and placed their helmets on and then they were ready to go. Nikita looked directly into Roger's face and said, "I lead. You follow, yes?"

"Yes. Of course, sounds good to me." Roger answered.

And... they were off. She hit the first turn a block from her apartment at almost full speed, made the corner and went back to pumping her pedals like she was in an Olympic try-out. Roger was thrilled to see this woman ride away with such power and precision. This was not her first time out. It took a couple of blocks for him to catch up with her, but Roger was a veteran cyclist and was going to keep up no matter what it took. Ten minutes into the ride she had picked up her pace and Roger stayed behind her on her back wheel and drafted off her. "This was freaking marvelous," he thought to himself. Nikita had skills. A few minutes later they had arrived at the Lions Gate Bridge, and they charged across and never changed their gait. The weather was pleasant and not raining so this was a glorious day for all Vancouver bikers, Roger thought. As time passed, Nikita slowed and let Roger pull up alongside her and said, "Do you want to feed ourselves, yes."

"Sounds great Nikita, any place is good with me." He said.

They stopped by a grouping of food trucks offering food from around the world. He stood waiting for Nikita to make her taste selection and he followed. She walked up to a truck that offered some Russian standards and she went about ordering some treats. "You eat Russian food also, yes?" She said.

"Perfect. Can't wait." Roger replied.

Minutes later they were trying all of the different dishes she had selected and were having a wonderful time. Although she seemed stern and hard, she was actually quite nice and her "Iron Curtain" was slowly dropping. They finished their food and went to sit on the nearby grass and watch the boats sailing by from shore. Another lovely day in Vancouver.

Once they had put their protective gear back on, they got to peddling up the slow rise over the second narrows bridge and it took its toll on Nikita. The Russian machine showed a spark of being human. She slowed down to a crawl by the time the two of them made it to the apex of the bridge deck. They stopped off to the side and allowed the view to overwhelm their senses. It was a beautiful vista from that vantage point, and it also gave Nikita a moment to rest and catch her breath without looking like she needed a rest. Less than an hour later, they arrived back at Nikita's apartment. They stood outside for a short visit until Nikita announced, "I'm hungry now. You take me for food, yes?"

"Wherever you wish, Nikita." Roger replied. He realized that his clothes were back in his truck parked several kilometers away so he piped up and said, "I only have the clothes I'm wearing so we can't go anywhere too fancy if that is okay with you."

"Nix. I show you place." She said.

They took their bikes up to her apartment and she quickly got changed, in front of Roger, to his surprise.

"What. You not see girl's underpants before?" she asked, with her head slightly tilted showing dismay.

"Yes. Of course I have. You just sort of caught me off guard, that's all." He said.

"Good. The way you stare this be first time, no?" Nikita said.

The two of them made their way down the street to a local watering hole that she selected. They sat at a table outside and began to relax with each other, taking in the sights and sounds of Vancouver's nightlife. They got on far better than he had hoped from all of the earlier communications. She was genuinely nice once she relaxed and let her "Iron" guard down. They shared a fine meal and a piece of cheesecake when the waitress came by and dropped off the cheque.

"Here, I can get that if you like?" Roger said.

"No. Canada men want intercourse for food. I not want intercourse. You are nice man but not my man. Understand?" She said.

"I completely understand Nikita. I was merely offering to pay for dinner as a friendly gesture between two new friends. That's all. No intercourse required, okay?" Roger said to her.

"Yes then. You pay." She said.

He squared away the bill and they retreated back to Nikita's apartment so Roger could fetch his bicycle and call it a day, however, when they opened her front door, she turned to Roger and said in a low whisper, "I cannot get your bike. It is out on the sundeck, and I rent my living room out to people every night for extra money, but I am not to ever go into that room, or they do not have to pay any rent for the month. The bike is on the deck now and I can't get it until 7:00 am. I'm sorry for this trouble." She said.

"Nikita, I can't leave without my awfully expensive bike. It is also my transportation back to my truck that is parked miles away from here." He whispered calmly.

"Nix. No Bike!" She barked.

"Well then, we have a problem. I will not leave without that bike so what other alternatives do you have?" Roger asked.

"You must stay night. Sleep on floor in bedroom." she commanded.

"Okay then. Good enough. I'll stay on the floor, and I will get up and go at seven." He said.

"Yes. This good. No hanky panky. Must behave, yes?" She said.

"You have nothing to worry about with me. I will be a gentleman. This, I can promise." Roger replied.

They made their way down a short hallway walking as quietly as they could to not wake up the renters. The room was nicely decorated in a cozy kind of way. Everything looked soft and inviting and gave you the urge to touch everything with your hands to see how it felt. She pointed to the floor and said, "You, here." Her index finger pointing down to the floor.

"You need bathroom?" she queried.

"I wouldn't mind a few moments alone." He replied.

"Please rush. I need to use." She said.

When Roger came out of the bathroom, he noticed that Nikita had aligned a grouping of pillows down the center of the bed. It was a king size bed so he was delighted to think he may be able to sleep on a bed rather than the hardwood floor. He walked to the middle of the room and stood for a moment just to be sure that he understood the gesture she was making.

"Your side," she waved her arm showing the delineation she had invented, "My side." She again used her hands to be sure to convey the message.

"Got it." He said.

Roger walked over to the designated sleeping zone and started to crawl under the covers. "Nix." She hissed. "Take off all your clothes. I don't want you get my sheets dirty from your sweaty clothing, please."

"Sorry, sorry, clothes off. Got it Nikita." He sheepishly replied.

She really couldn't surprise him anymore. She stood two feet away from him as he stripped down naked and turned away before getting under the covers, because he was feeling a little vulnerable at this point.

"Nix. She reached out towards him with some baby wipes and said, "Foots and bum please."

He took the wet-wipes and wiped his front and back privates and then balanced on one foot at a time to cleanse his bare feet individually. He stood naked in front of her as she scanned over his body like he was fruit at the supermarket and said, "You may enter bed now."

Roger stared at the ceiling wondering how many completely weird things had happened to him since he joined Lava Love. He knew he would get through this. Just fall asleep and get out of here in the morning. He rolled onto his side, and realized he could see a bit of her partly naked body through the crack in the door hinges that allowed a small peek-a-boo space that exposed all of the secrets. Her robust bottom was showing fully with a small eye patch and two pieces of dental floss that made up her G-String panties. He could see she was staring at herself in the mirror tossing her hair about and mumbling something in Russian and then the door swung open fully and she was standing before him with nothing but her panties on. She took two steps further into the room and said," Now we sleep. No intercourse for you. You understand?"

Roger was about to answer when he saw her moving around to his side of the bed. The area he had been designated to under Russian house rules. She pulled back the sheet and blanket that was covering Roger and climbed on top of him and covered them both with the blanket.

In Roger's head he was completely amiss with what was going on. Within a few moments she had stimulated Roger enough that his manhood was beginning to rise and then she got on him like a ride at Playland that she had bought fifty tickets to and began to squeak and squawk and get her monies' worth. For the first time in many years Roger was feeling a little shy because he had never met a girl this aggressive in bed before. His deceased wife was quiet and demure but not Nikita. She was a wildcat and Roger was absolutely sure that the renters were going to be knocking on the door for us to KEEP IT DOWN in there, but they did not.

Roger awoke in the morning to the rich aroma of freshly brewed coffee. "Things couldn't be all bad" he thought to himself. He pulled his clothes back on and made his way into the kitchen where Nikita was standing in her work attire curling her hair with an electric iron. She looked at him harshly and said, "We must talk. You are quite skilled at sex. I like it. Now you must get your bike and never come back." She walked closer to Roger and leaned in and gave him a sloppy kiss and said, "Now go!"

Roger found himself shambling down the hallway to the elevator pushing his bicycle, and as the doors closed, he thought…next.

Chapter Seven

Roger had decided to take a sabbatical from the dating scene. He hadn't given up, but he wanted to feel like a dad rather than a single dude trying to meet women. One of the discoveries he had made was, in order to engage with women, it took time away from his home life and his cherished time with Rose and Brooke. He was also feeling guilty about having his parents looking after his kids on such a frequent basis. Anne and Mitch were a big part of his support team, but Maxine and Clyde were his go-to couple, and he felt like he was abusing their kindness. They wanted Roger to find a new partner, love interest, possibly even a new wife, not just for Roger, but his parents knew that the girls could use the day-to-day support that they had been used to from their doting mother Michelle. She was a wonderful person that did everything she could for Rose and Brooke. She joined in no matter what the girls had gotten involved with and would forever be their greatest cheerleader. Michelle would volunteer for any bake sale, Girl Guides event, dance classes, soccer games, whatever the cause, she was a staple. The school knew they could count on Michelle as well. One phone call and she would be enlisted for driving kids to and from events, reading stories in the classroom, even participating as a lifeguard, if necessary. Michelle was dependable and loyal when it came to her girls and their activities. She was also a great friend to Roger. She was his rock, the person that he could tell his good and stupid thoughts to and someone to give him love and attention. Like so many men, Roger was guilty of trying hard to be macho all of the time and pretended he could do everything all by himself. He could not. This became clear to Roger once he was a single dad and wishing desperately that he had somebody to talk with. Roger realized quickly after Michelle's passing what he loved the most about her. It wasn't the cooking, cleaning, or sex, which he did enjoy, it was those heart-to-heart conversations with a person that really cared. Roger craved to be loved like that again and it was the catalyst that would keep him going out on dates: searching for a new best friend to be close and personal with.

When Roger arrived home that day, he walked through the door and was accosted by his daughters, who were both overly excited about parent-teacher night. "Daddy, you are going to love the artwork display I did in my classroom. I used lots of colours and I drew a picture of our house but it's a surprise for you so you can't know about it because it's a secret that I have told you...oops." Brooke said.

"My classroom is decorated for parents as well. We had to make some things out of egg cartons, but I'll keep it a surprise for you." Rose said.

Roger was filled with emotions. He felt himself welling up as he stood in the entrance hall with Rose and Brooke when he realized he had no idea that it was parent-teacher night. "What the hell kind of father am I when I don't have a clue what is happening with my own children." He admonished himself.

The girls were both very in tune with their father's feelings so when they saw even a hint of tears in his eyes, they went into "protect their daddy" mode. They were looking up at him and didn't hesitate to move in with a giant monster hug that always made daddy feel better. Roger dropped down to his knees and embraced the girls as if he had been separated from them for a year. As usual, Roger fought off his urge to cry and started asking the girls all about what other delightful things he was going to see at the school night. "Oh, my goodness," he exclaimed, "So many things to see and do tonight. I love your school so much."

"How much Daddy?" Brooke asked.

"This much." Roger held his hand up in the air as if he were measuring something way over his head."

"Holy cow Daddy. That's a lot." Rose replied.

"And what time do the festivities begin tonight?" He queried.

"From 6:00 to 10:00 pm?" Brooke said in a questioning manner.

"Perfect. Let's go see what Auntie Anne has made for dinner so we can eat and then get to the school. This is going to be amazing!" Roger said, infusing his voice with enthusiasm.

He scooped them up in his arms and whisked them off to the kitchen where Anne was setting the table and putting the finishing touches on her version of chicken pot pie. All the girls loved it because it had a crust and they all loved eating pastry. Roger put his girls back on terra firma and immediately headed over to Joy and Hope and gave big hugs to the two of them. He was conscious of the fact that Anne's daughters wanted his attention as well as his own girls, so he made sure to share his love with all of them. They sat at the large oval kitchen table that was surrounded by windows with a spectacular view of the Fraser River and the Port Mann Bridge. Each one of them gave a report on what they did that day and Anne, and Roger made all the appropriate noises and responses to keep the girls encouraged. Once they had completed the meal, it was off to the school for parent teacher night. This was Rose and Brooke's opportunity to show off to their dad what good and well-behaved girls they had been at school this year. Both of them adored hearing how great they were from their dad, and he loved telling them.

They got to the school by 6:30ish and Anne, with her two girls, went to their own classrooms and Roger stayed with Rose and Brooke to visit their teachers and classrooms. Roger had done this before, but he was taken aback when he entered Brooke's classroom. He glanced towards the front of the classroom and saw a stunning beauty at the front of the room smiling and chatting with other parents and holding hands with some of the shy kids. Roger was intrigued. He continued to watch her out of the corner of his eye while he was being given the grand tour by Brooke. He was careful not to stare, or even look in her direction too much, for fear of being noticed. He was sitting in one of the little itsy-bitsy chairs at one of the round craft tables looking at Brooke's accomplishments when she said, "Well hello there. I don't think we have met before. I am Miss Stevenson, the new kindergarten teacher. I took over for Margaret Smith when she left on maternity leave. And you are?" She extended her hand in greeting.

He was still reeling from her beauty. She might not have been the most beautiful woman in the world, but she was to Roger. He stood up from his seated position in the infant chair and looked at her face and said, "Roger. Roger Miller, Brooke's daddy." He smirked and knew he was blushing. "Not this shit again," he thought to himself. "It's nice to meet you."

"Likewise, Roger." She let go of his hand.

"I didn't know that…" he began.

"That Mrs. Smith was on Mat leave. Not every person has found out yet, but I knew that I would run into you or your wife eventually.

121

Oh my gosh, I'm so sorry. I forgot that your wife has passed. My bad Roger." She said.

"It's okay. She has been gone for two years now so the girls and I are learning new coping skills all of the time." Roger replied.

"A renaissance man." She said.

Roger couldn't help noticing that Miss Stevenson was a six-foot-tall knockout. She was the kind of woman Roger could never imagine being able to lure into his life. She was statuesque and slim. Her outfit had sheer sleeves in a light and airy type fabric in a paisley print. The skirt had a three-inch belt and was connected to the fabric that cascaded down to her ankles. It too was a soft material that enticed one to touch it and see if it felt as soft as gossamer wings. She completed the outfit with a pair of blinged out sneakers, obviously decorated by the girls in the class as a welcoming gift for her when Mrs. Smith left on leave. Her hair was honey blonde, halfway down her back with long bangs that she would sweep behind her ears as she was talking. Her teeth were straight, and her lips were nicely shaped. Overall, she was wonderful, he thought. "Mr. Miller," she asked him, "Are you going to sign up for our sports day activities? The kids participate in different games, and we need parents to help out with some of the organizing. Any chance we can get your name on that list?"

Before Roger had a chance to even consider, he heard himself agreeing to help out. Where would he find the time to participate? "Of course, Miss Stevenson. Where do I sign up?" He asked.

"It's Lori. Lori Stevenson but you are allowed to use my grown-up name. There is no sheet to sign but I will contact you when the time gets closer, and I'll let you know what tasks we need volunteers for, and you can just select one that fits with the time you can commit to. Does that sound okay with you Roger?" Through the strands of her fallen hair, her eyes glanced up through thick dark lashes to look for his reply.

"Of course. It will give me a chance to meet some of the other dads. Maybe even Mr. Stevenson." He added.

"Not much chance of that Roger. There's no Mr. Stevenson in my life except for my dad." She giggled.

"Yeah. That was a pathetic attempt at asking you if you are married. So, are you?" Roger asked.

"Not married but involved for a few years now. Does that have an influence on you being a volunteer?" She said.

"Absolutely not. I will join in gladly to spend time with my girls and get to know the other parents. Count on me Lori." Roger reaffirmed his sincerity.

"Thank you, Roger. You will be doing all of us a great service." Lori smiled.

By this point Brooke and Rose were ready to move on to Rose's classroom to continue the show and tell. They both grabbed their daddy's large, chunky hands and walked him out of the room. Roger couldn't help himself as he left the room, but he had to get one more look at this wonderful person. He turned his head ever so slightly and tried to disguise his last glance, but he was caught. When he peered off in Lori's general direction, she was staring right back at him. She gave him a pleasant smile and turned back to her other guests wanting her attention. Roger felt an unsolicited smile creep onto his face which his girls noticed and said, "What's so funny Daddy?" Rose asked.

"You two little angels are funny." He said.

Rose and Brooke were now beaming because their dad called them little angels. Even at eight and six years old they still loved compliments from their dad. Their hero. They made their way to Rose's classroom and did a replay on the visit with Mrs. Wade. She stood and chatted with Roger and told him how much she enjoyed Rose's company and her enthusiastic attitude that she brought to school with her every day. Rose was a joy to teach, she told Roger and he just gushed to her that other adults liked his kids. He knew that Michelle would be so proud to see the way these young ladies were turning out because he was proud of them also.

Later that evening, once all four of the girls had gotten off to bed, Roger talked to Anne about the replacement teacher. "You mean Miss Stevenson of course?" Anne questioned.

"Yeah. Lori Stevenson. I spoke with her for a few minutes tonight and she roped me into some volunteer work at the school." He said.

"Stop the car!" Anne belted out, "She managed to get you to say yes to something at the school. Well, well, well. And you got a first name. That is the first time you have ever known a teacher's first name. Who are you and what have you done with Roger?" She chuckled.

"It's not like that. She has a boyfriend." He said.

"Holy Kamaole! You actually asked her if she was single? I don't remember ever asking one of the male teachers at the kids' school if they were single. Let me think…no, it's never come up." Anne said.

"I didn't ask her. Well, I didn't mean to. We got to talking about this and that and she told me. That's it. I swear. However, if she were single, I would be interested in her. I thought she was a stunner. It has been a while since I felt something for another woman. But for a minute there sis, it felt nice." Roger adjusted his voice to a higher octave and said, "Always a bridesmaid and never a bride."

The two of them sat on the couch watching TV and laughed out loud.

"You never know what the future may bring Roger." She added.

***

Roger was upstairs in his office when Mitch showed up at the house the next day for a visit. Mitch headed to the garage beer fridge that Anne had purchased to keep her brothers happy. The two of them were so thrilled at this point of time in their lives to have a fridge dedicated to beer and other adult beverages that contain some percentage of alcohol. There were always a number of soft drinks used as mix in some drinks, but Roger and Mitch generally stuck to beer mainly because they loved it. Quick, easy, and available practically anywhere in the world. "Hey Roger, you wanna beer?" Mitch yelled upstairs to Roger.

"No dude. I'm good right now." Roger replied.

"So, bro, do you want beer?" Mitch asked, knowing the patented response.

"Yeah, sounds good." Roger said.

Mitch returned from the garage with the required quantity of beers for himself and Roger. He headed upstairs and went into Roger's office and sat down in one of the guest chairs in the front of the desk. "So, how is the wild world of dating going lately? Last time we talked you had gone out with the Russian lady, and you had already been cast aside from your evening of frivolity. Anything new on the horizon?" Mitch queried.

"I met one of the girl's teachers at the parent teacher night and I was pleasantly surprised. She was attractive and friendly. The real bonus is that both of my girls love this lady." Roger replied.

"So, did you make any plans to see her? What's the deal?" He asked.

"No plans. She was a lovely distraction for the evening. She told me that she is currently in a relationship with another man, so I simply backed off completely. Don't even know how I would feel if she was available because of the connection with both of the girls. It seems really weird to think about dating my daughter's teacher, however, I believe it would be worth a try and maybe go on just one date to satisfy my curiosity." He said.

"Your curiosity? Yeah right. So how hot was she?" He chuckled as he spoke.

"I'm not kidding Mitch. I don't know how weird it would be to date one of the kid's teachers, but I really liked her, well, what I know of her so far. We talked for a few minutes, so I really don't know her at all. Like I said Mitch, I would absolutely go out with her, at least once." He said.

"Well, with your dating record you typically only need one date to have something go awry and have her never speak to you again." He continued to laugh.

"Sure. All of this is pretty funny to you, but I am trying to connect with someone. I would like to have the company of a woman in my life again but there is so much more at stake now with the girls. That's why Lori, the teacher, was also appealing to me. My girls like her a lot. It will be tough finding a person that likes the girls, that the girls like her, and that she and I can co-exist. It's simple bro, if the girls don't like some potential mate I bring into their lives, it will be a short relationship. I just can't do that to them. They had already cried for almost a year when Michelle passed so, the last thing I want to do is have them go through any heartache again. I have to tread very carefully to attempt to not have their feelings hurt." Roger said.

"You're speaking of impossibilities bro. You can't protect them from that no matter what you do. And like so many kids, once they get a little older, they will start to have their own opinions about you and your significant other. This is something you cannot assure them or yourself of Roger. You will not be able to cocoon them for their entire lives unless you are considering locking them in the basement until they are twenty. I saw this episode on "60 Minutes" and it could be a swell alternative." He held up his hands mimicking a hand locking a door.

Roger giggled back at him. "Well, that's it then. Let's pop down to the hardware store, pick up some supplies, and get started on our user-friendly basement isolation unit guaranteed to stop young women from growing up." He said.

"I like the cut of your jib, Roger." Mitch responded. "Hide in the basement for approximately a dozen years and, presto, two girls that grew up completely safe from their father's future wives club."

"Ha-ha. Very funny Mitch. I'm being serious. I have to be overly cautious with online dating. So far it has been a bit of a bumpy ride." He said.

"Have you tweaked your online profile or is it the same one you started with? As you get more seasoned at this you are supposed to keep up with what you have learned along the way. It's not written in permanent ink, you know. You can amend your information if you think it could lure in some other fish. I'm just throwing it out Roger. I know you get fairly rigid about these kinds of things, but you must learn to be more flexible. Like in the Elvis song, 'I was an

oak, now I'm a willow, and I can bend.' You got to learn to bend."
Mitch said.

"Now you're quoting Elvis?" Roger said.

"He was the King! You better believe it baby." Mitch answered
in his best Elvis voice.

"Okay. I'll read through my profile and make some updates. It
can't hurt my chances at this point, right?" He asked Mitch.

"Not at all big brother. So, isn't there a game on we should be
watching? And I need another brewski, how about you?" Mitch
asked.

"You don't need to ask me twice." Roger said.

The two brothers made their way down the stairs and into the
large kitchen/family room area where Anne was sitting with a
couple of the girls doing a puzzle and the other two were watching
cartoons on TV before dinner. Roger didn't want to admit it to
anyone, but he was quite smitten with Lori Stevenson, however, he
knew that it would be a miracle if the two of them actually ever got
to go out on a real date. But he also thought to himself, "Stranger
things have happened." Minutes later Anne made the announcement
that dinner was to be served and that all should wash hands and
prepare for dinner. "Mitch, are you sticking around for dinner or are
you heading home?" She asked.

"Thanks sis but I gotta move along. Chanel has some stuff we must attend to tonight but thank you for the offer. It is always appreciated." Mitch replied.

"No worries Mitch. See you soon." She said.

***

After dinner, the group watched a Disney movie for the umpteenth time and snuggled under blankets in the family room for a spell. Then it was the kids off to bed and time for Roger and Anne to relax and decompress for the evening. Roger did go back to the dating site page to revisit the information and to see if possibly Mitch was right about making any changes to his profile, however, he couldn't do it. He could not convince himself to stretch the truth and try to be someone that he was not. It wasn't in his nature. He read over most of the data and decided that he really had represented himself exactly as he was, a single dad looking for romance and love. "What the hell does Mitch know anyway? He is still with the same lady that he started dating in high school, so how could he possibly know what women are interested in nowadays?"

Roger turned off the computer screen and went to bed.

Chapter Eight

Roger felt a certain sense of pride when he decided to check his dating site profile to find that there were even more seemingly bright and active women who had sent him positive feedback. Every time he got ready to pull out of the dating scene, he kept getting drawn back in by something. Positive feedback, you're great, can't wait to hear back from you, these are the types of comments that lure even the smallest of egos back into the game.

A woman named Mia caught his attention. She was of German background and had moved to Canada when she was late teens so assumed she would have a heavy German accent which Roger found all accents alluring. It was just so different to be speaking face to face with another person and they sound so completely different boggled his mind, but in a clever way. Intrigue was a good thing.

He had read her profile thoroughly and had noticed she was a bicycle enthusiast, which was most pleasing to Roger. A simple athletic endeavour that allowed you to chat or just ride in peace and quiet, always made it a lovely day out. Throw in a couple of breaks here and there, and the next thing you know, you've gotten to know that person a little better, usually. Roger was also elated that Mia lived in Port Coquitlam, which was a close-by neighbourhood so they could meet on their bikes and start their adventure from a local spot then head to their destination. Mia had said that at some point in her past she was a competitive cyclist and had ridden in some international races that Roger had actually heard of, which gained Mia even more credibility. However, in life the proof is in the pudding. He would give his final assessment once they had completed a ride together. The right weather and the right route would make for a smashingly momentous day.

Roger had also noticed that Mia was in her late twenties and nice looking. She had an athlete's build and seemed to maintain a low percentage of body fat, from what he could see from her profile pictures. He would find out soon enough. They agreed to meet on the following Saturday at a local eatery that was close to her house. Roger arrived early, grabbed a beverage, and proceeded to sit on the chairs outside while he waited for Mia to show up. Within a few minutes, a woman riding an all-black frame and tire bicycle with a black racing suit and of course, a black helmet, rode up and swung her one leg over as she glided the last twenty feet with poise and panache. She was eye-catching with very tanned skin. She appeared to be a person that spent many hours outdoors. She dropped her kickstand in one smooth motion and looked directly at Roger and said, "You're Roger?" She dipped her head in a yes motion at him. Roger nodded in agreement. "I will go get beverage and return so we can make some small talk and get out for a ride."

"Sounds great Mia." Roger concurred.

First impression was easy. She was a greatly confident woman when it came to her outward appearance and her bicycle skills but there was still so much more to find out. They planned out a route and she asked Roger if this was too much of a ride for a beginner. Roger was seething on the inside. He should not let her comment bother him at all, but his macho competitive side was raring to hit the trail and see who was still standing after a 100km day ride in the sunshine. "It's not a competition." he kept telling himself. "It's a date. It's supposed to be fun. Of course, that means as long as I am winning whatever the task/fun may be." She returned and had a mini cup of coffee and Roger inquired, "What type of coffee is that?" As he pointed to the cup in her hand.

"This is a quad shot of espresso just to jump start me. You must have some bike skills, Roger, to select a 100 km minimum ride with a person with whom you have never ridden. You definitely got some balls." She said.

She turned to face Roger, tipped her quad shot to her perfectly formed lips, and drained its contents. "I am ready! Are you good?" She asked.

"Yes." Roger stood up and tossed his almost full coffee into the trash bag, but he didn't want to be a bother when Mia was downing her quad shot. "No big deal," he thought, "It's just a run-of-mill $5.00 dollar coffee that I'm throwing away."

They stood up their bikes and she said, "I will take lead until we get onto the trails, if that is okay with you?"

"Sounds awesome Mia. I will be right behind you." He said.

She looked back at him over her shoulder and winked at Roger and said under her breath, "We'll see."

Within five to ten rotations of her pedals she was in full flight and was shifting up for more speed. Roger at first was pouring the coal to it but he could see she was slowly inching away from him. He could not believe it. Mia was playing snake in the grass but was actually a real athlete with some real biking skills. Touché. He knew that there was a long corner coming up with a 90 degree turn where she would have to ease up her radical pace to control her bike in the corner but then Roger would be right behind her again before they hit the trails. The first part that she had mapped out for them to ride had a steep incline for the first hour but then mostly long sweeping downhills with some sections that allowed experienced riders to push their bikes to tremendous speeds. As they started approaching the corner he could swear that Mia was speeding up not slowing down for a difficult turn when suddenly Mia locked up her brakes to the max and her bike began to shudder and shake as the rubber tires begged the pavement for assistance to slow down enough to take this first real test on the bike ride excursion but she mis-timed the turn and found herself having to lift up her lower leg knee to avoid it touching the hot pavement and scraping off any skin that may come into contact with it. As Mia completed the turn and rose back to a fully erect position, he knew that she had just escaped a terrible wipeout and even more so, a terrible embarrassment. Hitting the pavement on the first turn would not have been impressive. Memorable, but not impressive. Roger swung around the corner quickly but not with the same intensity that Mia had when he noticed that she was now riding at a reasonable pace and with a lot more control. This change pleased Roger because he did not want to race full-out all day. He wanted a bike ride not a triathlon. By the time they arrived at the trail's entrance the two of them had picked a speedy pace but not unreasonably quick. The two of them exchanged the lead position back and forth as they did the front-end hill climbing portion and Roger was blown away at the control and stamina that Mia was demonstrating. The only other woman he had seen as Mia's equal was his own sister Anne, who could have easily ridden in the Olympics. Roger found himself nodding and smiling with these new developments as they happened throughout their morning, but it was a good start to the day. They finally got to the apex of the ride and decided to pull their bikes off the trail and take a rest break. Roger was absolutely ready for a ten-minute sit down, as was Mia. As they sat and rested Roger asked Mia what she did for a living, and she explained to him that she had become a life-coach, assisting people with getting over things and helping give them a new direction to move on with their lives. She was excited as she relayed the information to Roger and seemed to genuinely care about her clients. Roger was impressed with her passion. Roger was also impressed with her bike riding skills. She powered up the incline without any hesitation or stopping for rest stops, which took Roger every fiber of his being to keep up with her to the top. This woman could ride a bike. Roger was also relieved that most of the remaining trek was downhill or flat grade, giving them the opportunity for a lot more conversation. So far Mia was turning out to be a delightful surprise.

They remounted their bikes and continued to follow Mia's predetermined route and had a wonderful time. They actually rode side by side a couple of times as the day went by and began to know each other a bit better. Overall, Roger liked Mia so far, which was a good thing. The big question would be later on, did Mia like Roger? Time would tell. When they began to return to the local streets that they lived on, Roger looked down towards a friend's house and saw that his brother Mitches' car was in Dave and Sue Anderson's driveway and was probably over for a visit. Roger shouted out to Mia, "Hey Mia, follow me back this way. My brother is over with his high school buddy Dave and his wife Sue's. We could stop in and impose ourselves upon them for a cold, intoxicating beverage, maybe?" He queried.

When they pulled down the driveway Mitch and Dave had their big fancy motorcycles sitting in the driveway in showroom condition. Dave and Mitch, as well as Roger, were all motorcycle enthusiasts. Roger had sold his bike years before because of a promise he had made to his wife Michelle not to ride until the girls were grown up and on their own. In Michelle's thinking that meant "Never ride again." Dave also had a street legal race car that always captured the imagination of men and women to see this older style car in factory condition. The car was a 1970 Cuda with the 440 cubic inch motor, which was ridiculously overpowered, but that was the nature of those types of cars back in the seventies. Mia pointed to the two glistening bikes in the sunshine and said, "Are these both Harleys?"

Dave immediately coughed in an incredulous way to make sure that Mia knew she had made a mistake of some kind. "No. This one, (As he pointed at his own Harley), is a Harley with all three phases completed. This one, (He pointed towards Mitch's bike), is a metric bike which can use any parts from any manufacturer there is. Plus, this bike is a third of the price of this bike." (He again pointed back at Mitch's bike).

"Sorry. It seems like I touched a nerve or something. But I am German from a town called Essen and we know the most superior bikes in the world are BMW motorcycles. Just ask any German and you'll see." She began laughing out loud at her own pun and the others got in on the joke.

"Yeah, they make top of the line bikes but some of the other machines just have a style that we covet in Canada." Mitch added.

"If that's true, where's your Harley?" She asked.

"My sons will need my bike's money for their university education. So, daddy gets this bike and shut up about it." He replied and gave her a smile.

"Understood." She said.

"How about everyone goes out to the backyard to the pool deck and relax? Can I twist your arms into sharing an adult beverage with us or if you wish, we have alternatives?" Dave asked the group.

They group headed to the backyard and Mitch took care of the introductions while Dave went to collect the required drinks.

"So, where abouts do you live Mia?" Sue asked.

"I am just a hop-skip-jump from here on Burke Mountain in one of the new developments. Been there for about five years now. How about you? How long have you been here at this house? I must tell you that I am horribly jealous of your pool deck and surrounding area. So beautifully kept and cared for. It shows that you both have a lot of pride." Mia said.

"We have been here for about ten years. Being at the end of a dead-end street simply means no speeding traffic down this street ever. It has been a nice and quiet place to reside." Dave responded.

Everyone had a drink now and Dave made a quick and pleasant toast to the group and to welcome Mia to their house officially. Sue piped up and asked if everybody had brought their swimsuits for a dip in the pool. Mia looked at Sue and said, "I have on only underwear under this outfit. Would it be okay if I just wore that to go into the pool?" She asked.

"Of course it is. We're all adults here and have seen people in their underpants, right?" She replied.

"Awesome." Mia stood up and made her way over to the edge of the pool and swooshed her foot around in the water to feel its temperature. "Oh, my goodness it feels like bath water. I can't wait to get in."

She just walked back over to the table that they all were sitting around and asked, "Is anyone else going in?" She asked.

"I am." Mitch said.

"Me too," replied Chanel.

"Yeah, I'll have a dip just to relax for a bit. How about you Sue?" Dave asked.

"No, I don't want to get my hair wet. Maybe a skinny dip later." She said back coyly.

Sue was just taking a big swig of Diet Coke when Mia dropped her bottoms and in the same split second removed her top and was now standing in the backyard wearing what appeared to be a G-string bottom cover and no bra to be seen. No sooner had she gone to semi-nude; Sue did a spit take on her pop that went the length of their pool. Sweet Sue was in a state of shock. It was like she had never seen a pair of naked breasts in her life. Mia was not shy, and she strutted across the backyard to the pool stairs and slinked down them into the water like she was a human on land but a mermaid when she entered the water. "Oh my god," she belted out, "This feels so amazing. Thank you, Dave, and Sue, for this beautiful break in our day. So deliciously unexpected." She disappeared again under the water and while she was under Roger, Dave, Mitch, and Chanel all returned in their swimming attire. It took a moment for the mermaid to resurface but she did and when she did everyone noticed instantly. Dave looked over at Sue and knew there was going to be a whole lot of judging in their house tonight but for now he hoped that they would just have fun with it. A group of adults just ogling one another for the sexual tension of it, or something like that. The second Chanel saw that Mia was topless she immediately said, "Oh my gosh, you lightened up on your pool rules I see. Thank goodness. I hate having to wear a top when I'm swimming around in a heated pool. She reached behind herself, pulled the upper and lower strings, and released her top that floated to the ground. Chanel was also a pro at entering a swimming pool in the most provocative way possible. On her way into the water Mia piped up and said, "Chanel you have lovely boobs. I'm so impressed. Are those real?"

"You bet they are," she said as Chanel slid under the water, when she reappeared from the liquid her nipples had gone hard and so had the boys who were all sitting together at the deeper end of the pool protecting their manhood's from anybody noticing they had grown a little bit in past few minutes. It was all so embarrassing for Sue; she needed a time out in the house to stop from looking at other girls' breasts. She had always had an issue with her own boobs over her life, but Dave insisted that she just leave them natural and that they were beautiful the way they were, however, Sue did notice that Dave always seemed to notice all other boobs that ever came through their little slice of heaven in the backyard and now it was two attractive women in her backyard showing the things that she promised herself to hide from the world at all costs. She crept up to the second floor of the house in one of the bedrooms overlooking the pool, so she could keep tabs on Dave and keep him safe from Satan, who, as it turns out, has a helper. Her name is Mia!

They all swam about and told stories and laughed and had a wonderful time. Sue finally worked up the courage to come back outside after a spell and sat down under the table umbrella and finished her drink. The rest of them had a mad time and loved the setting. It was a lovely space and a magical experience. Roger felt blessed to have such a lovely group of friends that would be so inclusive to a new person. Even Mia piped up and said, "I feel like I've known you guys forever. It doesn't seem possible that we just met today. Crazy, I tell you."

They all nodded in agreement and talked about moving on with their day, when Sue pleaded with Mia and Chanel to wrap up in a towel because all of the young lads in the neighbourhood had gone to the second-floor windows that overlooked the pool and she wanted to stop the peep show as quickly as possible. Dave rounded up the softest towels that any of them had ever felt. "Did they come this way, or do you have to do something to them to make them this bloody soft? It feels like an angora sweater." Mitch asked.

"Yeah. I use a heavy-duty fabric softener for a couple of cycles and, presto. Super soft towels." Sue replied.

"Amazing. They feel so good against my boobies." Mia said.

The group headed inside the house and all of the men of the neighbourhood could safely return to the main floors of their respective homes and go back to their lives. The swimmers got changed and gathered their things and headed for the front door. After the usual hugs and appropriate smooches, the two visiting couples headed on their way. Roger and Mia got back on their bicycles and peddled off and Mitch and Chanel got back onto his Kawasaki 1600 Nomad and off they rode into the sunset. Meanwhile Roger and Mia headed back to where the two had met in the morning and started their day off. When they arrived back at Roger's truck, there was no hesitation from Mia. She looked at him and asked, "Do you want to come back to my place and hang out for a bit? I have beer, wine, spirits, whatever you need. What do you think?"

"I think yes. Do you want to put your bike in the back of my truck, and we can just transport that way, would that be okay Mia?" He asked.

"Bloody rights. I all tuckered out from biking and swimming. I've done two parts of a triathlon. Only one part to go." She looked at him and winked.

He felt himself blushing again. He was so out of practice with women that he just ended up feeling like such a fool most of the time, but he knew it would all come back in time. Or he would find a new girlfriend. Hopefully.

They made the quick drive over to the new developments of Burke Mountain. He began to chuckle under his breath. "What's so funny?" She queried.

"This area used to be a riding school for young women. My sister Anne rode here for years and got a western style riding certificate. It is amazing to watch progress consume all of these old hang out spots we used to come to. This mountain is where Mitch, Dave, and I rode our dirt bikes around and there wasn't a house to be seen for miles and miles. It is kooky sometimes to see things change to the point of unrecognizable. Oh well, change is the only constant in life." Roger said.

"When I moved here it already looked like this, all grown up and developed. I really do like living here but I like anywhere in the lower mainland. It is all good with me. With my job I can set my own hours and work mostly from home except when I physically meet with a client." She explained.

They continued their drive until she instructed him to turn into that driveway, she indicated with her finger. Roger pulled into the driveway. He was starting to have a bit of an anxiety attack because for some reason he felt like they were coming back to her place to have sex. He only felt like this because of the casual attitude Mia had displayed over at Dave and Sue's house and now they were heading home to seal the deal and the comment about the third thing in their triathlon. He wasn't sure if he could resist her looks and straightforwardness. He was actually a little scared of Mia. Her confidence. He wasn't quite sure why, but he was scared. Mia exited the truck and went around to the back tailgate to wait for Roger to unload her bike. When he got down, he followed behind her to the door and leaned the bike against the front of the house. She looked at Roger in a curious way. "What are you doing Roger?" She faced him directly.

"I wasn't sure if we should end the date now when everything had gone so well, and you seem to still like me so I think I will call it a night and be on my way." Roger said.

"Yeah. I don't think so. You are coming inside, and we are going to watch a movie and sit with our feet up and I will give you a rub. How does that sound?" She asked.

"It sounds fabulous Mia. I would love to come in for a visit." Roger answered.

No sooner had they entered the house, she gave a quick tour of the up-to-date house with her hands waving around in the air and explaining where everything was located and she also added that there was a renter in the basement, but they shouldn't see or hear from HIM all night. They walked over to the sofa, and he plopped himself down and leaned back and relaxed as instructed. She walked into the open connecting kitchen, grabbed some beers, and put microwave popcorn into the machine to pop. Within minutes, the popcorn dinged, and she went and fetched it. She added real butter over the top of the product and hit it with a blast of salt. Yummy.

"I've got a movie you might like. It's called Grease. Have you ever seen it? You just have to. The songs are all so fantastic you'll be singing before you know it. Okay?" She asked Roger.

"Yes. I have seen it." He said. He didn't have the heart to tell Mia it was his deceased wife's favorite movie of all time. Roger had heard that music score so many times he could write all of the songs by hand if he had to, but he couldn't explain all of that to Mia. He just sat back and watched the movie as Mia gleefully sang along to every single note that was played. Quite shocking actually but he was not going to be a poopoo head and bring down the mood. After a brief time, Mia sat up and said, "Can we pause the movie so I can go pee? I'm sorry, maybe you have to go pee. Well, let's pause really quickly. Can you grab me another beer from the fridge Roger? Thank you." And off she went to her own bathroom and Roger made his way over to the fridge to gather the requested beverages. He swung the door open, and the fridge was well organized with things in little containers with labels and sticky notes and secret information plastered all over the place. Aha, there's the beer. There were so many red flags inside that fridge. She was definitely a fussy person and would be a handful to keep up to with her cleaning and organizing. It was a lot to try and take in, until Roger started to close the fridge door and just about shit his pants when the door swung shut there was a man standing in front of him wearing a super happy likeable face that immediately said, "Hey dude, you must be Roger.

Mia said she was going on a date with someone today." The man stated.

"Yeah. Roger. Who the heck are you?" Roger retorted.

"I'm Frank. I'm Mia's husband." He said.

A voice from down the hallway yelled back in a not too friendly fashion said back, "You're not my fucking husband anymore. I have filed for divorce. You have to sign the papers so we can get on with our lives, Frank. You have to let me live my own life now…please." As tears streaked down Mia's cheeks.

"Exactly Mia. I have not signed those documents so you should not be having strange men over to our house for a sex rendezvous. You should be respectful and wait until the divorce has been completed. What's your say in this Roger?" Frank asked.

"I have no comment, Frank. But I think that this evening has come to an end, and I must bid you both adieu." Roger said. He started to move backwards out of the kitchen to leave space between the two lovebirds and head for the front door.

"I'm still waiting for your answer Roger. Do you think Mia should be dating other men when she is still married? Does that seem right to you Roger?" He questioned.

"My answer is that I didn't come here to get involved in some family battle. I went for a really nice bicycle ride with Mia today and I was just dropping her off, so I am going to get moving along and Mia, give me a call if you can get all of this worked out." Roger said.

"Frank, you're such an asshole. Roger, this shit has been going on for a couple of years now, but I can't get rid of this leach. He won't sign the papers and he tries to ruin every single date I've been on. I was surprised that he didn't ride past us on the trail or was having coffee in the same café as us today. He has been doing this crap for too long now and this has to stop Frank. I MEAN IT! You are driving me nuts." She barked at Frank.

"You're so full of shit Mia. You know you still love me. You just bring all these guys home to make me jealous, well, it's working. You got my attention." Frank answered.

"I don't want your attention. I want you sign the papers and move the FUCK out of my house." She said.

"Our house. You mean our house." Frank replied.

"Frank for the love of sweet Jesus, please move on with your life. I can't take this anymore. You ruined my life as a couple and now you are trying to ruin my life as a single. I am going to have a moving company come by and start packing my stuff. I will be gone by the end of the week, Frank. This has to end and you're not willing to end it." She said.

"And you call yourself a Life Coach. You're so lucky your clients can't peek inside your secret 'life at home' box and see what a complete screw up you are. If they knew the real you, they would be running in another direction…looking for someone that can actually give some sage advice." Frank smirked a bit because he thought his remark was clever.

SLAP. Mia's hand hit Frank's left cheek with a powerful blow that he really deserved. The room went still. No one moved an inch. Roger wanted to stay the hell out of this, but it was too late, he was in it. Frank's demeanor was rapidly changing from argumentative, hurt, boyfriend into beast mode. Roger moved himself between the two combatants to try and diffuse the situation that was escalating. Roger was bigger in size than Frank, but he did not want to have to fight with one of his dates' husbands. What the hell was next? While that thought was going through his head, Frank, in anger, lashed out at Mia and out of pure instinct Roger grabbed his hand before it could make contact with Mia's face. He swung Frank's arm around to his backside and…snap. He had broken Frank's right arm. Roger released the hand he was about to hit Mia in the face with and spun Frank around and placed him on a bar stool that was sitting nearby.

He knew that in a couple of minutes Frank would start feeling a lot of discomfort and pain.

"Why the hell do you do that?" Mia asked.

"I stopped him from hitting you in the face Mia. I'm not going to allow any man to rough up a lady whether she is my wife, girlfriend, or just a female friend. I will not stand for violence against women. No how, no way." Roger explained.

"Well now how is he to pay his half of the mortgage if he is now going to be out of work. Thanks for nothing." She said.

"A minute ago, you were having a moving truck pull up tomorrow and remove all of your belongings for good. Do you remember that speech?" Roger asked.

"I don't feel so good. I think I'm going to…blah." Frank said as he sprayed hot vomit around the kitchen like an outdoor hose swinging wildly.

Roger grabbed him so he wouldn't fall onto the floor and eased him onto the sofa. He was already starting to melt down, not for just what had happened a moment ago, but what had happened for a while now. The waterworks started gushing down his cheeks, and he began telling Mia he was going to change. He would buy that life insurance policy. He would get a dog. He would call her mother more often. Roger was easing his way again back towards the front door to make his escape, but Frank yelled out though the tears, "Roger, did you fuck my wife? Did you play with those perfect boobies? Well, did you?" He asked.

"No Frank, Mia is still as pure as new snow. We never even kissed. But on that note, it sounds to me like you two have a lot of things to discuss so I will just be heading now and say thank you for a…day." Roger said.

As Roger was closing the front door, he could hear Mia trying to soothe her man back to life, however, somebody needed to get that boy an ambulance in a hurry. Frank was hearing all the things that he had been wanting to hear from Mia for a long time now. Kindness and interest. Things she had been holding back from him because of what he was holding back from her. Co-operation and affection.

Roger stood on their front door landing and thought to himself, "Maybe I should be a matchmaker. Date me once and your ex is bound to take you back."

A few hours later Roger was sitting in the theatre room in the basement of Anne's house when the police walked in with their weapons pulled and said, "Roger Miller, you are under arrest for assault and battery on a Mr. Frank Heinz. Anything you say can and will be used…"

Roger was taken into custody by the Coquitlam RCMP detachment and taken to the local station for questioning. Once the police had a chance to review all of the information and the proposed charges against Roger, they seemed to settle down fairly quickly after it had been affirmed that Roger was only trying to protect Mia from what Roger believed was potential harm by her estranged husband Frank. Even Frank gave a full confession on Roger's behalf that he was being a decent human being and simply trying to protect Mia. The fact still remained that Roger did break Frank's arm and there would most likely be a civil suit brought against Roger, but it would be difficult to make anything stick because of the circumstances of Roger's actions to protect a young woman who was potentially in harm's way, so the police had no real issue with Roger. Frank was going to be up on assault and battery charges for attempting to come after Mia, but it would most likely not be any jail time for the first offence and Mia was not going to press charges for the incident. She wanted to move past this occurrence and get back to living her life with Frank. Having Roger over to the house that day seemed to really light a spark under Frank and Mia's behinds to get them back on track as a loving couple rather than two lost souls. When she saw how vulnerable Frank was that evening, it altered her view of him from zero back to hero because he exposed his true self in front of her and Roger. Mia had decided while they were at the police station that she was going to find a way to make this marriage work. Mia was a fighter, and she wouldn't go down without a fight and Frank, for the first time in forever, felt the sense of pride a man gets when he has somebody that is in his corner rooting for him. Roger realized that his one-day fling with Mia may have been the best thing that could have ever happened to the two of them and he was delighted. Before Roger left the police station, he sought out Frank just to make amends and say he was sorry for hurting him, but Frank had brought this trouble upon himself and Roger did what he was taught by his parents to do, DON'T let men hit women. Ever.

A few days later Roger got some mail from Mia. He was ready to open the envelope containing the paperwork for something awful but no, it was an invitation to the Meadow Gardens Golf and Country Club for a "Renew the Vows" for Frank and Mia Heinz. Roger was so happy for the both of them. Then he promptly threw the invite away.

***

While Roger was in the RCMP Detachment, he did notice a well poised young woman in her uniform looking professional and friendly. He decided to smile and wave even though he was in the station currently as a suspect/criminal until proven Innocent or at least released from custody. Time passed while he sat on different benches throughout the building while waiting to be interviewed by the duty officers and so, when Roger had asked if he could be escorted to a bathroom, they concurred and walked him down the hallway to a men's room. Once he completed, he stepped out of the W/C and headed back down the hallway to the front, but this woman just happened to be in the hall at the same time. She stopped completely in front of Roger, thrust her bottom out and bent over to drink from the water fountain. While she was fetching her drink Roger had to stop and wait for her to finish because there was not enough space to get past each other at one time in the tight confines of the office hallway. When she had finished quenching her thirst she stood up and turned, accidentally, right into Roger as he attempted to slip by her undetected. "Oh, excuse me miss, I was just trying to get by you, so sorry." Roger explained.

"No worries," she replied, staring directly into his eyes.

He giggled a bit and then said, "What's a nice girl like you doing in a place like this?"

"Just living the dream. How about you? What brings you into our little slice of heaven today?" She said.

"Well, I'm embarrassed to tell you, but I have been brought here because I broke a man's arm for threatening a woman with bodily harm, so my instincts took over and I grabbed him and stopped him from doing anything stupid, however, it turns out I still did something stupid, like breaking the dude's arm." Roger answered.

"Who said that chivalry is dead? Bring on a modern hero." She laughed.

"I don't think your sergeant sees me in that light. Currently I am a criminal in custody. I don't want to seem forward but, what's your name?" Roger inquired.

"Holly. Holly Christie. And how about you? What's your name?" She asked.

"Roger Miller. My friends call me Roger but my family still calls me idiot and a few other notable names but that should be enough for you to get started." He said.

"So, idiot, are you a local man or from parts way out yonder?" She smirked.

"You know what they say Holly. If you are going to get arrested by police, most people will do it within three miles of their own home. Wasn't sure if you knew that little gem of info. But feel free to use it as you wish." Roger said in a laughing manner.

"Well Roger, it's been nice chatting with you, but I must return to my desk. You know, work and all of that stuff, trying to catch criminals. I am going to give you my business card just in case you have any questions or just want to discuss crime as a subject, I would like to hear from you. Maybe you could show me some of your self defense moves. I hear they're mighty effective." She passed him the card and winked. She held her fingers up in the "call me" type way so Roger got the message loud and clear.

"Sounds awesome Holly. I will call you." Roger said. As Roger exited the Police Station the next morning, having been there for most of the night, he still felt like it was a win – win situation. He had helped Frank and Mia find each other again and he might have found a pretty cool lady cop to ask out. He stepped outside the front door and realized; my truck is over at Mia's house. Roger sat down on a bench in front of the building and called an Uber. He couldn't let the family know that something else completely insane had happened on one of his dates. Besides, dad was just starting to forget about the "Idle Times" sinking.

***

Roger pulled up to Holly's apartment building at 6:30 pm for their 7:00 pm dinner reservations at The Boathouse Restaurant in downtown Port Moody which was nestled up against the edge of the water beside Rocky Point Park and all of its festivals and activities. It was one of the city's busy spots over the summer months because its location was perfect, especially for a romantic interlude. Roger's hopes were high.

Holly looked fantastic. It was difficult to tell this was the same woman from the police station a couple of weeks ago because of her stunning transformation. Her hair was brown, down to her waist, smooth and silky like chocolate, with large open curls throughout. She was wearing a fitted dress that came to her knees and was fashioned from a fabric that had a certain peek-a-boo effect as she slinked through the front doors of the restaurant. She stood about five feet, six inches tall so she was right in Roger's wheelhouse. She was not afraid of colour because her dress could have been seen from miles away with a bright yellow background and the bold blood red flowers making their way through the print. Spaghetti style shoulder straps completed the dress which allowed her beautiful olive skin to shine like she had just been oiled up for a Ms. Olympia competition. Her makeup was subtle but stunning. She had adored herself with some jewelry, but every piece deserved to be part of the ensemble. The host approached the couple and said, "If you could please follow me, I will take you to your table now." He led them to a table beside the fireplace with a view of the picture windows encompassing the splendid vista in front of them. "Your waiter will be over shortly and will bring your menus to tell you the specials." He said.

Roger clasped Holly's hand in a gentle manner and said to her as he leaned in closer to her, "I know that one of the specials of the night is the outfit you have put together this evening. I feel a little embarrassed because I can't stop staring at you. You are stunning Holly." Roger preached.

"Oh my gosh Roger. You are such a flirt. I didn't know about this side of you but let's face it, we did meet at the police station, so it is tough to get a real read on people when you are there." Holly replied.

"That is true Holly. It is a place where it can sometimes be a bit tough to really be yourself." Roger said.

Soon the waiter came and took their drink and appetizer order to get things started. Within minutes hot scrumptious food was taking up the available inches on the dining table while the two chatted and laughed like old friends who were getting caught up after a long time apart. Roger was loving every part. The room, the vibe, the music, the company, this was working out really well until…the topic of equal pay for equal work. Roger immediately piped in and said whole heartedly to Holly that he was 100% behind women making the same wages in the workforce if they are doing the exact same job. Roger watched his mother Maxine fight tooth and nail to climb the corporate ladder at IBM over the years but even though they preached a delightful story, it just wasn't true. Men climbed the ranks faster than women and men got paid faster and higher than women. It was total baloney, but it was a fight that Roger was well versed in and probably didn't deserve a full lecture on it while out on a dinner date and he had already confirmed that he thought it was unfair practices, at any company. It was simple, equal work means equal pay, or at least it did to Roger, however, he had never really met Holly before today.

Holly got up on her virtual high horse and got to discussing the fairness to women in the workplace and gender biases. She started with those two isms to create her theme and just seemed to build from there. Before Roger knew it, they were ordering dinner and he still had not asked her any questions about her, but she continued to go down the path of the world is tough because men have ruined everything already. "So little time, so much to save," Roger thought to himself. Clearly this HOT topic was one that Holly had given a lot of thought to and had come up with many ideas and potential solutions that could be put into place if we could only elect the right leader. "Like a woman?" Roger piped in.

"Exactly Roger. It is so refreshing to speak with a man that has an open mind when it comes to these tender topics. You are such a great listener Roger I am just having a wonderful time talking with you." She said.

"Me too Holly. Just terrific. So, do you have any hobbies that you are into? Basket weaving. Painting carousel horses. Teaching underwater treasure hunting? What does Holly do for fun?"

Before he could finish the question Holly wanted to know if Roger had any women on his construction team and if yes…do they make the same as their male counterparts. Luckily for Roger he only hires trades as required on the projects so that it was totally out of his hands, so he thought.

"So, if you need a plumber for some work, would you hire a male or female?" She asked.

"I would hire the person best suited to that exact project, and who can get it done on time, and come at the requested price. If those qualifiers were all met by a woman, then she will FOR SURE get the work." He said.

"That's a conclusive answer." She agreed.

"I'm sure it would be the same for you Holly. If your detachment required another Detective on staff, I'm sure that you would follow all of the protocols and procedures to find the best available match for that position, right?" Roger asked.

"Well don't get me going on how many women make Detective and then can maintain a leadership role in a RCMP unit." She continued.

Roger felt like a politician's son. You just gotta sit there and take it. It's part of the job. Roger was beginning to figure it out. He may date for the remainder of his life to find the right person, but it would be worth going through some of these interludes to find an updated version of true love. Currently he needed to do the right thing and show all of them an enjoyable time. And why not? Not in a sexual way. In a fun way. That way it's easy for both parties. Fun times like in an old Elvis Presley movie, and everyone hangs out and sings like it's their first time to ever do it. Well, that is when Roger vowed to do it, no matter how silly it may seem to others, he was resolved to see all of these encounters through. He was becoming resolute in his goal. He started to feel a weight being lifted off his shoulders. He was going to allow for things to turn out organically. Go on some dates and have some fun and meet new people. It didn't have to be let's find a nice girl and get married anymore. Roger had already done that. It was time to go out on adventures with new people and hopefully find a fabulous new lifelong friend. Roger was at peace.

He zoned back into the non-stop rantings from Holly, who still occupied the chair across the table from him. She was a lovely woman but certainly not his type of partner. He continued to smile and take in the comfortable ambience that filled the restaurant that evening with the waterfront views and terrific food selections. Roger was okay with just letting it happen, and to stop trying so hard to find the next Mrs. Right.

Holly finally took a breath in her own political debate with herself over who knows what topic she was covering and asked Roger, "So are you going to have some dessert?"

Roger mumbled for a moment. He wasn't prepared to speak because it had been so long between sentences, but he managed to get out, "Yes, the cheesecake please." He quickly answered.

Holly had begun to soften her stance on how women are repressed in everything they do once she had consumed a second glass of Chardonnay and could see that Roger was just not a fighting type and was a reasonable person with an understanding of women's rights and issues and the willingness to listen to outside opinions. However, Holly also knew that Roger was not the one for her. The two continued their quiet encounter and enjoyed the experience as it was, rather than a prelude to a kiss.

The waiter came by the table to settle the check. He placed the small folder onto the table beside Roger and said, "Sir, when you are ready."

Roger knew that Holly was about to blow a gasket. Put the bill down beside the man. What the hell was this waiter thinking? But surprisingly Holly merely glanced at the bill and said, "Excuse me, could we have separate checks please."

"Are you sure Holly? I am more than happy to pay for the both of us to share this meal together. It would be my pleasure." Roger said.

"No. I am an independent person that does not need a man to come and rescue me from a dining room table every time I go out, thank you very much." Holly stated.

"I am deeply sorry for this inconvenience, Miss. I will run your bill through separately." The waiter responded. The waiter disappeared into the backdrop of the room and Roger and Holly continued to discuss some of the places that they both had on their bucket lists for travel when the waiter returned to the table looking very sheepish and clearly had a feeling of angst about his findings. "Excuse me miss, but your card was declined. Do you have any other cards that you would prefer to use?" he asked gently.

"Oh, my goodness. After all this talk about it tonight and then it had to happen to me, right? It just goes without saying that my credit card that I have used for a decade has decided to stop working tonight when I am out with a man. Just freaking great." Holly said.

"Miss we also take cash if that is easier." The waiter added.

"No. That won't be necessary. I am also going to enjoy a piece of that humble pie out in the kitchen that I've been smelling all night. In the meantime, could you please add this bill to the gentleman's bill for me." she said as she passed the bill back to Roger. Roger dug out his credit card and whisked the waiter away to stave off some of the embarrassment that had been mounting within Holly, but it was too late for that.

"It's just a silly accounting accident Holly. No harm, no foul." Roger said.

"Well Roger I must admit that you really are a gentleman. Most men would love to throw that one back in my face, but you are a calm and respectful person and I thank you for that." Holly replied.

The drive back to Holly's house was a quiet one. The two of them knew their destinies were not going to be together but Roger's epiphany earlier that night had made him feel different about dating. He felt like he had accepted what he was doing and realized that this was one of the ways he was going to try and capture his unicorn. He had to keep trying. They pulled up in front of the building and they said goodbye. She got out of the car and turned back towards Roger's open window and said, "You really are a good man, Roger. I wish you success with your future." And she went inside.

Roger drove home with the windows down listening to the local oldies radio station and enjoyed the rest of the evening.

Chapter Nine

Roger decided to start doing more research before he went on future dates with the women that had agreed to go out with him. Checking out their Facebook account for instance, to see what some of these potential dates have been doing. He wanted to know more about them, but he often felt like he was spying on them by reading through all of their social media postings. However, if they posted the information or images, they must have decided that it was safe for others to see. That included him.

The weather was warm, and Roger wanted to get out with Rose and Brooke to do some family activities, but he also had the urge to go away on a weekend excursion with a woman and do some grown up things, which did not include his daughters: otherwise, they would end up catering to the juvenile ideas of entertainment. As fun as that could be, Roger was looking for something a little more sophisticated. He had been in contact with Jennifer Newsome, who lived close by to Roger's neighborhood and they had been trying to find a time to go out and meet for coffee before committing to something on a grander scale. They made plans to meet at a local brew house, beer that is, at the halfway point between their respective houses. Jennifer arrived on her bike, as did Roger, and put her kickstand down. The two of them exchanged pleasantries and headed inside to order a beer from the menu. They both got distinct types of beer and headed back outside to an area in front of the brewery with adorable little tables, umbrellas, and chairs. The space was beautifully decorated, and the furniture was arranged in an inviting layout that felt conducive to basking in the sun, drinking refreshing beverages. The place was not too busy, so finding seats was easy. Once they plopped themselves onto the oversize lounge chairs that were scattered about, they laid back and allowed the alcohol and the sun to do what they do best…relax people. Jennifer and Roger spent the next couple of hours lazing about on the cushy pillows while getting a comfortable vibe from each other. Roger got up to get another round of drinks and when he came out into the blinding sunlight he looked over at Jennifer and had a wow moment. He was extremely careful to be sure that she had not seen him have that Zen response to her charms. It was too early. Too soon. Roger gave his head a shake. Was it the beer and too much sun? He looked over at Jennifer and began to really look at her. Her golden-brown skin and long legs wagging about in the air like a silly girl that doesn't mind what others may think of her. She was clad in bike shorts and a stylish sports bra that she filled out magnificently. The fabric was bright with brilliant colours that made her look feminine and friendly. She seemed to be smiling at all times. Roger placed the drinks down in front of Jennifer and sat down beside her, then it happened. She looked at Roger and said, "Could I try your beer?

I've not had that flavour before." She picked up the beer and again looking into Roger's eyes said, "You don't mind?"

"Of course not. Help yourself." He said.

She picked up his beer glass and tipped the liquid back until she had finished almost all of the glass, lowered it down, looked at Roger and said, "I like mine better. Let's get two more."

Jennifer then leaned towards Roger and said, "Come close to me. I have to whisper something to you."

Roger leaned in and started positioning his ear to hear this secret when she grabbed his chin between her thumb and index finger and held him steady and…burp! She burped and blew Roger in the face. He began laughing out loud because it used to be one of Michelle's trivial things that she would do. He was always thinking, "Who does shit like that?" But she did and that was part of her charm. Then, from outer space, Jennifer gives him a burp and blow on their first date. What are the odds of that happening, Roger thought to himself? This extreme act of familiarity towards him made him take a greater interest in Jennifer instantly. From that moment on they began to "hit-it-off" and enjoyed each other's company that wonderful sunny afternoon. After a couple of hours, they had decided to call it a day. Jennifer had plans in the city that night with her parents and Roger knew he had all four girls waiting for him back at the house. They exchanged handshakes but when Jennifer went to mount her bicycle

Roger squeezed her hand and gave her an open hug. She leaned into Roger and gave him a kiss on the lips and said, "Let's do this again Roger. I had a fun time. God only knows if you can pull this off a second time or are you a one-trick-pony?" She gave Roger a healthy elbow in the ribs and said, "Later."

Roger collected his riding gear and mounted his bike. He was definitely intrigued with Jennifer and started to plan the next possible outing.

***

After much deliberation, Roger asked Jennifer out on a real date with all of the trimmings. He had selected the Lift Restaurant in Coal Harbour, Vancouver. It was a lovely setting that overlooked the Royal Vancouver Yacht Club and Stanley Park seawall with the Lions Gate Bridge as the backdrop. Most of the walls were able to be opened up on the warmer days of summer and with their long, billowing draperies, the winds drifted in and out of the main dining area and created picturesque scenes. There were small, round tables and chairs and lower profile soft loungers throughout the space. It looked like a multi-million-dollar home in an Architectural Digest Magazine. They entered through the front doors and were greeted by the hostess who promptly escorted them to their waterside table. The air was warm and smelled of evergreen trees and a hint of ocean breeze. Mother nature was truly showing off Vancouver's beauty on this evening.

As the night progressed, Roger and Jennifer ate and drank an abundance of delicious treats and leaned back into their chairs after the meal was done, exhaled a big breath and relaxed. Roger had his hand resting on his own knee when he felt Jennifer cup her hand over his in a sign of approval. Jennifer could sense that Roger was a decent human being with long-term boyfriend potential. That made her smile. As the evening pushed away the light to darkness, all of the decorative lights that enhanced the Lift's ambience came twinkling to life and made for a spectacular evening presentation for the two diners that night. They both knew that this was special.

Roger asked Jennifer if she was okay with him paying the bill and she confirmed it with a yes and a smile. She really was turning out to be a pleasant woman and didn't seem too militant about opening doors for her and being, what he was taught, was gentlemanly behaviour. They collected their belongings and made their way back to Roger's pickup truck. Roger walked around to the passenger side and opened Jennifer's door and placed his hand in a position to assist her getting into the truck, but she coyly sidestepped his balancing tool and slid her arms around his waist and hugged him as hard as she could. She liked this guy, and she was going to make bloody sure that he was aware of this fact. They smooched beside the truck for a couple of minutes, but Jennifer didn't want to appear too eager, so she embraced his large body one more time then released his waist and climbed up and into the cab of the pickup. "Okay Roger. I'm ready." She announced.

The two of them held hands as they drove down the highway back to Jennifer's house. She found herself doing something totally out of character because she realized that she had pulled Roger's hand towards her mouth, and she kissed it as they drove through the night. She couldn't even remember the last time she demonstrated that level of affection towards anybody. It was light years away. "What the hell is coming over me," she thought to herself. Play it cool. Don't have this guy thinking you are ready to give up the farm on the first real date. She knew better than this. But there was something about Roger. They continued their conversation about fabulous overnight outings in the lower mainland of Vancouver and they both agreed that Harrison Hot Springs Hotel and Spa might be a nice spot to go to and spend a weekend together. It was not too far from the city, and it still had an out-of-town feeling when you were at the resort. Much of that was because of the way the building was situated on the property that created a destination resort vibe by the front façade facing onto to the lake, which was exceptionally large and stretched out for many miles of open water but surrounded by a ridge of low mountains that created an edge to the entire vista. The two decided that Harrison was the place to try an overnight encounter. Roger said that he would look after the planning to get everything booked and paid for, and Jennifer simply said yes. By the time Roger had been able to book a room at the resort it wasn't for a few weeks but that was good because it would allow Roger to spend a couple of full weekends with his girls and not be distracted by going out on any dates.

Roger pulled his truck into the turnaround at the front entrance of Jennifer's apartment building and came to a stop. He opened his door and got out to help Jennifer exit the vehicle on the passenger side. When he came around and opened her door she had decided to sit and wait and allow Roger to help her get down out of the cab. Roger was delighted that she was not going to be too militant and let him help her down to the sidewalk. She stood in front of him for only a moment and then leaned in for one quick kiss on the cheek and off she went through the glass entrance doors. It happened so fast Roger barely got to say, "See you in a couple of weeks. I will send you the itinerary for our Harrison excursion." he said as the automatic glass door closed behind her.

***

While Roger was planning out his romantic weekend with Jennifer, he had decided to pull a favour from an old friend, Bob Henkel, who owned Sky Helicopters in Pitt Meadows, which was less than one hour away from Harrison Hot Springs as the crow flies.

Roger was going to see if he could get a helicopter ride on the weekend that the two of them were planning to take together. He had hoped that on Saturday they could stay the night at the hotel, and then go for a few hours in the helicopter on Sunday morning. Needless to say, Roger anticipated that Jennifer would be thoroughly impressed with the room and then a flying excursion to boot. He was feeling good about the arrangements he had solidified for their weekend away.

The plan was to pick up Jennifer at her apartment and drive up to Harrison Hot Springs on Saturday morning. They could wander around the town for a couple of hours and check into the hotel at 3:00 pm and go for a relaxing swim in one of their many available pools. Roger figured that they could enjoy an afternoon dip before they were to get ready for dinner in the Copper Room with a live band and dancing until the wee hours. Roger had attended other events here in the past with his family at Christmas a few times and even on New Year's Eve when Mitch, Anne, and him were much younger. Nonetheless, the family had a certain familiarity with the resort. For many years previously, Harrison Lake was the official spot for the Annual Sandcastle Building Contest that took place each summer in August and would draw thousands of guests to the little city and flood into all the bars and restaurants and make a small town feel like a big town for a couple of weeks per year. It was chaotic but still maintained its charm as a lakeside resort.

When the two got into town that day Roger dropped Jennifer off at the Lobby Entrance and gave his truck keys to the valet. Already he could start to feel the burdens of life lifting off of his shoulders. The Bellboy attended to them with a cart for their luggage, put everything on board, and scooted down the main hallway to the elevator core. "DING" the empty elevator announced its arrival and the three of them got on board. Seconds later they had been whisked to the top floor of the main building and followed the bellboy down the hallway to their suite. When the bellboy opened the door to the room, he said out loud, "This is my favourite room in this building." He gave a quick demonstration of the room and its attributes, turned on some lights and put the bags in the bedroom. "Is there anything else I can get you Mr. Miller?" He asked.

"No, thank you." Roger reached out and gave the young bellboy a twenty-dollar bill, and he nodded and started to head for the exit door. As he walked out Jennifer slipped a ten-dollar bill into his hand, and she gave him a friendly thank you nod. The two new friends went straight to the balcony door and whipped it open to let the cool, fresh lake air into the suite. The room was exquisite for its view and convenient location in the town of Harrison. Right in the middle of the beach and surrounded by all of the local eateries and bars that made up the town of Harrison Hot Springs. Jennifer grabbed a couple of bottles and began blending some things together to make drinks for her and Roger. She returned to the deck with a tall glass filled with a greenish liquid and Roger said, "Oh I know this one. This is a Margarita, right?" He hoisted the full glass and let it pour down his throat and some managed to spill onto his shirt, but he didn't care. Not that day. He just wanted to relax with another adult and possibly be a bit intimate. They stayed in the room for a few hours and started to get ready to go for dinner in the hotel restaurant, "The Copper Room," for their 7:00 pm reservation. They both got dressed up in nice clothes. Jennifer wore an A-line wrap around dress that always hugs a woman's curves beautifully. The dress was white bamboo and appeared soft and supple to touch. She adorned her outfit with all silver jewelry accessories from necklaces, bracelets, earrings, and an anklet, with her hair in an updo and just a couple of long, well-formed ringlets hanging down to balance the look of her radiant face. With her shiny red cheeks, from all of the sun that day, Jennifer looked alluring. Roger looked on with an approving gaze. He had put out some effort also. He was wearing a white raw silk suit with an electric blue shirt and white, high gloss loafers. It looked as though he was going to attend a white party, where all of the attendees wore white clothing to the function. He finished the look with a light brown leather woven belt with a silver buckle. The two of them stopped at the door to their room and looked in the full-length mirror hung beside the exit, and they looked at each other and themselves and they were happy with the results. They were all dolled up and ready for some fun. Within minutes they had arrived at the Copper Room. The Hostess took them to their table and got them seated comfortably. Moments later the waiter came and confirmed the drink orders and they now felt like they could just sit back and relax. All the heavy lifting was done. Roger raised his glass in the air towards Jennifer and said, "Here's to the two of us having a nice, quiet evening. Cheers." He said. "And of course, here's to you looking the way you do. You are a vision, Jennifer."

"Oh Roger, you're making me blush. Stop it." She replied coyly.

The waiter came to the table to describe in detail all of the specials, but it was already a done deal when Jennifer found out that the kitchen was featuring a seafood extravaganza and would have all the different seafood varieties available to try in a Spanish Cuisine style and heat. They both ordered the seafood special and bottle of Chianti to help wash it all down. When the food basket came to the table there was no room left on the table. The seafood cornucopia had so much in the basket that the two of them had a bit of a laugh at first because they felt embarrassed at the amount of food that had been delivered to the table. The bowl had a zesty and steamy essence to it when it sat on the table. It looked and tasted spicy, which was exactly what they had wanted. Something different.

A good amount of time had passed when Roger and Jennifer had discovered that they had eaten all of the seafood and drank all of the wine. They had discussed the possibility of dessert but had decided to go back to the room and see if anything tasty popped up. They returned to the room and decided on a movie to watch. They both got into their cozy clothes, grabbed some sugary treats, and plopped themselves down on the sofa with some pre-made popcorn. The excitement was building, the two of them were finally alone, no interruptions. Roger came to from his slumber a few hours later. Jennifer was out cold and sleeping with her head on Roger's lap. The excitement of the day had taken its toll on the two of them and it would seem that they were not able to stay awake and fulfill the hanky-panky plans they had formulated. When they awoke on the sofa, they quickly moved from the sofa to the king size bed and continued to rest. Roger had made plans for him and Jennifer to take a helicopter flight around the local area and up the valley to Hope and swing back down to Pitt Meadows for fuel and then drop them off back at the beach across the street from the hotel in the late afternoon. The views were going to be second to none. Roger was expecting smooth sailing because the turbulence can bounce you around quite a bit when you are airborne. Before you know it, you end up feeling seasick. It is simply caused by motion, but it can hit some riders hard. Most people never go up in a helicopter long enough to get sick because it costs so much to rent a whirly-bird for anything over a couple of hours worth of airtime.

Roger and Jennifer walked out the front door of the Harrison Hot Springs Resort and could see the Bell helicopter sitting on the beach with its rotor spinning around slowly across the street. They both trotted over the crosswalk and made their way to the closed doors on the helicopter. The pilot was sitting in the front left seat and signaled for the two of them to open the back door and let themselves in, put on the headphones so they could hear each other, and the safety belts to keep them both secure in their interior positions, as the helicopter was flying. Within a few minutes the pilot had run through the safety check with Roger and Jennifer, and they were ready to head out for an exciting day until it happened, gurgle gurgle, sloppy slop. Roger knew that sensation. It was the sensation that tells you that you are going to be in or near a bathroom for the rest of the day. "Was it something I ate?" He thought to himself. Roger was not a betting man at the best of times, but he knew all too well that he could be in trouble today with the internal twists and turns his guts were taking, and they were about to lift off and be airborne for the next two hours. Jennifer was all agog about going on a helicopter ride as well. She had never been in one before so she was quick to tell Roger that she would scratch this off her bucket list when she got home today. The helicopter was literally brand new. The back of the rear seat configuration still had factory protective plastic on it to keep it clean and safe. Once the headphones were on your ears it felt like another world. So quiet, so peaceful. Jennifer was looking out the side window as the machine lifted off the ground and into the air, "and away we go," she said to herself. No sooner than she was watching things on the ground get smaller than she had an intestinal urge with which she wasn't happy. Her tummy started to bump and thump inside, and she could feel her internal body heat go completely out of whack. Something wasn't sitting quite right. The heat was rising. Was it something she ate last night? A sense of Inner fear came over her when she looked out the side window and could see they were over a thousand feet off the ground. "Not too many emergency bathrooms up here," she said to herself. She continued to look out at the amazing view drifting on by the windows, but her head was now playing a new game with her. How long can she hold it?

Within twenty minutes of lift-off, they had already made it to Hope and were flying over its own little airport. Roger thought there is no time like the present, "Hey Bob," he said over the headsets, "is there any chance that we could land at that airport right there?" He said pointing down towards Hope Airport.

"Sorry Roger, when I entered my flight plan, I did not identify any stops except for Pitt Meadows. We are actually not permitted to put down anywhere because my rotor scares the shit out of every type of barnyard animal there is so we have to be careful, or I could get a major fine." Bob answered.

"So how soon are we scheduled to be in Pitt Meadows?" Roger asked.

"Not for at least an hour Roger. There's just nothing I can do about it." Bob explained.

Suddenly Jennifer spoke into her headset, "Copy that Bob, however, I am really not sure if I can make it that long, if you catch my drift." She said.

"What's going on with you two? You are both feeling a bit watery inside? What did you both eat last night?" Bob quired.

"We had the Spanish Seafood Platter. It seems to have a couple little surprises hidden inside some of that hot and spicy sauce that they covered the meal with. I just do not feel 100% right now and I know that I will need a washroom soon. How about you Roger? How are you hanging in there?" Jennifer asked Roger.

"The pressure is slowly starting to build. I know that I am on a time limit now." Roger replied.

"Me too Roger, me too." Jennifer said.

Only minutes had passed when Roger could feel the lower rumblings of his colon and could only begin to count the minutes until trouble. He was sitting as still as he could believing that less motion was going to change the fact his bowels were full and now, he could sense the dinner coming back to make another appearance. He sat there wondering how this day could possibly get any worse when it happened, Jennifer barfed from one side of the rear passenger seat to the other without missing one inch of its high-quality leatherette. She couldn't stop it once it had begun. She controlled herself for a moment but then hit the floor with another round of steaming hot vomit. And there was an added bonus now, the helicopter interior was beginning to smell really funky. Roger felt like shouting out, "Can someone open a window?" He chuckled to himself. Roger looked over at Jennifer and she was not doing well. She had broken the barf seal, and it was coming hard and fast. Roger was thinking to himself, "Holy shit. I hope she is okay." He then opened fire with a beautiful arching puke stream and re-sprayed the back of the pilot's seat and added more volume to the floor's already polluted gloppy mess. It was disgusting. The second that Jennifer saw the river of puke from Roger, she conjured up another fresh batch and barfed all over the seat again. It was a losing battle. There was nothing to help clean up the mess and it was now rolling around in pools on the floor and making its way towards the door seals across their bottoms. Slowly the barf found its way under the seats, and it crept up to the front of the helicopter on the floorboards until it was strategically positioned all around Bob's feet. It was now only a matter of time until this gooey matter was under his feet and then it would happen, just as sure as Santa comes down the chimney every year, Bob was going to see and feel this and hopefully it would not make him puke instantly all over his controls and instruments. Just when it looked like things could not get worse, Roger lost control of his bowels and was now off-gassing on the passenger seat and filling his trousers. It was completely out of his control now. Roger realized that he should probably be heading to a hospital at this time, but this humiliating date wasn't done with him quite yet. Poor Jennifer was also unable to restrain her bowels any further and they became as active as Roger's. The helicopter's cockpit stench was at a new level of hideousness. The pilot continued saying, "Oh my god. For the love of Jesus."

Bob aimed his helicopter for an airstrip in Pitt Meadows and headed down in an emergency fashion. All the way down Bob communicated with the tower to follow all of the protocols but Bob was like a horse to the barn. He wanted his feet planted flat on the ground and now. The tower okayed Bob to land beside a hanger off to one side of the runway and shut down his engine. Bob struggled to stay calm and follow all of the procedures when all his mind wanted to do was to get out of the cockpit of that helicopter and breathe so could ingest some clean fresh, puke-free, air. No sooner had Bob turned off the rotor, than he swung his door open and leaped out of the helicopter and made contact with the earth right before

Bob began puking all over the landing strip. He did manage to keep himself together for a long while before succumbing to the aroma of one of mother nature's lethal combinations, puke and shit. It took a bit before they could really all look each other in the face. This was a new level of humiliation and Roger couldn't remember feeling this weird in his entire life. Lucky for the group there was a bathroom in one of the hangers nearby, so they had a place to go clean up, a bit. Jennifer and Roger were covered in fluids, and they had no clothes to change into and their replacement clothes were back at Harrison in his truck. They were in a bad way. There was no choice. He would have to get back into the helicopter and fly back to Harrison with Bob. "Jennifer, do you want to fly back to the hotel with me, or do you want to wait here, and I can come back and pick you up?" Roger asked.

By this time Jennifer was shutting down. She had taken all the embarrassment she could for one day. She wanted to get showered and changed immediately. Her insides were doing better but her outsides had been crushed. Even as she was discussing arrangements, she was still sitting about in soiled clothes. She couldn't suppress the tears any further.

Roger instantly called his sister Anne and told her to come and pick up Jennifer and take her home and bring a change of clothes for a five-and-a-half-foot tall woman. "I can be there in thirty minutes.

Is that too long or do we require an Ambulance type response?" Anne asked.

"Jennifer, are you okay to wait here? My sister Anne is on her way, and she will bring you a change of clothes and drive you home. I can drop off your bags tonight." Roger said.

She shrugged and continued to stare at the ground, so clearly, she was having a rough time processing the weirdest helicopter ride in the world with a guy that has seen you covered in barf and shit. It was all a bit much for Jennifer to overcome.

Later that day Anne picked Jennifer up from the Pitt Meadows airport and drove her back to her apartment. They had exchanged a few words but had not got on like new besties. It was left that Roger would contact Jennifer about the bags, but Jennifer then insisted, "It might be better if you bring me the bag when it's convenient for you, I'm in no rush." She said.

It would appear that Roger wasn't going to get another date with Jennifer anytime soon! Roger believed that Jennifer Newsome was not going to be in his dating future. The humiliation mountain is just too big to get over and forget about it.

***

For the next couple of weeks Roger kept close to home and did not venture out into the harsh world of relationship terror to get his heart kicked around a smidge more than normal. No matter what happened, Roger had to believe that there was a nice person also wanting to get into a full-time relationship somewhere out there and he intended to find her. One date at a time. Roger had made the mental commitment to have a few more encounters before the end of summer. If he were lucky, he could have a full-time girlfriend by the fall and would have a date for winter holiday activities. A new special angel for Christmas.

Chapter Ten

Summertime was winding down in a hurry it seemed, and the cooler air would be arriving soon. Roger always thought of this time of year as back-to-school/labour day because it marked the return of children to the classrooms. Roger knew he would have to go to the store and pick up school supplies for the coming year. It was the girls' yearly ritual.

Roger looked at the calendar and felt he could easily squeeze one more date in before the end of summer vacation for the kids. And why not, he was on a hot streak. He hadn't been arrested for at least two weeks now, so Roger was feeling a bit punchy.

He ended up sending a message to Shay-Shay McKinnon to see if she wanted to go into the bush and do some ATV riding. She was a self described outdoors person and was up for anything that was outdoor-related. It turns out that Shay-Shay was raised in Revelstoke on the outskirts of a logging camp, so she was familiar with roughing it. She was the one girl with five brothers, all older than her. There was a twelve-year difference between the youngest and the oldest and Shay had been treated like one of the guys her entire life. There was no time for make-up and fancy hairdos growing up in the bush. She had become hard because, most of the time, she would use the two-person outhouse right beside her brothers or her father. Shay could swing an axe, take down a tree, build and light a fire, and forage for food in the woods. Shay-Shay was an extremely independent woman that was ready for confrontation and Roger had never seen this type of spirit before. He was lured into Shay-Shay's profile because she seemed so self-assured for a young woman in her mid-twenties. Roger wasn't trying to find a wife that day, so he made arrangements to go on an ATV ride, but they were going to ride out from her dad's house out in a town called Mission that was about thirty minutes from Port Coquitlam. They had planned to meet at her place and ride off into the surrounding bush and trail areas. There were so many trails and adventures around every corner. There was always some direction to head off into and you would still find something new every time.

When Roger got to her father's place, he quickly found a place to park his pickup and get his machine off-loaded. Within minutes of being at her dad's place, they were packed up and ready to ride. Roger decided to bring along his twelve-gauge shotgun and some rounds just in case there was a zombie apocalypse while they were out. Quickly, they were loaded and ready to go on an outing. Shay took the lead position and darted off into the woods with Roger close behind.

Roger was feeling quite bold on this day because his date was with a Black woman. He had dated Black women previously but never for a long-term relationship. Certainly not going into the woods and riding ATVs for the day but Roger was up for anything. He couldn't wait to follow Shay through the woods and see where they got to that day. He was excited. Shay-Shay was a perky type of person who preferred to smile rather than frown at all times. Although small in stature, her five-foot, four inch tall one-hundred-pound frame was up for anything. She was a real outdoors person and could catch fish, hunt for food, make a shelter, build a fire, and was completely independent in the woods. Surprisingly, she was a real looker. She had big silver braces covering most of her teeth at this point in her life but eventually, the braces would come off. Her hair was fashioned in cornrows with a tight add-on weave that she wore down her back in a ponytail. Her body was small but exceptionally well muscled, making her appear like she was a bodybuilder getting prepped for a competition. The other attribute she demonstrated was she seemed to know how to do so many guy things. She could shoot, she could ride, there were so many checks in her checklist column; Roger was impressed. She even chopped her own firewood at one of the stops they made. She was capable and Roger found that attractive. Her eyes were mahogany brown, but she adorned some light blue contact lenses, and they really popped when she had a dark glow to her skin colour. Her cornrows were massive and had been pinned on top of Shay-Shay's head, but the mere bulk of hair was difficult for Shay-Shay to keep the hair on the top of her head. She would pile up the hair, but it was an act of futility trying to keep it on the top of her head.

As the day rode by, Roger and Shay-Shay were having lots of fun. They just kept puttering around her father's property and going back and forth and up and down all of the paths that weaved a lacework pattern on the ground where they had been riding. Finally, Shay waved Roger down so they could take a break and have a conversation without their motors running all day long. They drove across an open meadow, and they came to a stop in the middle of the field. This would give them the chance to talk without interruption from the ATVs for a spell. They chatted about all kinds of things. He had no idea that Shay-Shay had one of the county's biggest and brightest stars working with her in "Sir Spuds." He was a twelve-hundred-pound male that had garnered her "Best in Show" more than once. He was an incredibly special pig, so he had been told, over and over again. All of this bacon talk, and Roger was starting to get a little peckish. While Roger and Shay discussed their lives outside of the farm, it gave them a chance to connect with each other. So far that day they had only been running the ATV's all around the acreage and not just getting to know one another. "So, have you ever dated a Black girl before?" Shay asked.

"Yes, I have. A few times actually. I have found Black women to be as enchanting as white girls my whole life. How about you? Have you ever dated a white man?" Roger put the question out there.

"No. Never. I'm not allowed to yet. When I have moved out of this house for good or my daddy isn't paying any of my bills in the future, then I am permitted to date white guys. Until then, absolutely not." Shay said.

"Well then what the hell am I doing here right now? Is this some kind of bizarre family experiment that your family is trying out on white folks?" Roger said.

"No. Not at all. It's just that he knew my brothers would be around the yard today so I wouldn't get up to any hanky-panky stuff. No sneaking off to the barn for a quick hay loft rendezvous. I have been a bit promiscuous in the past, but I wanted to see what it's like to kiss a white boy. I know the lips will feel the same but white guys act so differently than other races of men. Just an experiment, that's all." Shay-Shay said.

Roger looked to his left and then to his right, he stepped closer to Shay-Shay and wrapped his arm around her snuggly and kept her close to himself. He leaned in closer once he could see that none of the family tree were hanging around waiting to pounce on any man touching their baby sister. The two of them stood side by side in an awkward position beside the ATV's and did some light necking.

Roger could tell from the series of positive hums coming from Shay that she was enjoying her white guy opportunity. Roger was giggling a bit because he kept looking over his shoulder towards the main house, but he couldn't see any sign of Shay-Shay's dad or brothers. Roger knew for sure that if her brothers saw Roger pushing his tongue down Shay's throat, there would be hell to pay. He decided to not push his luck any further and halted the smooching. He wasn't going to allow his luck to run out on that issue. Shay asked Roger if he wanted to continue to ride around the perimeter of their property on the ATV's and just ease along. Roger concurred instantly with the new riding idea and began preparing to keep moving. Shay-Shay's hair was heaped on the top of her head, but it was falling off to the side slightly so she repositioned her hair and tossed it all back and then began to reposition her helmet so that all of the hair would sort of fit under the safety helmet also. While Shay was making adjustments with her hair and helmet a large and bulky portion of the hair slipped past all the watchful eyes and her unbelievably expensive weave fell into the chain and sprockets and became lodged into the gears, grinding them to a halt. Completely stuck. "Could just one of these dates start off real nice and maybe even finish nicer than it started? Could this ever be possible?" he pondered. He dismounted his ATV and looked at the hair twisted into the gears. This was NOT coming out. This would have to be cut out with scissors and worked on like a high school project. Roger was on his knees beside the machine trying to release her hair while doing the least amount of damage possible. Before long, one of the brothers looked out the window and could see Roger and Shay-Shay messing around with the ATV until it became clear that she had got her hair trapped in the machine cogs. Finally, the entire family was out in the driveway taking turns trying to release one strand of hair at a time. None of this grab and pull maneuver. It had to be carefully undone. It was going to take hours. Her father said, "Enough of this Sweet Shay. Let's just have your boyfriend cut it off and we can all move on with our day."

"I'm sorry sir, but why would I take the responsibility for your daughter's hair removal when I had nothing to do with it getting stuck. I was thinking that if you take your time and remain patient with it, you can remove all the hair with no cuts necessary. It will take some time." Roger added.

"Screw that. Here, cut this hair right along here, (his hand pointing to an area that he wished to have altered), and I'll hold the weave down firmly." Her dad added.

"Okay," Roger acknowledged, and took the cutting blades edge and plunged them through the thick and knotted pieces of hair and tried to liberate the shorter pieces of hair that were connected to her head with glue and weaving techniques. With some chopping and sawing, Roger had separated Shay-Shay from the chain and gears on the underside of the ATV. Roger was relieved because it got her hair out of the teeth of the machine so she could begin returning back to normal. But there was trouble. Shay-Shay held the discarded clump of weave hair and became angry with the sense of loss and waste. "Shit," he thought to himself, "Never get between a Black woman and her hair." Roger vowed.

Shay-Shay ran the gamut of emotions as she stooped over her ATV in the yard that day pondering not just whose fault it was but who's going to pay for this very pricey casualty. Heads would roll, and Roger was always up for a nice sock on the chin.

"Shay-Shay, I feel just terrible about what has happened here. I knew I should have double checked your gear before we continued to ride and to have been sure that everything was safe and secure. I'm so sorry. Would it be okay if I give you some money to cover the cost of the damaged item?" Roger said.

"Well, I think I would be okay with that. Thank you, Roger." She answered with composure.

"Whatever you need Shay-Shay, I've got you covered," Roger said.

Shay sat still, twisting her fingers as if they were her own secret abacus, until she came to a conclusion. "I'll be alright with seven hundred dollars." She said.

"Perfect. I'll e-transfer the funds right now." Roger stated.

"Holy shit Roger! You are such an amazing guy. I can't believe you just did that. I know it's not your fault Roger. I'm the idiot that wanted you to see my new weave, even with helmets on all day. I never bragged about being smart, but smart enough to have met a man like Roger Miller. Your kindness leaves me speechless." She posed and covered her face with her fingers open for effect.

Roger kept feeling that he had dodged a bullet. He was anticipating a couple thousand dollars for a replacement weave, but this was easy, and it wasn't going to destroy his life financially. He wasn't a rich man, but he had decided that this was a worthwhile investment.

***

Shay-Shay and Roger did manage a couple future outings but there was no "true love spark." So, if at first you don't succeed…

***

That was a brave week for Roger. He went about his business as usual, but he could tell his dating confidence was beginning to grow. The same list of fears and stupid questions didn't immediately race into his mind and cloud his judgement with irrational thoughts about how every dating encounter would end in disaster. He wasn't that far off currently however, but there were many more fish in the sea.

He knew that eventually he would find an amicable match, move towards a real girlfriend with feelings, and hopes and inspirations.

Roger had responded to Cathy's request that the two of them make arrangements to get together and meet. She had picked a local eatery in Port Coquitlam called Earl's which was a chain of restaurants. They had several locations, but they were like McDonalds in the sense that their product and interiors were exceptionally conformed and their reliability in the marketplace was, of course, their consistency. No matter which town you went to, at Earl's you would receive the same quality and service every time. They had started with a couple of locations in BC and now they were scattered throughout the province. They were current, hip, and knew what the young diners were looking for, value for money. Their internet connection was second to none so when the younger crowds would flood into their establishments, they could get great tech and great food. Earls had it all.

Roger and Cathy decided to meet at Earl's in Poco at 8:00 pm on a Friday night. Roger was feeling up because he saw Cathy's profile picture online and she looked beautiful. Pale white skin with big, well-formed eyebrows and a petite nose. Her eyes were strikingly blue with huge eyelashes and a platinum blonde, short cut hairstyle. She was quite a vision but physically she was about five feet tall and possibly one hundred pounds, so Cathy was a bit on the petite side. Most of Roger's life he had been with mostly tall and thin women for some reason. He never seemed like he had a type but when he was remembering all of the women he had dated, he really had aimed toward tall, thin women consistently. He was getting to know himself better and there was nothing wrong with that. This could help Roger look for what he really wanted and that was a tremendous asset to him at this point in his dating quest.

When Roger entered the restaurant, Cathy was already there and standing by the front hostess stand. Cathy made a friendly wave gesture as Roger was led away by the helpful hostess staff and they escorted him over to an open table and informed Roger the waitress would be there quickly to take their drink order. Roger looked back over at the front entrance of Earl's and could see that Cathy was still on the phone but again gave Roger the "I'll be there soon," nod and continued to chat with her invisible guest. None of this bothered Roger anymore. He was becoming jaded by all the strange things that women do but he wasn't going to make a scene. The one thing that Roger had developed was the ability not to take any of it too seriously and realized that he was on a date, not a mission to the moon. Pretty simple stuff.

He patiently sat waiting for Cathy to come to the table but to no avail. Roger decided that he would acquire a libation to help keep him calm and tranquil. Minutes later, Penny the server, returned with a skookum size beer and some nachos. Oh boy, this looks really good. He picked up the beer and drained half of it in record time. "That was tasty," he thought to himself. Restraint, control, he reminded himself. He didn't want to finish the appetizer before Cathy had ever even made it to the table. That just wouldn't be right. He began to pace himself. One sip, a few nachos. This new method was a sure-fire winner until Roger finished the beer he was drinking while waiting for Cathy. Not to worry, he would just order another beer and Cathy would not even realize that he had already downed an entire beer. She would never be the wiser. Roger was quite impressed with himself when the second cold beer arrived, and the remnants of the previous glass were removed from the table. It simply never happened.

Cathy made her way over to the table. She smiled brightly and said, "I'm so sorry but I've got a couple of projects that I am working on, and wouldn't you know it, everybody needs to speak to me tonight. So sorry. I promise I will be only a few more seconds, really." She assured Roger. She went back to making phone calls and seemed very excited whenever she began speaking to other parties on her cell phone. Before long, the nachos were exhausted as in…gone. Roger was a bit hungry, so he finished off the nachos and beer and decided to maybe get another Appy until Cathy was back at the table to stay. He ordered some Calamari and another beer. If all went well, the appetizer and the drink would all arrive at the same time, and she would never know that he had been eating and drinking all night, without her. Oh well, he was allowed to have fun on these dates as well. Penny, the waitress pulled up to the table at the exact same time as Cathy and put the Calamari down beside the beer. "Oh, would you care for a drink Cathy?" Roger asked.

"Yes Roger, I'll have whatever you are having please." She said.

Roger lifted his head to face the waitress and said, "Thank you. Could you please bring another beer for the lady, thanks?" He said.

"Of course. Is this going to be the same or different checks?" She asked.

"To be safe let's put them on two different tabs but if there is any trouble in the waters ahead let's just put it all on one bill and not tell anyone, shall we." Roger said.

Roger slowly picked away at the calamari but before you knew it, they were running out again. Oh shit, Roger was running out of beer again. Where the hell is Cathy? He pivoted his head looking through the bar trying to locate Cathy but could not. Ah ha, there she is outside the front door on her cell phone again. She had a serious look stamped onto her face so Roger knew that it must be serious. It could be that this is just the way it is always for Cathy. Maybe she was in high demand at all times. No freedom for Cathy.

"So, hello there finally." Cathy said to Roger. She was standing beside the table with her finger scrolling through her phone list at breakneck speed. Roger marveled at how someone could be able to give such hyperfocus to two things at once.

"Well hello Cathy. It is nice to meet you in person. It seems you are in high demand this evening with all the phone calls. Are you going to have time to sit down and relax for a bit tonight?" Roger said.

"I hope so, but I am trying to launch one of my new beauty mascara products and there are always a million trivial things that didn't happen and a million things that still need to happen. It is the price you pay to be an entrepreneur." She said.

"It is all good with me Cathy. Did you want to see a menu or hang out for a while longer?" Roger asked just as Cathy was receiving another cell phone call, which she had to take. "I have to take this Roger. I'll be right back, I promise." She said.

"Can we borrow your salt?" came a voice from the next table.

Roger turned to see three attractive young women with one male friend pointing to the salt and pepper shakers on the table. "Do you mind?" The male friend asked again.

"No. Not at all." Roger picked up the shakers and handed them off to the next table and went back to his beer drinking.

"So, what are you celebrating?" One of the ladies asked.

"Nothing really." Roger answered. "Actually, out on a first date. So far, she hasn't been able to spend more than one minute at the table, but I feel like there will be an opening coming up. We'll see." Roger said.

One of the women said, "If he were my man, I wouldn't leave him sitting around by himself where other predators could get to him. I would want him on a short leash, let me tell you. Most likely at home on the sofa." she said with a giggle.

"I love sofas." Roger chimed in. He leaned in towards the three ladies and their friend and continued to communicate with them in a friendly and harmless way. They all were getting better acquainted when Cathy returned to the table and sat down. "What did I miss?" She blurted out.

"Nothing my dear. I was just considering having a cocktail. Would you care to join me?" Roger asked her.

"Sure, that sounds great. What are we drinking, Roger?" She said.

"Currently I have a beer, but I am open to new things Cathy. What's your fancy?" He asked.

"How about a couple of tequila shots to get the blood boiling?" she said.

The waitress was walking by at that instant and said, "Two tequila shots, coming right up."

Roger and Cathy actually managed to say, "how are yah," before Cathy's phone began to ring for the umpteenth time that evening. Within a moment Cathy was back outside on her phone making deals. Roger stood at the table and waited for the shots to come. Poof, they were there. He looked around the interior of the room and decided he was not going to wait for Cathy. He was going to do his shot without delay. Down it went, it was scrumptious. Roger looked around the room as if his mom were going to catch him using swear words until he knew that his mom wasn't coming to scold him, so he picked up the second tumbler of tequila and downed it also. Roger noticed that his legs didn't want to cooperate with him and allow him to move around the room safely anymore but what the heck? He was in a good mood, and he could always catch a cab back to his sister's house at the end of the night. He was playing it cool and enjoying the atmosphere of the restaurant for a change. Time for Roger to enjoy himself for a while, even if he was alone all night.

Cathy returned to their seat and continued to play the role of company magnate. The phone kept ringing and she kept answering. Roger had realized that night he would never date an influencer again because she would spend the entire evening doing just that, influencing. Taking pictures, scrolling through lists, reading crap. When does your workday end? Do you go home and do all of this stuff all over again? He was fascinated but he was also not into that kind of stuff. Roger knew that a woman like Cathy was best suited to be around younger men who understand any of the jargon he had heard during the evening. It was hard to imagine but Cathy made Roger feel like he was really old, and he was, compared to her.

Roger got the bill and paid it and headed for the door. On his way out he made eye contact with Cathy and smiled and nodded in a friendly way towards her, and then he left. In the back of the cab that night on the way home he came to the conclusion that he had not actually spoken directly to Cathy all night. They exchanged some words, but they had not said anything that would allow the two of them to know each other any better at all, and they had not. This was going to be a date worth adding to his memoirs. "The one that got away?" he guessed.

When Roger returned home that evening, he removed Cathy's name from his potential list to the dating morgue, never to be called again.

Chapter Eleven

Fall was upon them. All of the retail stores couldn't wait for Halloween to be over so they could get their Christmas displays out of storage and set up for all to see. The spookiest night of the year had been converted into a one-evening event and the second those kids got home and unpacked their bounty of candy; the holiday was officially over. No more waiting around for a week or so. Halloween ended that night at midnight and Xmas was in full swing the following day in Vancouver. That also meant that all of the schools would start with their winter line-up of activities. All the craft and bake sales and whatnot, but of course, this would bring the annual school Christmas concert back to life. All the students would begin warming up their music skills, whether it be singing, playing an instrument, or acting in a version of Scrooge, it was that time when kids demonstrated their artistic talents. The tough part for all of the parents was that they had to go and watch, no matter what they conjured up. A true testament of spirit.

"Daddy, can we stay after school today and help Miss Stevenson? We're going to learn new songs and build things. Is that okay?" Rose asked.

"Have you spoken to Auntie Anne? Has Anne approved the change in schedule?" He turned his head seeking Anne's whereabouts. She eased into the kitchen area from down the hallway and nodded. "You're good with drop/off and pick/up for Rose and Brooke?" Roger posed the question to Anne.

"Absolutely. I'll be out this afternoon and will pick them up on my way home. It works perfectly for me." Anne said.

"Terrific. Then it's settled. Anne will pick you up after school so you can start to work on all the Christmas stuff that needs to get done before the big show, right Rose?" Roger said.

"Right Daddy." Rose confirmed.

Even though Roger had really only met Lori Stevenson once, he still couldn't get her out of his mind. There is always something that attracts a man to a woman, for whatever silly thing it may be, but it is always there. For Roger, he had noticed Lori's long, thin fingers and for some strange reason he had thought about her hands a few times since the last meeting. She was also tall and attractive, that didn't hurt too much either and, most importantly, his daughters adored Miss Stevenson. Kind of makes it easy when your girls want to bring her home to stay, right now. Children do not understand the complexities of a relationship, but they do know what they like. And currently, Rose and Brooke really liked Miss Stevenson, so they were ready for their dad to bring home "Misses Right" immediately, no questions asked. Who knows, she could end up being a big meanie that made children go to bed early and eat all of the vegetables on their plates or no dessert. It could happen. Roger resigned himself to believing that everything happens for a reason and if he and Lori were to be an item, then it was going to happen without any prompting from him, or his girls. October flew by and seemed to be over before it began. One week the leaves were changing colours, and the kids were making turkeys out of handprints and next thing it is time to go out trick or treating. Every year the top-rated conversation was - what to be on Halloween night. A witch, a ghost, a goblin, or a zombie. It was always quite a debate for costume decision time in the Miller household. At least none of the young women had got to the next phase of life when the costumes change from goofy and fun to mature and having to be approved by an adult before it leaves the house. Thank goodness they were not at that age yet. Year by year Auntie Anne would go down to the costume store after Halloween and buy all of the left-over outfits left on the shelves. Anne figured it was the easiest way to not have a bunch of disappointed kids standing around on Halloween night not knowing what costume to wear. She had an entire wardrobe which would make the girls squeak and giggle for the duration of the evening and then back they go into the costume box for another 365 days when it was time to bring them out again the next year.

Anne still adored Halloween night. She would stage all the electronic blow-up figures in her yard, the ones that would wield big swords and make horrible noises to scare kids, but it never seemed to work. Every year there were always a bunch of kids at the end of the night hanging around Anne's house and looking forward to next year's events. So much for scaring them off. She also gave out full size chocolate bars and full bags of potato chips. "Who does that?" She did it every year and every year the crowd got bigger, and the line got longer. In order to keep the little tykes busy, Anne's oldest daughter, Joy, dressed as a Mad Doctor went outside and chased people around with her imitation chain saw. It made such a wonderful sound and appeared quite realistic when she would come out, swinging madly to and fro and yelling, "Who wants a piece of this?" Anne's home was the hit of the street every year and the four girls were proud that all the kids at school knew where the house with the big candy bars and big chip bags were.

Thanksgiving came with its usual fanfare provided by Maxine and Clyde. Maxine insisted on having a full-size family dinner for twenty people every year, without fail. It started in the 60's at Maxine and Clyde's place and had evolved to Anne's place when she purchased a luxury home with a dining room set that could accommodate twenty people for a full sit-down dinner. It was a beautiful, handcrafted set of furniture and Anne had all of the accoutrements to dress the table to be fitting for her Royal Majesty. Every little serving gadget that could be used at a table setting was on that table every Thanksgiving and Christmas. Year after year Anne's table never disappointed. No matter what the holiday was, the table was decorated for the occasion. The only thing the table had not been subject to was craft days and Anne was never going to let that happen.

The family all sat in the family room and listened to Roger regale them with his difficulties from the dating world. He did mention that there were no downs because he always believed you were never going to find the right girl sitting at home on the sofa, unless she is led to the sofa to actually meet you, of course. Roger was enjoying his life right now and even the dating experiences were turning out to be an interesting distraction to his life. He had not really moved anything to the top of his priority list currently, except to raise his daughters and spend time with his family. Roger was living what seemed to be a carefree life on the outside, but in his core, he pined for love. Grown-up love. His kids, or the nieces and nephews, couldn't provide Roger with what he was looking for. They were a wonderful distraction, but he was at the point where he was eager to move towards having special time alone with a grown-up lady.

Winter descended on the school parking lot at Citadel School that November morning. From out of nowhere, the city had received several inches of the white stuff that was found on every bald tire in the lower mainland. It would seem that many of the "described shitty tire's" were from Roger's neighbourhood. He knew that as the day moved on, if the snow kept falling, it was going to make the drive home that afternoon a total shit show. It was tough enough to get around Vancouver at the best of times, so the additional white flakes simply brought most things to a complete halt. Roger had changed his plans that day to be sure he could pick the kids up from school so they wouldn't have to trudge home in the snow through the unplowed sidewalks. They loved the snow and had no intentions of ever coming inside the house once it began falling. Roger eased his pickup into the school parking lot and began the search for his and Anne's kids. He was looking enthusiastically around and then he spotted the entire group of them. Rose and Brooke were together with Joy and Hope, and they were standing beside Miss Stevenson's car. Her car was not running, and snow was piling up on top of the vehicle, so Roger jumped out of the truck to consider the situation. It would appear that Miss Stevenson had a flat tire. No sooner had Roger given his assessment than the girls all started to chirp up, "Our daddy can fix anything. No matter what." Rose and Brooke trilled out. "Daddy, you need to fix Miss Stevenson's tire so she can go home. He's really, really fast. (The little heads turned to Miss Stevenson and gave her an all-knowing smile.) 'You'll see." Roger actually didn't want to do this task, but he also knew that otherwise, Lori would have to call someone to come and fix the tire and by the time they arrived, he would be done. Pitter patter let's get at her. Roger jumped into action, opened Lori's car trunk, and removed the spare tire with assembly required to accomplish the task. Within minutes the car lurched into the air and off came the damaged tire, on went the spare and before they knew it, the car was fixed. Lori stood back under the cover of the school's overhang with the kids, and they sang the new Christmas songs they had been learning, while Roger made short work of the tire replacement. He approached the group smiling and said, "these keys belong to you Miss Stevenson. The spare is not very safe and should only be driven – slowly - for a short distance, so please get yourself to a tire shop toot sweet." Roger said. He extended his hand towards her and dropped the car keys into her hand. "Thank you so much Roger. That was very gallant of you. I feel like I owe you a favour now." She said.

"You don't. It is my pleasure to help you. It keeps the girls happy to see me getting along with their teacher. Could you imagine how they would be if we were together?" He burst out laughing. "I tremble at the thought." He said. Roger suddenly felt awkward with his remark and wanted to rescind it but that was all water under the bridge. He made a comment about relationships that he probably shouldn't have but there was no turning back. He kept his head up and pushed on by having the girls all get their things together and got them all into his truck to head home for the night. Timing was going to be perfect because by the time he got them all home it would most likely be the dinner hour. As Roger grabbed things and piled them up inside his truck, he did take the opportunity to look over at Miss Stevenson for one more moment to reassess her overall presence and he was definitely a fan. She was an attractive woman with panache. Roger kept thinking to himself that maybe one day their paths would cross at the right time in life. Stranger things had happened. Lori turned and waved goodbye to Roger and the bevy of young girls he had with him, but he knew he was smitten with Lori, and although he didn't know how all of this would go in the future, he was hooked. "See you later Miss Stevenson" he called from the driver's seat.

"See you later Roger," she said, waving goodbye to the group but maintaining eye contact with him.

Once the group was settled into their seats the little girls could not control themselves any further and said, "Shame, shame, double shame…now we know your girlfriend's name." The girls all giggled in unison.

***

A week later Roger was called to duty once again to help with a fundraiser to be held at a local golf club in Coquitlam. The facilities were beautiful, and always in immaculate condition. The Westwood Plateau Golf & Country Club was a destination facility and the views from the golf course holes were considered to be some of the "Best in BC." And they were right. Some of the holes sneak up on you, not with the skill required, which was really hard, but with the vistas that distracted you as you played your round of golf. It was a steep and difficult course for any golfer on any day, but it's the BC SuperNatural feeling that the forest gives off in some of these places in the province, and they will take your breath away. Add in all the perennial and annual flowers and you got yourself a visual phenomenon. This year the school decided to raise some money through donations before the Xmas Show to gather toys for kids in the local area of Coquitlam. Roger always felt that if there were kids without toys, something needed to be done about it. This year they were to have a bake sale for the daytime volunteers and attendees, but they were also going to do a silent auction for some wine, spirits, and breweries from all of the local merchants that wanted to generate positive interactions with people from the neighbourhood. The positive thing was many of the golf members had kids in the nearby school, so it felt a bit more intimate to be at the golf facility rather than at the school. The booze side of the auction was to be managed by Roger and his brother Mitch, who loved getting up on a stage and being the center of attention for a while, along with some other parents wanting to do their part. Amongst the cast of characters scheduled to help was Tony Tanti, who Roger thought was the current boyfriend of Miss Stevenson, whom he kept an eye open for to see what kind of man she liked.

Shortly after, the day of the event was upon them. Roger was setting up for the evening portion of the auction with other volunteers when a large, steroid-using Italian man sauntered in and asked where he should be to help out with the volunteering. "My name is Tony Tanti." He said.

"Hello there Tony. Please fill out a name badge and you can start helping by unpackaging all of the items that are in boxes so we can put them all out for display purposes and for people to bid on. Does that sound okay?" Roger asked him.

"Yeah, sure." He said and got to work.

Before long they had set up all of the booze for auction and were done setting minimum prices on everything and getting more into the decorating of the items to make them look good and inviting for their guests. Within an hour the place was jammed packed, and people were dancing, eating, and having fun. The local press was there to take photos, so all of the donors felt they had got a good bang for their buck. As the evening went on, Roger noticed an odd tension between Lori and Tony when they were near each other. She seemed scared. "Roger," he said to himself, "You don't know this woman. You do not know how she acts. Maybe she is always like this with her significant other." There it was again. Subtle but noticeable. She appeared to be a bit frightened of him. Roger completely understood. Tony was six foot tall and two hundred and fifty pounds of amped up bodybuilder. This man could crack walnuts between his bicep and forearm. Tony had a mesmerizing air about him and yet he seemed shy. He wasn't pushing himself to the front of any of the duties that the volunteers had been asked to accomplish but he wasn't a wallflower either. As the evening progressed and the items began to warrant some traction and garner some bids, Tony had decided at some point to have a few drinks to lighten his mood. Unfortunately, this didn't seem to mix well with his huge doses of stanozolol and made him a total creep for the next while. He moved away to an area where he was alone and unable to hassle any guests except for the one that brought him along, Lori. He drunk ranted at Lori for a while until Roger overheard a couple of comments from Tony to Lori and that was it, he volunteered himself as a punching bag to this goliath of a man to ease the savage beast and he did something he wasn't expecting, he started to laugh. "How many days a week are you able to come over and…hang out?" Tony said as he began to laugh.

Roger and Tony had an odd moment for sure, but it was clear to Tony that Roger was going to become competition. Roger still had to be sure that Lori felt safe with him. He needed her to say so in front of Roger and Mitch, so others knew Tony's intentions. "Should she be going anywhere with this guy tonight? Ever?" She looked directly into Roger's eyes and said, "Is Anne still here? I need to talk with her right now please." Lori said.

"I'll go find her, Lori." With that Roger whizzed away and began slipping through the large groups of people gathered for the auction. Now, where to find Anne. He was headed around the edge of the room looking inward trying to scope out his sister then, avast, he spotted her. He quickly approached Anne and apprised her of the current situation with Lori's living arrangements. He escorted Anne back to Lori and made a hasty retreat so they could speak uninterrupted. Roger assumed that something was amiss, but he was not making any speculations. He needed Lori to decide if Tony could be trusted. He went back to the auction area and continued his duties. He hoped that Lori would make the right decision, whatever that was to be. He only had spent minutes with this woman, so he was not trying to build a life on it but…maybe he was trying to build a life on it. He prepared himself for whatever may happen next and knew it would be a fun ride if Lori was in the picture. Only time would tell.

The auction was a hit, and all the volunteers began the chore of taking everything down and putting things away. The people simply merged from one area to the next cleaning up and putting things away until there was nothing left to do. The head of the committee gave an encouraging speech to the troops at the end of the night and, of course, asked everyone within ear shot to please continue to volunteer as much as possible in the future. People began to gather their belongings and head for the exits when Roger approached

Anne and asked, "What is happening with Lori and Tony. I have not seen the two of them together all night so I really can't tell what the heck is going on."

"Lori will be coming to my house for a while until she can sort things out. She can stay upstairs in one of the spare bedrooms and we can let her get equalized in her life and work. She needs space between her and Tony for now. They can try to work things out from a safe distance from each other. Let it happen organically." Anne said.

"Okay then. I will walk her to her car and make sure she gets away safely." He said.

Many guests and volunteers were still milling about and preparing to leave when Roger spotted Lori standing outside of the big double wooden doors on the club entry, speaking with Tony with slightly raised tones back and forth. Roger bounded up the stairs, walked out the doors, and stood nearby, but not between them. They were clearly discussing the living situation details with each other, but Roger was determined not to be an influence. Lori had to make all her own decisions that night and decide what would work best for her future. Finally, Tony reached out and put his hand on Lori's arm and said, "Lori I do not want to play this same game every night with you. You are always about to leave and then you never do it. I have tried to tell you over and over that you can come and go as you please. If you don't want to live with me anymore, just say so and we can make new arrangements." Tony stated.

"I don't want to live with you anymore." Lori said. I am going to stay with Anne for a while and sort things out. I will let you know when I need my things." Lori responded.

"This is such crap. I've heard all of this before. Come get into the car please and let's go home." He said as he reached out his arm and held Lori by her shoulder. Lori quickly turned her body away, so he was no longer resting his hand on her at all when she said, "I'm leaving with Anne. We can talk later. For now, this is my decision." Tony attempted to close his hand on Lori again, but Roger simply said, "She has made a choice. It's not one that you like, but she has made it nonetheless." Roger now repositioned his body between Lori and Tony and held firm. If Tony was going to make a move, he figured it was going to be now. Tony took a couple steps backwards and realized that there was going to be a changing of the guard and it was taking place right now. "I don't want any trouble. I will speak to you when you have had a chance to think things over," he said pointing at Lori.

The behemoth slowly made his way across the parking lot. He entered his car, started the motor, and left. Roger breathed a sigh of relief once the man was gone because Roger never wanted to engage in a physical battle no matter what. He was huge and he was on juice, so he was armed and dangerous, so-to-speak. Anne appeared from inside of the building and turned to Lori and said, "Lori darling, could you be so kind as to get into the minivan? The smell of empty containers and juice boxes is from empty juice boxes and containers," she said as she laughed heartily. "Not to worry, it's a smell that I know you are used to." Anne said.

When they arrived home from the Westwood Plateau event with Lori Stevenson, Anne knew she would have to be honest with the girls, but everything in life is about timing. She slipped Lori into the house and skirted her past the kids' rooms so they would not see her until the morning, and they could deal with the aftermath at that time. Lori whispered "Goodnight" to Anne and headed off to bed. Anne had already fetched some sleeping attire for Lori to use for her temporary situation and she closed the door and went to bed.

The following morning had some realities that had to be faced and Anne was just the person to make that happen. Anne seldom "beat around the bush," as they say. Anne just gave it to you with both barrels. "Daddy, why is Miss Stevenson at our house for breakfast?" Rose questioned.

"Miss Stevenson will be staying with us until all of the rats are removed from her house. She has Tony still there to make sure that all of the rats are found and gotten rid of in a humane manner. Her house is in BIG trouble, so it will be a while. And, you know what else?" she quizzed. All four of the girls were at the breakfast table shaking their heads in unison. "We are not going to tell anybody that Miss Stevenson is here because we don't want her getting into big trouble with the school board with the rat thing going on right now. We have to stay quiet. Can all of you," she pointed directly at the four girls, "keep this jumbo-size secret from everyone you know? We must not tell a soul. Can you do that?" She got down to their eye level and looked at them all again. "A jumbo secret, okay?" Anne finished.

"Of course, we can." Brook added.

"Who do you mean?" Joked Joy.

"I promise not to tell the school police." Hope said.

"Why are all you looking at me? I'm not going to tell anyone, I promise." Roger added.

Miss Stevenson sat at the end of the table and did what most people would do in the midst of this crisis, she started to cry. Before one fallen tear had made its way down a cheek, the girls were all over Lori and covering her in hugs, kisses, and support. Lori smiled for the first time in forever and felt a family warmth that she had so desperately missed over the years. The second Roger saw the waterworks factory starting up, he immediately made a hasty exit and headed off to work on a project in North Vancouver that day.

He didn't really want to be around for any of that sentimental stuff. He was still aching inside himself but today was not the day to work out of his problems. He closed the door behind him as he left but he could not stop himself from thinking it, "Lori Stevenson is staying in my sister's house!" He smiled as he considered all of the potential possibilities.

He was driving when he got a call from Mitch. "Well Mr. Smooth. This is the way you do it. You just have young and attractive women moved directly into your house I see. This will cut the driving time down and save a fortune on gas and eating out at restaurants. Very clever Mr. Bond." He said in his best sinister voice. "I simply want to learn from the master." Mitch said in a mocking way.

"I know, right? Totally weird to have breakfast with her and all the girls at one time. Holy shit. Brooke and Rose are just as happy as Hope and Joy. They were all having a love fest when I got the hell out of there and figured I would see and hear more later when I return from work." Roger said.

"Oh well brother, hopefully this will go well for all parties involved. And right before Xmas. Mom and Dad are going to be over the moon in love with Lori in one visit. Most importantly bro, there is another guy out there right now that I'm sure still feels like he has dibs on this woman so tread lightly and check the back seat every time you get in the car, at least for the next while. Tony didn't appear to be a quitter. If he has the discipline to body-build, he has the ability to stick with things. I'm just saying, watch your back. This is not over that easily." Mitch said.

Roger knew he was right. Be cautious and mind not just Lori, but his own girls. He didn't want them being used as some pawn in a mind game that Tony might plan out. Stay the course.

As he drove to his North Van meeting that day, it was the first time in years that he couldn't wait to get home for dinner that night. Would she still be there? Or had she come to her senses and realized it was all too crazy. He hoped not and kept driving.

When Roger arrived home that evening, he was about to pull into the spot that he always parked in but couldn't because there was a VW Bug in his way. He recognized the car and smiled. Home sweet home.

Chapter Twelve

Surprisingly, Roger thought that he would see Lori a lot more at the house, but such was not the case. The first week, he saw her a few times in the kitchen in the evening, but she was elusive by necessity not by habit. Every night she came home and graded papers. Then she had to plan out activities for the next day and this took time, a long time, for her to prepare. Roger just assumed that over time he would start running into Lori at the house regularly, but he did not. He knew he had to be patient with the situation and not try to turn this into a dating opportunity for him, rather than an opportunity for Lori to get her life on track. She already had issues with Tony and now she was living in a stranger's house, which would be overwhelming to anybody. He knew that she deserved space to be left alone and sort things out for herself.

As they got closer to Christmas, Anne began to decorate her house, which took at least two weeks to set everything up. Anne had four Xmas trees just inside the house, as well as three outdoor fully decorated trees. She was all things Xmas. This created a bit of a diversion for Lori as she trudged through the last part of the school days before the two-week Christmas holidays; attempting to get all of her responsibilities wrapped up before the break. At Anne's house, everything was full speed ahead with baking cookies, shopping, buying, and wrapping presents - it was all systems go.

Anne loved the Christmas holidays, and she was determined to make them memorable every year for the children by spoiling them terribly. She didn't care that everybody knew what a horrible parent she was just by giving in to their every whim and desire. Anne's attitude would never falter. Give them everything, allow children to have fun and use their imaginations and be around positive thoughts from positive people. It sounded like most parents' goals.

After dinner one evening, Anne and Roger were still sitting at the kitchen table when Lori reappeared and sat down to chat with them. They were a bit shocked because they really hadn't had the chance to chat casually with Lori since she had been there. She kept herself exceptionally busy with her work and she didn't seem to have time to do anything else. Roger began to wonder how hard it was to be a schoolteacher. Another one of those circumstances, you really don't know the job of an elementary school teacher until you walk a mile in her shoes, or at least listen to one of them. She explained how so many things worked and the relationship between all of the teachers and how things really get done versus what the public is aware of. It was fun to sit in the kitchen at home and have a pseudo date-night with someone, even though they lived in your house. Roger was impressed with Lori's dedication to the field of education. She was enthusiastic about her work and started to open up to Roger and Anne as they sat in the kitchen and had a real chance to get to know each other better. It turned out that Lori was quite the scholar because, after she graduated from University of Toronto with a degree in Education, she decided to move to Vancouver, BC and attend UBC for her Teaching Master's Degree. Since she was a young child, her true passion was teaching English to foreign students. She had been fascinated with Japanese culture ever since she was a child growing up. She read Shogun four times. All things Japanese were of interest to Lori. She absolutely loved the structure of their culture and the discipline. They were a race of people that understood the real meaning of respect, right down to how to respect your elders. As she painted these mental images for Anne and Roger, it was clear to see that this was a hot topic for Lori. She was so expressive and passionate about her findings regarding Japan that Roger and Anne could feel her spirit soaring as she fantasized about having the opportunity to teach and live in Japan. She lost herself in thought for a moment and didn't realize she had stopped talking out loud and was folding a piece of paper on the dining room table into an origami. "Oops. I can't stop. I am currently obsessed with all things Japanese." Lori stated.

"Have you ever been there?" Anne enquired.

"No. I haven't had the time or the money yet. I got my master's a couple of years ago and then I've been trying to save some money while I am working but I am just taking whatever work the school board gives me so I can get by and try and save enough money to go to Japan for at least one year and try it out. Who knows, maybe it turns out to be a complete disaster, but I would love to watch students learn English as I learn Japanese." She said.

"Do you speak any Japanese?" Roger asked.

"I can say some words and a few phrases but no, I have that on my bucket list." Lori said.

"Best way to learn is by being immersed in the culture, full time." Anne said.

"I know Anne. It is the best way, but not only do I need money to get there, but I would also want some companionship while I was there. I can't imagine going to Tokyo to live by myself. My fear is that it would be too lonely to go through every day. I know I would need someone from Western Culture that would understand me, and we could go through it together. I also don't even know how long I would want to go for. A week? A month? A year? It would be tough to decide when to set sail back home for my own country. However, for this conversation I know that two years is the length of time that I have been thinking about over the years. It would give me enough time to tour around the country and see all the sights before returning home." Lori said.

The three chatted about Lori's plans for the future for a while and then said their goodnights and headed off to their respective bedrooms for the night. Roger was realizing he really didn't know much about Miss Stevenson at all. They had been thrust into each other's lives because of the children but not through any dating site. This arrangement wasn't arranged, and it made Roger wonder why this situation had not gone to hell, like so many of the previous dates. That was it. It wasn't a date but merely two people living their lives and meeting by chance, not being forced into something. It seemed to be working out quite nicely. Maybe this new living arrangement could turn into something positive for Roger. Hopefully, he could get to know Lori a bit better before they ever went on a date. "Slow the process down and make good choices." That seemed like good advice to him.

The following morning the kitchen was a whirlwind of activity with everybody coming through to fetch breakfast and coffee. The four girls took their positions around the kitchen table and ate their cereal. They laughed and giggled about everything, the way young ladies should behave, having fun. When Lori entered the kitchen, she went over to the coffee pot and filled a large mug to the brim and began sipping it down while making all of the expected yummy noises that people make. All the girls went silent and said to Lori in unison, "Good morning, Miss Stevenson."

"Good morning, ladies." She responded. "All of you ladies are doing such a wonderful job of keeping our secret quiet. I am so proud of all of you." Lori said.

"It's okay Miss Stevenson. How soon before we can tell everybody that you two are in love and are going to get married?" Brooke asked.

Roger did a spit take on the mouthful of coffee he had just taken from his cup. He and Lori started to laugh but knew that you needed to be truly clear with children or mistakes could be made. "Just to be clear - we are not a couple. We are not dating. We are really good friends, and we're really glad that Lori is at our house right now, but we are not going to tell anyone because there is nothing to tell. She is living with us right now so Lori can decide where would be a good place for her to settle down for a while. She is deciding where she wants to be for the long term, right Lori?" Roger said.

"Absolutely right Roger. I love it here so much, but I need to be sure that I satisfy my own heart and my desires to seek out and do new things. Always be growing, right girls?" Lori said.

"Like a tree Miss Stevenson. It's always growing." Joy said.

"Exactly Joy. Always growing." Lori responded. "On that note, we all have to get moving along to school." She grabbed her coffee and a muffin sitting on a tray on the kitchen island and said, "I'll see you at school ladies. See you two tonight," she said, nodding her head towards Roger and Anne.

"Have a wonderful day!" Anne shouted back at her. "Okay ladies, we need to leave the house in five minutes so please start making your preparations." Anne instructed.

"See you tonight," Roger said as he walked out the front door. He kept thinking about what Lori had been talking about that morning with the family. It was noticeably clear that she was passionate about the idea of living and working in Japan but, what was the real hold up. What would keep her from buying a ticket and heading there to take a chance? Roger was no expert on working visas for out of the country, but he had a lawyer buddy that would most likely know. He instructed his in-car phone to dial up his old pal Paul Reeves. Paul was a smart man that went to University for Chemistry and when he graduated, he went back to another University to take Law. When he finished school on the East coast he flew to Vancouver on the West coast and went to UBC to complete his law degree. After a few years under his belt in patent law, he decided to open his own small chemical business and took his life in a different direction. Through his journey, he met a Filipino lady with style and a heart of gold, and they got married and settled down. Even though Paul was not a practicing lawyer anymore, he was deeply knowledgeable and remembered most of the things that lawyers are supposed to know. He was an awesome buddy because he loved sports and beer and gave legal advice for free, or at least for a case of beer. They spoke for a while and Paul said he could look into the requirements for living and working in Japan. The best way to know is to do the research. Then weigh out the facts and make solid decisions. Paul agreed to find out what he could and get back to Roger with his findings.

Roger then contacted his travel agent friend, Sheila. She was Japanese/Canadian by birth but resided her entire life in Canada. Her mother and father were from Japan and her Grandparents on both sides were Japanese, so she had many resources to find out information. What Roger was really curious about was, how much to fly to Japan? And how much does it cost to live in Japan? He knew that these were key factors to find out for Lori that might help her make that big decision one day. Roger thought about how crippling fear is to so many people. How many things are not done because of Inner fear? It seemed crazy to Roger to at least gather the relevant details to see what a future in Japan could look like. Sheila and Roger spoke about the information that he was after. Roger was also good friends with Sheila's husband Ryan, and they had spent much time together playing competitive Texas Hold'em Tournaments. Roger's deceased wife, Michelle, was good friends with Sheila and the four of them had taken several adventures together and had socialized frequently over the years. After

Michelle's passing, Roger wasn't getting out much anymore so on the rare occasion when these old friends would hear from him, they were eager to help out and come to Roger's rescue. They knew he would do the same for them.

He hung up the phone and began thinking about how insanely different life would be in Japan. He wondered if it could even be possible for him. Two daughters. Entire family in Vancouver. No back-up team. No way! He marveled at the thought of the ultimate freedom to go and do whatever you chose with no strings attached and live in a new place and learn a new language. He felt himself having heart palpitations just thinking about how scary that would all be and yet, at the same time, exhilarating. He was envious of her potential and position in life, but he was a father now. His priorities had changed and became solely focused on Rose and Brooke. That would take up the rest of his life. Lori, however, was footloose and carefree. No husband. No children. The idea of Japan spun around in his head for the day. He couldn't wait to hear back from Paul and Sheila and get their take on the destination.

Later that night while eating a family meal, Lori arrived late from work and joined the festivities in progress. She sat down right away and had on her work clothes. Roger could not resist saying how pretty she looked. Black slacks, a fitted white shirt, red framed glasses, and attractive, sensible red pumps to finish the look. It was very Karl Lagerfeld. The little ones couldn't resist telling Miss Stevenson that she was the most beautiful teacher at their school. Lori blushed from all of the fawning attention. Although this was not her usual dinner conversation, it was nice to have a cheering section at the table that night. A person could get used to it. They continued with the dinner and when everyone was finished, the girls got up from the table, cleared the table and loaded the dishwasher, as one of their daily responsibilities, among other tasks. Roger and Lori continued to chat at the table after it was cleared. They touched on simple and risk-free topics so as to allow themselves to not expose their vulnerabilities. Lori was smart. She knew exactly what would happen if she became more deeply involved with Roger. She would become their "sort of mom" from then on. There were still so many things that she wanted to do in her life. Did she want to put her dreams on hold to fall in love with a man and his two kids?

The two chatted on and enjoyed the camaraderie but Lori had school paperwork and Roger was ready to flake out in a vertical position on a sofa somewhere in the house.

"Goodnight Lori." He said.

"Goodnight Roger." She replied.

Roger retired to the sound-proof theatre room in the basement to watch NFL Football. As he sat alone in the dark that night, he realized that Lori was still a young woman that needed to rise to her full potential, and although he was becoming aware of feelings for her, he certainly could not be the reason for her to not go for it. No matter what it may be. Roger knew he didn't want to be her reason for not doing something. He didn't want that responsibility.

***

Sheila got back to Roger within a week of him inquiring about plane tickets to Tokyo, Japan. He was remarkably surprised that the prices seemed reasonable to fly halfway around the world for under $3,000 CDN. For the fun of it, Roger did ask about first class plane tickets to Tokyo, and they were $15,000 CDN but, like anything on the internet, there are deals to be had if one chooses to do the research and find the golden nuggets, (or tickets in this case). She did inform him that the availability was usually fairly open but, like all things related to the airline industry, you had better get a ticket and then see what happens on the day of the flight. There really are no guarantees when it comes to flights leaving from a major airport. Sheila did ask Roger if the tickets were for him and a special someone but when he explained that he was just fact-finding regarding travel to Tokyo for Lori so he would know how much it would actually cost to fly to Japan. He assumed that Lori's lodging would be paid for and arranged by the University of Tokyo, from what he had gleaned from their website. Roger checked with Sheila about special inoculations that travelers may have to get to go and

231

live there for more than a year. She talked extensively about insurance and forms and documents required to live and work there but none of it seemed too difficult to achieve. Like always, it just takes time to fill out all the forms correctly and then double check them, so you don't run into some kind of snag along the way. But once all the forms were completed and received approvals from the Japanese Consulate, it would be clear sailing to process them. The final details were things like the place of business address and the residential information and anything else that was required. Roger knew there was so much more to be discovered but he wanted to be informed if and/or when he discussed any of this with Lori, while sitting around the dinner table. He always liked having some information, so he didn't sit on the edge of the sofa all night being amazed by everything, he was not up-to-speed on and feeling like a silly goose. This time he would be well informed as to what Lori might go through to make the arrangements in order to move to Japan. He had no idea if that were still one of her key goals, but it wouldn't hurt to find out as much as he could about all of the organization and hurdles that could be coming her way.

By chance, Roger also heard back from his ex-lawyer buddy Paul regarding his findings about living and working in Japan. It turned out that when Paul Reeves checked into finding out the facts on this task, he was given some very odd information. When Paul spoke with one of his old colleagues at Williams & Stern Law, he had specifically used Lori Stevenson's name in mentioning that she was trying to get a work visa for Japan and to see if Connie could help him with this task. She immediately knew who Paul was speaking of because she remembered seeing Lori's approved paperwork and had one of the secretaries in the office send it off to her by Registered Mail, which had to be signed for as proof of receipt. She seemed to think it was several months ago, but she could clarify who had signed for the mail with Canada Post. She went through all of the details with Paul, which clearly demonstrated that she was aware of this person applying for a work visa. Now the question was who signed for the mail and where did it end up?

Hours later Paul heard back from Connie with an answer. It was signed for by a "Mr. Tony Tanti." He went to their local post office and retrieved the Registered Mail after he signed for it, however, apparently it never made it into Lori's hands. Tony had completely omitted telling Lori anything about the positive news in the mail. It turns out that the University of Tokyo was extremely interested in having Lori come and work at the university for a minimum two-year contract with all expenses paid and the university was to supply the accommodations just off campus with many of the other guest educators that worked at the university full-time. There was a village just for educators working at the campus, and it had its own shopping and transportation to assist the professors with their busy routines. Paul knew that Roger would be disappointed to find out that his friend Lori could have started her journey already, if only she had known about it. Paul also knew that this was going to cause some trouble for Roger because he was going to be the bearer of unwelcome news if he told Lori about his findings. It wasn't law. Roger did NOT have to tell her. The trick would be how to allow Lori to find out this horrible news without him being involved at all? If he had Paul or even Connie contact Lori, she would know that Roger was snooping around in her business, and she never asked anybody for any help. Yet, Roger was torn because this information was something that Lori would really want to know because of the impact it may have on her future. On her life. It seemed funny to Roger that they were just talking about Japan and the dream job, and it turns out she had already been awarded the opportunity, but she just didn't know it yet. He knew he had to spill the beans in order to help Lori fulfill her potential. Yes, he was guilty of snooping into her life, but look what he found out! Miss Stevenson shouldn't even be working in Vancouver. She was supposed to be living and working in Tokyo. He couldn't sit on this information. He would reveal the facts as he knew them to Lori after dinner that night. There was no time like the present. This was a secret that could change Lori's life forever and Roger was not about to allow Tony "The Gorilla" Tanti to keep it from her. She needed to know that her services were highly valued and sought after in the country that she dreamt about living in. He realized that this was going to create a real hate/hate relationship with him and Tony for life. Roger knew that once Tony had been exposed for being a liar, his time with Lori was over. It would mark the last time that Lori would ever trust a word that came out of him. As Roger drove his truck home that day, he was nervous about how he was going to reveal all of his findings to Lori without seeming like a creep. Oh well, the truth shall set you free. He was going to expose his findings to her and let her decide how she wished to proceed.

***

When he arrived home that evening, Roger was a little relieved that Lori wasn't home yet, but he had to give his head a shake. No matter what, he had to tell her his findings and then it would be up to Lori to choose the best plan moving forward. Roger had to keep reminding himself that he was not responsible for Tony being a bit of a nut-bar. He knew that he was still going to have to explain why he found all of this out, but it was worth it. He had nothing to lose at this point so he might as well come completely clean with her. "Tony is the bad guy, not me." Roger kept telling himself.

He went upstairs and cleaned up for dinner. As he came down the open staircase, Lori was just coming through the front door and was immediately bombarded with four little girls adoring her and giving enough attention to keep Lori going another day. They all squeaked and giggled and disappeared into the kitchen area of the house. As Lori was skirted off, she glanced at Roger and smiled and gave a mouthed, "Hello," to him as the girls engulfed her completely. They sat down for dinner and had their fill as the group talked about the things that had happened that day. The girls were almost bursting with excitement because Xmas was getting ever closer. That meant two weeks off from school and lots of Christmas presents. The other tradition to look forward to was the family Christmas dinner with all the trimmings, well, sort of. Over the years the family had decided that turkey was not really that popular amongst everyone and so they no longer bought the seasonal standards but instead, moved to Beef Wellington one year, and Prime Rib the next, and so on. From that year onward there was never a turkey cooked at Christmas again. With that change, it did take newcomers to the family ritual a bit of getting used to not seeing the turkey dinner with all of the trimmings. The really good news was that there were no leftovers to speak of every year to clean up because it was all eaten, and you don't need stuffing for a prime rib.

The girls got up and cleared the table, loaded the dishwasher, and washed up the pots and pans after dinner and went to watch a Christmas movie together. In the meantime, Roger asked Lori if she could afford some time to discuss the burning issue on his mind about Tony. She seemed dubious but agreed to find a quieter part of the house to discuss this personal matter. Roger laid out what he had done to find out information for her and then he relayed his findings back to her from his personal references. He explained that the University of Tokyo had written and prepared a contract for Lori to sign so she could become a member of their esteemed faculty and that she was to start in September of that year. As Roger explained all the details Lori kept calm and listened to the entire story before she made any comments. She was seething when she found out that Tony had lied to her. He decided her future. He was making plans for her without her permission. She wasn't happy with Roger prying into her personal life but if he hadn't, she would never have known that she had achieved one of her bucket list goals: to teach abroad. Lori was spinning, because on one hand she had accomplished something she never thought possible, and on the other hand she was so furious with Tony that she wanted to hurt him. She had no idea how she would achieve that yet, but she would work at it. Lori began a torrent of stories involving Tony and all the odd and weird escapades that he was involved in, but Roger knew that Tony was still taking steroids and that made him an extremely dangerous man. He listened intently as she described in detail all the peculiar things that Tony did to try and control her life. She had no idea about being accepted by the University of Tokyo and began to wonder what else she was in the dark about. As the evening slipped by, Roger was happy that her rage and negative attention had been directed at Tony, not him. She had truly omitted Roger from any hurt and upset feelings that she was experiencing and aimed all of her hurt and anger towards Tony. In a word, ideal. The two began to discuss how Lori could get back to the university and explain what had happened, maybe they would understand. She was panicking because she had no idea whom she should speak with to get this rectified as quickly as possible. Maybe Lori might be able to salvage the contract they had proposed to her in the first place. Roger felt safe encouraging her that she would have the opportunity to clear up all of the mess in short order.

Lori started speculating on contacting the police and having Tony arrested for Canada Post Mail tampering. It would be on record that he had signed for the registered mail but there really was no way to prove that he did not give the envelope to her. Just because she didn't go to Tokyo was not proof that she was never told about the opportunity. The two of them realized that it would be hard to make that accusation stick. The more important thing to work on was communicating with the university admissions office and letting them know what had transpired from Lori's end. They both agreed it would have to be handled with great tact, because Lori didn't want to be the overseas professor with a big bag of shit connected to her. Lori definitely did not want any negative attention brought her way while she was attempting to find her way back into the good graces of the university. She felt that she could go back to her contacts and explain the goings on and see if they could reinstate the offer. It certainly was worth a try. In the meantime, she knew to stay away from Tony at all costs. "If you see this man coming your way, immediately go in the other direction." Distance was her ally. Roger continued throughout the conversation to express his regret in snooping around in her private affairs but because he did so, this critical information had bubbled to the surface and actually allowed Lori to know what kind of man Tony really was on the inside. He was a liar and Lori had caught him red-handed and Roger was delighted that Tony was exposed.

Over the next couple of days, Lori confronted Tony regarding all the facts that had been collected on his behalf and requested an explanation. He tried to convince Lori that it was actually Roger who had screwed up her chance at teaching abroad by having her move into a students' house, but of course, that had happened after Tony stole her mail. He was caught red-handed and had no one to blame but himself.

***

Roger answered a phone call from a number he did not recognize as he scooted down the highway on his way to a project.

"Hey asshole, do you know who this is?" The voice asked.

Roger's blood ran cold! He knew that all of this crap was coming but he wasn't sure when the tsunami would roll in. He had spoken with Tony at the Westwood Plateau fundraiser, and he recognized the voice. "Take the high road," Roger said to himself.

"Well, hello there Mr. Tanti. How are things with you?" Roger asked.

"You know how they are Roger. You stuck your nose into the wrong persons' business. Now you are going to pay for that mistake." Tony said with agitation in his voice.

"Mr. Tanti I can assure you that I truly have no idea why you feel any hostility towards me when I have done nothing to warrant such a threat. We worked well together at the fundraiser and went our separate ways. Lori moving into my sister's home has nothing to do with me. That was a choice she decided to make, not me. So, okay Tony, why are you pissed at me?" Roger replied Innocently.

"Lori is pissed off at me because of you! She isn't taking my calls. She thinks I sabotaged her life." Tony said coldly.

"Did you?" Roger said.

"Up yours. Ever since you appeared in my life everything has gone to shit; so, I'm holding you personally responsible for derailing my life. I promise you Roger, one day when you're not expecting it, I'll get my revenge." Tony growled and hung up.

Perfect. Now Roger had a gorilla-sized, heartbroken moron that was fixated on him, simply perfect! The problem that Roger was faced with was he had two daughters and nieces all at the same address that they shared, and he couldn't put them at risk. What if this oaf decided to go through with his threat and showed up at Roger's doorstep some evening and brought a weapon with him? He would be completely responsible for bringing this menace to their house. He knew they needed a family meeting immediately to create a strategy. Roger called his dad and explained the situation. "Meeting tonight and all should attend. Threats of violence. 7:00 pm at Anne's house." Roger felt like they should discuss the matter as a family and have Lori present to find out what they could expect from Tony. Should they be taking his threat seriously? Did he have a history of violence?

Should Roger go to the police?

***

The entire family attended the meeting. They all understood that it was urgent and important. They could not remember the last time that any of them had been threatened with violence against them; however, that did not remove the current threat against Roger.

Lori began to explain their history as a couple and gave a better background on Tony and how she saw him as a person and as a predator. Lori never described any real hitting as such, but she also

241

added that he was a 250 lbs. chunk of muscle so even if he banged into her, he would usually leave a bruise on her. She seemed convincing with regards to his violent tendencies and that Roger was the first guy that he ever took the time to track down and personally threaten. She went on about how, in the beginning, it was fun to have this Greek god-style body available to you day and night but after a while a diet of egg white and oats for breakfast and broccoli and fish for dinner every single day of every single day. Even if you are on holiday. He would find the restaurants that would sell any of the hit-list items and were good. It was a strenuous, robotic lifestyle. When people are too rigid, they can extract the fun out of many things. That was Tony in a nutshell. But a violent killer, absolutely not. She would not believe for a second that he would do something regretful. It wasn't in his nature.

After digesting Lori's information, they decided not to call the police and allow Lori the opportunity to talk some sense into Tony. They all agreed to maintain a watchful eye for Tony or his vehicle. If anyone saw him in the neighbourhood, they were to call the police ASAP.

Lori then discussed with the family openly the information about her circumstances regarding the University position. She was still deeply hurt that Tony had lied to her, but she was also crushed by the fact that she never even got to respond to the university.

Once they got done all of the business side of things, the family all shared some beverages. Anne's house was starting to look very Christmassy, and Maxine loved Christmas more than any other holiday. The gifts, the wrapping, the gatherings, she took in as much as the family would let her. Anne's house roared with the activity of children playing and grown-ups chatting. Everybody talked like they hadn't seen each other in a year even though it was a daily occurrence. Grandma quickly gathered the children in Anne's massive kitchen, and they all got together to bake cookies, which she basically made and had ready to create the ruse that they actually made the cookies. No mind, they all loved Christmas cookies of any kind. As Grandma occupied the kids, the adults could all sit and relax.

Clyde spoke to Lori regarding the possible botched paperwork for the university position in Tokyo. He knew that someone in the administration office could help them, so he was going to use his contact list to see if anyone could pull some strings. If all the paperwork was done, then it was just getting someone to reinstate the documents and he believed he had someone that could help. He would at least make the call and see if anything good could happen. The next thought was if there was a way for Lori to obtain the position at the university sometime during the semester, even though it had already begun. There were many questions that needed to be answered but they were not going to find out anything tonight. The good news was the family all had an opportunity to be sure that they were all on the same page. Currently, Lori needed help and the family was going to give her any assistance they could. They all felt somehow that Lori had been cheated out of her golden opportunity and they were all going to rally around her to make things happen. Time would tell.

****

Christmas was now in full swing, and all the stores had their decorations up and were looking festive. All the kids were well rehearsed for their Xmas shows and presentations to take place and Anne had finished making her home look like a page out of a "Better Homes & Gardens" Christmas Edition. Anne loved Christmas as much as Maxine did so the two of them had a friendly competition between them every year for "Best House" design for the season. "Too close to call," the family would all proclaim and stay out of the way, so no one got called into the kitchen for refereeing. Miss Stevenson had been working diligently with the younger students to get them ready for their songs to be performed during the school Christmas Show. The kids had been practicing a lot, so the teachers felt confident that the children would put on a great show this year. All the parents made their way into the assembly hall and took their seats on the little wooden stacking chairs that were placed into orderly rows for the performance. Every year the show was different with regard to the songs they would sing but every year it was the same because you had lots of children wishing they did not have to be up on stage singing in front of their parents. Nevertheless, the show was terrific, and the songs were performed enthusiastically because the kids really gave it their all this year. Miss Stevenson and the other teachers, who put so much effort into the show, knew that the real reason the Christmas Show came off every year seamlessly was due to the dedication of the faculty. Lori was feeling relieved that the show was done, and she was also feeling immensely proud for having been able to wade her way through the turbulent times of her own personal life, while still getting the work done with her students to put on a nice Christmas Show. She felt great and was eager for the seasonal break from teaching so she could begin enjoying the spirit of Christmas.

When the group arrived home that night, the four girls ran inside the house, straight to the bedrooms so they could change into pajamas for the next two weeks. Mitch and Chanel had already headed for home with William and James. They all knew they would see each other frequently over the course of the next two weeks. Maxine and Clyde headed for their humble abode to call it a night. The girls all piled into the family room and took their positions on the floor and furniture to sit and watch some Xmas cartoons. Anne got out some snacks for the kids and a bottle of wine for her. Minutes later, Roger arrived in the TV room to join the festivities while carrying a cold beer. It was official. The Christmas break was upon them.

***

Over the next couple of weeks, the family came and went from Anne's house like in previous years. Anne's house became the central location, and everybody worked with that as their base. Lori was participating in all the activities as a valued part of the group, rather than a sideline spectator. Roger was delighted to see how wonderfully Lori fit into every situation that was thrown her way, and she really did seem like she belonged. Roger was elated. He also kept noticing how attractive Lori was, even in her housecoat and slippers, while lounging around the house during the day. Regretfully, he did wish that he could find a chance to flirt with the girl. He was no idiot and realized that the rare opportunity for romance was indeed going to be elusive over the winter break. Roger just kept thinking to himself that this relationship continued to stall over and over again, to the point where Roger started thinking that it was NOT to be. So far, at every turn, there was something in the way of Roger and Lori spending time together to even attempt to create a romance. Roger knew he couldn't be selfish and worry about himself at a time like this. He needed to think about his girls having a fun winter holiday.

Christmas dinner was here, and Anne was the hostess this year. From the sidelines, Lori wanted to get into the spirit of things and told the group that she would gladly make the customary pumpkin pie for dessert. The family was delighted and were happy to scratch that task off of their to-do list. What the family didn't know however, was that Lori had never made a pumpkin pie before and had no clue. She had no idea that once you mixed together the ingredients and poured the liquid into the pie crusts that they needed to go into the oven at 350 degrees for an hour to cook. Lori thought you just mixed them together and put the pie in a fridge to help the ingredients chill and set up. This of course wouldn't happen, no matter how long you left it in the fridge. So, after a magnificent meal had been prepared and served, it was now time for Lori to shine with her homemade pumpkin pie, however; when it made its way onto the table, the group noticed that the pie seemed a bit wobbly and was going to be difficult to eat with forks, maybe spoons. The family burst into laughter because, for the first Christmas ever, there was no pie and ice cream, and nobody knew for sure if Lori's pies would cook and turn into what they all knew as pumpkin pie. The oven was engaged, and the crusts of pumpkin soup went into the oven. We would have our answer in the next sixty minutes or so. And sixty minutes later they had their answer. It didn't work at all. The big question on everyone's mind was where Lori found that pumpkin pie recipe. It was not a Julia Child standard go-to recipe. After one hour of baking, the pie was still liquid, and the family had to find an alternative for dessert that night. Lori did have to hide her face for almost one hour because of the embarrassment, but she was quickly forgiven once the Nanaimo Bars had made their way into the family room. The evening wore on and excitement levels subsided enough that all the girls could finally go to bed. Once they had been put to bed for the night, the adults then grabbed all of the hidden gems and brought them out and placed them around the tree. For one more year the younger children may still believe in the miracle of Santa Claus, and for another year, the family was all together and sharing peace, harmony, and love.

The following morning the girls were up and running around by 7:00 am and Anne had already prepped and started the coffee. They would wait for all the bodies to be in attendance before they began the ritual of tearing open the presents. Mitch, Chanel, and the boys arrived first. Soon after, Grandma and Grandpa showed up with arms full of presents. Before long, the chaos that was Christmas had begun and was in full swing with everybody ripping open the mysterious boxes and smiling with happiness from their contents. Anne and Maxine made sure that Lori had plenty of things to open so she would not feel left out of the festivities. Finally, Grandpa approached the big tree in the family room and moved in closer so that he could reach the envelopes that had been stuck into the tree with peoples' names on them and began to pass them out. Clyde completed the task but still had one envelope in his hand and he got everybody's attention before he made an announcement. "Lori," he started, "the Miller family got together this year and we did something we haven't done in many years, but we wanted to bless you with good luck and," he passed her the envelope, "good fortune. The family has amalgamated some funds that we understand will pay for your travel to and from Tokyo as well as give you a few months of spending money." Clyde said. "This is our family gift to you this year. One day in your future, you will need to pay it forward to someone else. For now, we all wish you the best success in teaching at Tokyo University at the start of the next term. Congratulations."

"What are you talking about Clyde? What position at the University of Tokyo? Could someone fill me in please." Lori said.

"I spoke with my friend at the Consulate, and he was able to pull some strings so if you want it, you can head to Japan and start your new teaching career next week. All you have to do is say yes and pack your stuff. It's time for you to prepare for your next adventure."

Mitch couldn't help himself, so he began singing, "I'm turning Japanese, oh yes I'm turning Japanese, I really think so."

Lori steadied herself against Clyde, she was looking like she may pass out from all of the excitement, and…she did. Down to the floor she began sliding until Roger scooped her up in his arms and placed her carefully onto the sofa where she could recover. Anne collected a cold compress to place on her forehead to try reviving her somewhat. Before long she was making noises again and looking around the room like she had never seen any of the family before, but not long after, she was back to life and sitting up and drinking coffee.

"When is all of this supposed to happen?" She asked.

"Your flight for Tokyo leaves on New Year's Eve Day at 4:00 pm from YVR. When you arrive, there will be a car to collect you and your things and take you back to the university facilities, where you will be staying for at least two years. The rest will be up to you." Roger said.

"I don't know what to say. I have never had anyone show me this level of kindness before. I am so overwhelmed. "Lori said.

"We all want you to succeed Lori," Maxine said as she wrapped her arm around Lori's waist in a show of support. "So, get out there and succeed."

"I need a minute," she said to the group, "I need to go cry by myself for a minute and then I'll be okay." She turned and headed off to her room to decompress from all of the goings on that morning. She was shocked and amazed.

On New Year's Eve Day Roger, Rose, and Brooke all piled into the truck and drove Lori out to YVR airport to drop her off for the start of her next adventure. Roger was feeling odd that this lovely woman he was just getting to know, had to find her own way in her life and that meant her, and Roger were going their own separate ways. They exchanged small talk for a moment and Rose and Brooke squeezed Lori so hard they tried to break her in half. A few more tears and goodbyes and it was time. Lori leaned in close to Roger and whispered in his ear, "You have been the best NON-boyfriend I've ever had. Thank you and your family Roger. I will never forget you."

Chapter Thirteen

Roger loved a challenge, so he was determined to get right back up there on that dating horse as quickly as he could. He ended up having to work so much during January, before he knew it the month was over, and he hadn't done anything on the love-interest front. Roger always had to do the mental checks with himself, girls, job, family, check. Prioritizing was a key element in his life, but he had longed for mature lady company, and it had been an exceedingly long time. The last time he was with a woman was Nikita from Russia and he had felt like he was pushed around and not pleasantly treated. He was definitely hoping to find someone a bit less aggressive than Nikita.

Plans were made to have a simple lunch date at a neighbourhood restaurant where he had eaten with his family many times before. They made tasty food at affordable prices, and it wouldn't appear like he was trying to impress her with his taste in high-end dining. Her name was Tracy, and, from her profile, she was an attractive young woman. She did, however, make sure she was not hiding the fact that she had two sons and a daughter all under the age of fourteen, which was not surprising to Roger because he too was a single parent. Having kids in tow is common in today's adult dating scene.

They met at noon at the local bistro and when Roger entered, he saw Tracy waving to get his attention and draw him over to her table. He was pleased with her beauty. She was lovely to look at with dark, tanned looking skin and raven-black hair and dark eyes. She was petit and definitely had a tiny bit of a tummy, probably from having three children. She was wearing a midi-length dress that was a floral print fabric in dark rich colours. It was a wonderful match to her hair and skin tones. She sported a pair of fashionable sneakers to finish the outfit that looked nice and also had a touch of practicality to them. They made their introductions to each other and sat down to eat. Roger was delighted to have such an attractive woman to look at across the table from him and hoped that the two of them might find some mutual interests and likes. They began to discuss a wide range of topics and Roger and Tracy really seemed in sync for a couple that had just met for the first time that day. The conversation just flowed so perfectly from one topic to another, making Roger feel like this lady would get along with his entire family, if given the chance. She was smart, kind, and pretty. A lethal combination. The two chatted away for about an hour when she excused herself to leave the table to freshen up. As she walked away, Roger noticed the four young children at the next table were starting to get a bit noisy and began to tease each other for a variety of reasons, like kids do, and he smirked, giggled, and thought, "Kids will be kids." He glanced again and saw that there was no adult sitting at the table with the children, but assumed there was somebody there with them and went back to drinking his coffee. Seconds later, he saw a projectile of some kind come flying over his table and land on an unoccupied table next to his, at which time Roger turned to the table of kids and said, "This is a restaurant not a playground. Please refrain from throwing things around while you are a guest here."

"Sorry mister," the oldest member of their group replied.

Moments later something else went sailing by and set down even further away than the first projectile. Roger spun his head around to face the children and said, "That is enough! People are trying to enjoy themselves and DO NOT want to be hit by some flying object from your table. I asked you very nicely to please stop doing that. Do we all understand each other?" Roger quired.

"We are not allowed to speak to strangers, mister." The oldest boy replied.

"Very funny. Where are your parents or guardians?" Roger asked.

"Our mom is in the washroom right now. When she comes back you can talk to her." He said sarcastically. All the kids at the table began to laugh and found this exceedingly funny. At that time, Tracy was coming back to the table and saw that Roger was speaking to the kids at the next table. She could instantly tell something was amiss. What had been happening while she was away?

"Are these kids causing trouble?" she asked.

"They are simply acting like kids. They were throwing food or something around and I asked them to cease their activities." He said.

She stood for a few seconds looking at the group of children and said to them, "I asked you all to behave while we were at the restaurant today. I told you I was going on a date today with this nice man and I needed you all to act maturely so we could sit and visit but, as normal, you can't just be good for a little while. Mother is disappointed in all of you right now."

"I thought your profile said you had three kids?" Roger blindly spewed out.

"Okay you caught me. I lied. I have four children under the age of fourteen and I'm a single mom. I said I had three because in my mind I thought that seemed a more reasonable number. Most men hear you have four kids, and they are running in the other direction. When you came in today, I thought you looked handsome and after we began talking and found out how nice of a man you were, I didn't know how I was going to tell you the truth, but I thought we would cross that bridge when we came to it. So, yes, I have four children and they are all sitting behind you." She finished.

"Well, let's not be strangers." Roger said. He stood up and looked at the three boys and one girl and asked them all to come over to their table so they could all get to know one another better. The kids all moved to Tracy and Roger's table and began to make lots of noise and bug and tease each other. Within a few minutes, the boys were arguing about who got to use the PS5 gaming system when they got home and the daughter, who seemed to like men, wanted to sit on Roger's lap and eat his last few fries, which Roger agreed to instantly. He was a sweet man and was not going to make a little girl feel upset, so he was okay with it as long as Tracy was good with it. The daughter, Denise, was elated to be sitting on his lap and munching down the last of his food. She was delighted and Roger could see that Tracy was pleasantly pleased that Denise was opening up to somebody else besides her. She explained to Roger that she was married right out of high school, to a man that was training to be a medical doctor, so she did feel like she had it made and was in a state of shock when her husband finally finished all of his education and promptly left Tracy for another woman. Another doctor from the same hospital that he had been working at during his schooling. Tracy was devastated, but she was also left high and dry and had spent all the years since he left her and the kids battling in court to try and get some alimony so she could survive, however;

he was willing to fight for every dime that he could. Her life was turned upside down with no home, no money, and no husband to help raise the four kids that he wanted so badly. She realized later that he wanted a family, but he also wanted to be the rich doctor without a care in the world. The only way for him to achieve that lifestyle was to have a wife and kids when he was really young and had the patience to put up with the children and all of the responsibilities of having a family. Once he was free and clear and had officially completed his training, he was gone. Tracy was left to fend for herself and the kids, and he moved on with his new life. She couldn't get help from any family members because they all lived in Tampa Bay, Florida and did not have disposable income to throw her way to aid with the raising of her family. She was in trouble and had to go out and get a job as a cashier at a local supermarket to make by but could not afford the bills of four young children all going through school. She continued to tell her story to Roger, and she was welling up, so Roger was hoping to change to subject to something a bit lighter, but it was clear that Tracy was having a tough time in life with money and the responsibilities of a young family. He felt terrible for her, but he was sure that he was not going to be her white knight and was not going to be the one to save her.

He sat and thought about how many times he had heard of people acquiring an education only to leave their significant other once they made the big leagues on their pay cheques. It was crazy to think that someone could do that to the children. Leave them all to make it on their own. He hoped that Tracy would be vindicated and would somehow get a large settlement out of her ex-husband so she and her family could live their best lives. He also knew that it was not going to be him that was going to get her to the promised land, whatever that may be.

Tracy had tried to be flirty with Roger during their conversation, before the big reveal about the kids, but she seemed to be done once the truth had come out. It was clear to Roger that Tracy, like him, was interested in having some adult company, but it was clearly going to be too complicated. He didn't even want to pretend for a second that there was any chance of romance between the pair. Tracy might have been in need of some company, but Roger was not her guy. He could barely manage Rose and Brooke on his own, let alone have four more dependents needing his attention and money. Roger waved to the waiter to bring the bill. He passed the waiter his credit card and said, "Please add the four kids to my check." Tracy smiled at him while nodding in a happy manner. She wasn't expecting Roger to pay for her kids, but she sure was pleased that he did.

As they finished up, they all stood to leave, but Denise wanted to hold Roger's hand on the way to the car. Her tiny hand stretched her fingers around one of Roger's oversized digits and off they went to Tracy's car in the parking lot. Roger helped load Denise into her seat and then he buckled her into place. As he reached down to do up the buckle, Denise extended her arms around his neck and hugged him hard and said, "So are you going to be my new daddy?"

Roger leaned over and kissed her on the cheek and said, "Denise, you already have a daddy. Your mommy and I are good friends, but I am not going to be living with you and your brothers in the future. I want you to know that you are precious, and I hope we see each other again someday." He patted on her head and said goodbye.

Roger made his way back to his truck and climbed in. He sat in the cab for a minute digesting the events of his lunch and chuckled to himself, "If we got together, we would have three boys and three girls all in one house. Sounds like the makings of a Disney movie."

As he drove away that day, he kept wondering if he would ever have a straightforward date with a woman from this dating site? So far…not so much.

***

"If at first you do not succeed, try, try, again." This was becoming Roger's mantra. He was determined to find a wonderful person to spend some quality time with and he was sure she was out there, maybe not in Vancouver, but out there. He reached out to a woman named Lisa. She was under thirty years old and was a self-professed athletic person. She was into everything to do with exercise. Her profile page was more like a dare to compete than a chance to meet. He didn't want to be schooled by "Super-Athlete-Girl," so he picked out an activity only a handful of people on earth can be good at, Segway riding. It turned out that you could rent Segways by the hour at the University of British Columbia, UBC, and ride around on the university grounds, which are massive. It seemed like a pretty safe thing to do, and they had a tour guide that was available to ride along with you, to show you the highlights and answer any questions arising from the Segway machines. They looked like they should be really easy to use, but like everything in life, it takes time to get the hang of it. Once you have climbed aboard, you feel like you are standing six feet above everybody as you move about the sidewalks and paths. When you pass people, it seems crazy high compared to the pedestrian traffic. Roger and Lisa met in one of the parking lots near the Segway Rental area to collect their machines and be given the safety instructions before getting under way. Roger usually didn't like to use bike helmets but, for some reason, he thought it would be a particularly clever idea to wear one during this experience. Once they met the safety requirements for the machine rental, they paid their fees and were on their way. Lisa had acquired a map of the UBC grounds so they could scoot about and not get lost. Within a few minutes of using the Segway, Lisa was bombing around and controlling her Segway as if she had done this activity a million times before. She was able to fully manipulate the machine like she had been riding forever. It was really something for Roger to watch this young woman completely take control of this new device and make it appear like it was as common to Lisa as one of her legs. It was astounding. The weather was a high, overcast sky and a touch cool, so they were both wearing leg coverings and sported lightweight jackets to keep out the cold dampness of an early spring day. As they rode along, Roger could not help noticing what a terrific figure Lisa had. She filled out her Lululemon tights beautifully and had powerful looking legs like a personal trainer. She had long, blonde hair that was carefully pulled back in a ponytail and fitted through the opening in her baseball peak cap hat. She hadn't applied a ton of make-up to her face and still looked alluring. He was happy to see that she was smiling most of the time and seemed to really be enjoying their Segway experience. Roger was pleasantly surprised at how easy it was to ride alongside of each other and they could easily chat without feeling like they were in peril at all times. It made the day go so much nicer when they could be side by side and still hear the conversation back and forth. They came across an ice-cream stand and stopped to top up their useless calorie intake for the day, besides, Roger couldn't help himself when they had Birthday cake mint cookies and cream flavourings with sprinkles. This was one of those amazing moments in life when you are having fun, and it just keeps getting better by using other body senses to complete the effect. They sat down at a tabletop and talked for the next hour about their jobs and interests. Roger figured out quickly that Lisa was a doer. She was a person that needed to be on the go at all times. She couldn't go home every night and look after children, at least not at this point in her life. She filled Roger in on her travels around the world and talked about her ambition to go to many more destinations before she settled down to have a family, which she was clear that she wanted a family, but she did not know when that was going to happen. Certainly not at this point in her life and Roger had two daughters that needed full-time care and attention, so he was already starting to wonder if there was any future potential with Lisa. He knew he liked her looks and attitude, but he was not about trying to coax women into bed for one-night stands. Maxine had raised a far more responsible type of man than that. Roger was keenly interested in female company, but he wasn't going to attempt to make any woman feel cheap. With that in mind, he knew that this was another lovely day out and about in Vancouver with a pretty woman, but their future looked bleak. He knew that she was at a different time and place in her life, and her wants and needs were different from Roger's. It was too bad because Roger did like this woman. She seemed friendly and energetic with a positive outlook. Great traits to have in any of your friendships.

"How are you doing?" Lisa asked. "Are you good to keep going for a while?"

"Absolutely," Roger replied. "We can use the Segways for another two hours, so hopefully I can get my skill set of operating this crazy machine into high gear."

"Okay. On the map it showed a bunch of pathways over there," as she waved her arm and pointed her index finger to an area to the south of where she was standing. "There are a ton of paths and lookout spots along the way, so it should be quite stunning." Lisa said. She leaned her head downward and her machine leaped into action and began to race across the campus to seek out new unexplored pathways. As time went by that day, they were both starting to get used to the Segways' weight, size, and capabilities and were able to manipulate the machines in a highly efficient manner. Before he knew it, Lisa was racing along and hanging off the side of the machine doing donuts and attempting to pick things up off the ground while she was motoring, which again, showed Roger how much of a daredevil this woman could be. Lisa turned onto a path that had some thick and heavy evergreen trees lining the side of the pathway but was straight for a long distance from where they stood. She wanted to race along at breakneck speed and freak herself out. The two headed onto the path, leaned into the machines, and let them go at full power and they raced beside each other. Lisa did a mock-type voice of a horse track race announcer for effect. "Coming around the final turn, it's Lisa riding Rocket Launcher and close behind is Roger on Sea Slug, but he seems to be falling further and further behind," she said giggling as her Segway inched ahead of Roger's machine on the straightaway. As she delighted the two with her commentary, they noticed a large group of people on the path ahead in the direction they were racing at a high speed so before they knew it, they were closing the gap quickly and Roger panicked and attempted to take defensive maneuvers to not crash the group, but when Roger's front wheels hit the edge of the curb, the Segway leapt into the air high enough that Roger's head bashed directly into a low hanging tree branch and knocked him off the machine. He landed on his back on the ground on the grassy edges all around the pathways. "I'm so glad I am wearing a helmet today," he thought to himself. He stared up at the sky through all of the tree branches that reached out from the tree trunks throughout the campus grounds. He realized that he was feeling weird as he lay on his back and wondered how hard he had actually hit his head even though it was in a helmet.

"Roger. Roger, are you okay? Can you hear me, Roger?" Lisa asked as she cradled his head in her hands. The cobwebs in his brain were slowly clearing as he tried to sit up on the ground, but he still felt too dizzy to sit up, so he knew he wasn't going to stand up for a while. He put his head back down and just relaxed and breathed deeply to give himself time to regain his bearings. As he laid there on the cool grass, he had the thought again about this dating site and his luck with it so far. He knew that eventually he was going to go on a normal date without all of the drama he had continued to face.

"How are we doing Roger? Is your head feeling any better?" Lisa said while kneeling beside him on the ground. He was coming in and out of reality. One second, he was at the UBC campus and the next he was on stage performing a scene from the Lion King, and that didn't seem right. He heard the faint sound of sirens coming from somewhere, but he couldn't make out the direction from which it was coming. It was getting louder and louder by the second. "Holy shit! That siren is for me!" Roger thought to himself.

"Just relax Roger. The paramedics are here to assist you. Everything is going to be okay," she said as she stroked Roger's head.

Through a fog, Roger felt some male hands touching him, sitting him up, and asking a battery of questions. As the two men continued to work on Roger's vitals, one of the paramedics announced, "Oh my God. This is Grouse Mountain. I would recognize that face anywhere. So how have you been G.M.?" The paramedic asked.

Roger was still coming in and out of consciousness and was beginning to realize that he had clobbered himself much harder than he had originally thought. He felt like a fool as he lay there trying to figure out how he managed to crash his head into a low hanging tree branch so hard that he couldn't get himself off the ground. The paramedics evaluated and asked questions and probed Roger, but they were concerned and had decided to take Roger back to the hospital for further examination. They brought out the gurney and placed Roger on top and then strapped him down for the ride to the hospital. Lisa had asked Roger for an emergency contact person, and Roger, somehow, was able to come up with a name and number. Lisa called Mitch and let him know that Roger was heading for VGH for observation for 24 hours, just to be on the safe side. They rolled him to the back of the ambulance and lifted him inside. Once he was strapped down and secured the lights began flashing and the siren began wailing and they were off.

Lisa stood at the scene for a moment, wondering how she was going to get the two rental machines back to the owners on the other side of the campus, but she figured she would just take one back and have to walk back and retrieve the other Segway. She too had some awkward experiences on the dating site, but she wasn't ready to give up. Like Roger, she was in it for the long haul, and she knew that finding love was not easy.

The ride to the hospital was quick. The entire trip had the two paramedics teasing Roger about being one of the premiere dating bachelors in the city of Vancouver. "Every time we see you dude, you are with some new smoking hot babe. How do you do it Roger? You should be authoring books to help other men find the perfect girl." The paramedic said.

"I had the perfect girl, but then this imperfect world took her from me and now I spend my spare time trying to fill in that emptiness. It might look like fun boys, but I can assure you, it is not." Roger said and then fell back to sleep.

When Roger came to, he saw Mitch and Anne standing in the hallway just outside the room, speaking with Lisa, trying to glean all of the information they could regarding the accident and how he ended up in VGH. She explained the pathway they attempted to go down with the low hanging branches and how a group of tourists thwarted Roger's ability to drive down the middle of the path and when he went off the beaten track, he managed to hit his head on a branch, but thank goodness he was wearing a helmet. He was knocked to the ground, but the safety equipment had lessened his potential injuries immensely. Lisa stuck around for a bit to be sure that Roger was coming back to health before she left. She came into the room and kissed him on the cheek and continued on her way. He could not believe his dumb luck when it came to dating beautiful women. He was beginning to believe that there might really be a curse on him. All of these dating failures couldn't be a mere coincidence, could they? He closed his eyes and drifted in and out of consciousness for the next twelve hours. Finally, a doctor came into the room and gave him a clean bill of health and released Roger, so he was free to go. Mitch was waiting at the front door and once Roger was out of the wheelchair and into the car, he said, "Let's go to UBC Segway Rentals so I can retrieve my truck."

"Sounds like a plan, Roger. Are you sure you are okay to drive?" Mitch queried.

"Yeah, I'm alright. The only thing bruised was my ego. Got to tell you though Mitch, my ego has been taking a beating lately and that has got to change." Roger stated.

"How so? Are you planning on giving up on the dating scene?" Mitch asked his brother.

"I'm going to go down fighting Mitch. I know there is a match for me somewhere out there. I just gotta find her." Roger said.

Chapter Fourteen

Emily contacted Roger to arrange a date with a slight twist. A local bar was hosting an art night, where patrons could attend an evening of painting on canvas and have a beverage while they created their works of art. The bar set up an easel for each of the guests to stand or sit behind and an instructor would stand at the front of the room and assist the painters through the process. The instructors demonstrated a stroke or application process and then the class would do the same thing until the paintings were completed. Step by step, the instructor would walk the class through the piece until it was a masterpiece to take home and hopefully, it was good enough to hang on a wall at home. (Easier said than done). The thing about professional artists is that they make everything seem so easy and effortless, however; it is not. Most of the Jr. Picasso's finished pieces found their way to where most of these collections belong, in the trash. The wonderful thing is, it's a lot of fun for the evening, and you get to chat between instructions, so it allows lots of time to get to know someone better, which is the result Roger was hoping for. The event was planned to begin at 7:00 pm and he made sure to be there early to reserve two seats side by side, which was easy to accomplish. He grabbed two sets of everything required and found his way to the two assigned chairs and got set up, which meant putting his stuff on the counter by the canvasses. He decided to wait for Emily to arrive before ordering any drinks for himself, to see what she wanted to order. The group of participants began to grow, and the friendly people just kept coming through the door and heading to their workspaces to prepare for the activity. There were so many smiles and friendly greetings to one another that Roger was really taken aback by this display of kindness. He was quietly impressed so far. In about ten minutes the room was filling fast and most of the guests had introduced themselves to one another and were preparing to get the evening festivities started. Roger couldn't help noticing that an attractive woman had arrived with a couple of girlfriends and was at least eight months pregnant. He was looking in her direction and caught her eye, so she instantly came over and introduced herself to Roger and began chatting about nothing in particular and then he asked her outright, "When is your due date?"

"I'm actually due tomorrow but you know how these things go, right. Do you have any children?" She extended her hand to greet and shake his.

"Roger," he replied, "I have two girls, eight and six. How about you?"

"Jane. And this is my first." Jane replied.

The two continued to talk at which time Roger found out that Jane was married, and Jane found out that Roger is widowed. She was an attractive, robust woman with a wonderful smile and an alluring aura. She just seemed like the kind of lady you would want on your friend's list. They talked until the area of the bar that they were occupying had a hush come over it, somehow, and people were stepping out of the way as you would if a celebrity entered the room and was heading for the stage to perform, it was a spectacle. Emily appeared and had stolen most of the available air because she was dressed differently than most people. She had styled her jet-black hair, standing straight up from her hair products, a piercing in her eyebrow, nose, and ears, large bosoms with a crop top, mini skirt that barely made it, and knee-high black patent boots with four-inch platform soles. It was quite a look and she clearly shocked all of the other women that had attended that night. She was wearing a plethora of silver rings, bracelets, and chains to complete the effect. Her makeup was strong and dark like a comic book heroine. Mysterious. Emily was almost six feet tall and higher with the boots. Her body was trim, and she clearly had worked out in her lifetime. Surprisingly, she had no visible tattoos. She smiled and it immediately changed how she looked, drastically. Approachable and confident. They introduced themselves to each other and ordered a drink, but within minutes of their greeting, the instructor was ready to begin so all of the participants took their seats, and she commenced her lesson.

The room's volume increased significantly when the group put brush to canvas and the class began to make what they believed to be mistakes and the laughter, and the self-deprecation got started. It looked so simple when you watched the instructor's capable hand move paint across a canvas with ease and grace, and then when the participants attempted the same maneuver, it never seemed to turn out the same way. Roger and Emily hadn't only just met but they were engaged in some heavy laughs, which was an amazing icebreaker for both of them. Roger was dealing with his own insecurities because he hadn't spent any time in his life hanging out with women that looked like Emily. This was a bold outfit, and she was completely comfortable in it and held a confidence when she went about her business. So far, she was a unique person.

Roger was also drawn to this art class because of its subject matter, which was sand dollars. The people could choose between doing sand dollars on the beach, or on their own ideas with some ocean looking things to tie the theme together. Both versions appealed to Roger because they were something that really connected Rose and Brooke and himself in a unique way. He figured even if the date went poorly, he would still end up with a sand dollar portrait of some kind and his girls would love it.

The woman running the class allowed the group to take a quick break and return back in ten minutes to resume painting. Emily went off to the restroom and Jane seized the opportunity to come over and razz Roger about his latest Mona Lisa. She was giggling and being funny and clearly flirting with Roger when Emily returned to her seat.

"And who is this?" Emily asked.

"This is Jane. Jane, this is Emily." Roger said.

"So, you know this woman?" Emily inquired with raised eyebrows.

"We met earlier tonight." He said.

"You met her tonight while you were on a date with me?" Emily said.

"No. You weren't here yet and Jane came over and introduced herself to me. That's it. End of story." He continued.

"Interesting. Meeting a woman on a date that starts with meeting other women at the bar first. Let me guess, you got here two hours before the class commenced? Just to scope things out?" Emily asked.

"Emily, that is just not the case here. I am here to meet you. That's it." Roger said.

"Okay then," the instructor bellowed, "Let's all get back to our paintings."

They got back to their seats and continued to follow the tutelage of the instructor. Emily was still painting but not with the same enthusiasm. She kept giving sideways glances at Jane and seemed to be upset with Roger's actions. 'If you're on a date with me, why are you talking to other women?' She was having a challenging time getting past this incident. For some reason it really bugged her.

Soon after the paint lesson had restarted, Jane was doing her best Van Gough imitation when there was a large puddle of liquid forming underneath her as she was holding her belly and proclaiming, "I think my water has broken!"

No sooner had this development taken place, than Jane began to moan and claimed that she was having contractions. Jane was standing in the puddle and had not moved an inch since this started. Roger could see that Jane was looking odd and a bit ashen so he instinctively walked closer to her in case she passed out, so that someone would be there to support her. As he stood beside her, she made an attempt to move forward and slipped, as anticipated, so Roger pulled a chair and scooted it under her as she was slowly getting lower to the floor. She could now lean back in the chair and take the weight off her feet temporarily as many of the other women were calling 911 to get help. Roger was on one knee beside Jane's chair and was holding her hand in a show of comfort while waiting for the paramedics to arrive when Emily looked over and saw this show of support and she approached asking Roger, "What the hell is going on with you two? Now you're holding hands and rubbing her belly? What's next, are you riding in the ambulance to the hospital?"

"I am just trying to make her feel okay until the paramedics get here. That's it. No secret agenda. Only common decency." Roger said.

"Well, it all seems a little too close for me. This broad shows up here tonight and the two of you can't seem to separate for a minute. Makes me feel like you are not fully committed to this date because you're too busy thinking about all of the other women in the place. If you're with me, then you stay with me. I don't want to see you flirt with every girl in the place." Emily stated.

"I'm sorry Emily. I don't want you to feel like I'm ignoring you at all. I have been looking forward to this date and the chance to meet you so, for the record, I am having a wonderful time. This painting thing is a really cool idea." Roger said.

As Roger was mentioning this to Emily, a pair of young paramedics arrived on the scene to assess the situation. No sooner had the men turned the corner with the gurney, they then saw Roger and said, "Hey! Grouse Mountain. What the hell are you doing here? Oh my God, is this your girlfriend? We didn't know you had a pregnant girlfriend GM. This is so unbelievable dude." One of the men said.

Roger piped up immediately and said, "No guys, this is not my girlfriend. She is just a lady that is having contractions in a bar where I am taking an art class. Not my girl, not my child."

The two paramedics looked at Roger and noticed the steam coming out of Emily's ears and realized there was more going on here than just a woman in labour. In seconds, the first responders went about their process with great efficiency and skill and had Jane strapped into the gurney and ready to travel. They grabbed the rolling bars and moved the patient out the front door of the bar and to the back of the ambulance. Roger was walking beside them all while holding Jane's hand and giving moral support until they got to the back doors and the paramedic said, "Okay Roger, just hop in and sit down so you're safe."

"No guys, I'm actually on a date right now, so I can't leave to go to the hospital with you guys." Roger got out.

No sooner had he finished that statement, then the driver swung the back door shut and gave the double tap to the back of the truck and he climbed into the driver's cockpit and began to drive with the siren and lights blaring, back to the hospital to care for this pregnant woman, who was about to have her first baby. Roger looked out the back door window at the pub as it diminished in size as they drove away from the scene and realized that his date, Emily, was still in the bar with no idea that he was now sequestered in the ambulance, heading to the hospital with his new acquaintance, with no idea how to get out of this dilemma. He couldn't phone her because they had not exchanged numbers as of yet. All of their communication had been online, so Roger had no way to let Emily know where he was, or what had happened to him.

Back at the bar, it only took a moment for Emily to figure out that Roger had left with the paramedics and his old girlfriend, so she was now abandoned in the bar halfway through an art class. She was a tolerant woman for most things, but this one had really ticked her off. She could tell when she saw Roger and Jane together there was something there. She couldn't put her finger on it, but she knew something was off. She spun around in her chair and faced the two canvases that Roger was working on creating his seashell sand dollar painting for Rose and Brooke. Emily was actually impressed with what a wonderful job he had done on the pieces, however, she was hurt and now had no intentions of doing anything nice for Roger. She removed a large brush from the container filled with discarded paint brushes and dipped the tool into the black paint and went about adding some finishing touches to his two works or art. Emily's message was clear and understandable.

***

When Roger emerged from the VGH emergency entrance he was still spinning. Somehow, he had managed to completely screw up another date that he was on with Emily and had been kidnapped into helping with Jane and her first ride in an ambulance to a hospital. When they dragged Roger into the building, however, they couldn't allow him to go into the operating room because that was reserved for family only, which he was not. He had been trying to escape ever since the ambulance had shown up at the pub, but with everything going on, he was pulled into a situation that he wanted to get out of immediately. He decided that he would go back to the bar and see if Emily was still there or if she had vacated the premises.

As he entered the bar, a number of people began clapping vigorously because of his heroism from earlier that evening. A few of the people from the art class asked him how Jane was doing and wanted to be sure that the new baby was okay. He didn't know. He forgot to ask anybody at the hospital if Jane's delivery went okay. He would have to find out at another time and place. He soon realized that Emily had left the building earlier in the evening and gone about her business. He checked with the art instructor, who was still packing things up to leave, and inquired about his two sand dollar paintings and would it be okay if he took them with him when he left that night. She said of course, but I'm not sure you are going to want them anymore. "What is that supposed to mean?" Roger asked.

"Your girlfriend, after you left, had a bit of a meltdown here and we had to have the security guards escort her out of the building and off the premises. She was fit to be tied because she was so mad that you chose a pregnant, married girl over her. It didn't sit well with her at all." The instructor said.

She walked Roger over to the bin of discarded artwork dreams and saw his two little canvases peeking out from the pile of scrap paintings. He reached in and pulled them from their early grave; however, when he was able to see the entire front façade of the canvas, he could see a note left for him in black, oil-based acrylic which read, "**FUCK YOU ROGER,**" on both paintings, to be sure they were both destroyed.

Roger brought them out to his pickup truck in the parking lot and climbed inside and shut the door. He looked at the artwork that had now been destroyed and he began to sob. He was really wanting to give these two paintings to his daughters…now he couldn't.

Chapter Fifteen

It was a Friday night and Roger was at home with Brooke and Rose. They were watching some kind of children's movie about cats, which the girls could stay glued to for hours and hours, going, "Awe, they're so cute." This can be a lot of fun for a few hours but, after that, one needs to move on to adult-type activities, like drinking. Roger was always conscious not to drink too much in front of any of the girls so they wouldn't see how much he loved drinking a variety of beverages. More so if they contained alcohol. Once the girls had settled on another classic kids' movie, Roger thought he would excuse himself and go online and seek out new potential relationships. Today was different. He was going to try something a bit more radical by selecting to engage women that were the exact opposite of him. He was purposely going to find a person that had nothing in common with him at all. He figured after over a dozen attempts to find love; he might be looking in the wrong places. Maybe women from his own province were the problem. They needed to be from someplace else and they needed to have nothing on their profile that matched Roger's. It seemed a touch wonky to try and find Miss Wrong but why not, he hadn't found Miss Right, which was for sure. This new tactic might just be the revised plan he needed to find the woman of his dreams. If not, it would be another swing and a miss mentality.

His search began with the simplest thing there is, her name. He was now only interested in women with names that he couldn't pronounce or had never even seen before. Where were they from? Who knows? He wanted to be seeking a type of woman that would challenge everything he had ever known before. Let's just find out if opposites attract after all. Roger scoured through all of the available woman's names on the dating site, looking for the anomalies. There it was, staring back at him like a lighthouse, warning ships in the night. Her name was Sloane. He had no idea where that name even originated from, but he didn't care. This girl was perfect. He had nothing in common with her and he had never seen or heard the name Sloane before in his life. She was perfect. He sent her a message to ask her on a date. Something simple he thought. He asked her to meet him at the Gillnetter Pub in Port Coquitlam, right on the edge of the Fraser River. It sported a huge interior and twenty-plus outdoor tables that were under a glass roof so the light would shine through and brighten the ambience of the space. All the workers at the Gillnetter were long-term employees, so they knew what they were doing, and they were quick and efficient, so within minutes you are seated with a drink in your hand, the way it should be. Roger arrived early and took a seat on one of the bar stools to wait until Sloane got there. He had seen one of the pictures from her profile, but he wanted to be completely surprised by how she looked and especially, how she acted. When Sloane entered the bar, he was really looking, trying to determine if this was the girl he was supposed to meet. She was at least five foot ten inches tall and had shoulder length brown hair with sculpted eyebrows and a sharp, pointy chin. It appeared that she had not combed her hair that day. Her dress was midi style and bright white and fashioned from cotton. Even from a distance, it was easy to see that Sloane did not appear to be wearing a bra or panties under the dress. When the outdoor sun would cascade its beams through the room, it would make Sloane's dress seem semi-transparent and one could easily see through it. Roger walked over and introduced himself to Sloane and then the hostess took them to their seats. They browsed the menus, made some appetizer selections and drinks, and then continued to exchange small talk. He was astounded that he was getting along so nicely with a person that was to be the exact polar opposite of himself. 'Kooky,' Roger thought. As the evening progressed, he observed that Sloane did not shave her underarms or legs. He was trying to think back in his life if he had ever dated a woman that didn't shave her body entirely and realized that he was not going to be judgmental regarding this issue. The "NEW" Roger was completely open to all things novel, so throw caution to the wind and go for it. She had excused herself to visit the washroom and, as she walked away from the table, Roger could see she had a tattoo of something on her back, but he could not tell exactly what it was portraying. The new Roger was incredibly open to people with tattoos. No big deal. As she returned to the table, he saw other tattoos all over her body and thought it could be fun to see the complete collection one day. After noshing on some tasty treats, the two of them had decided to date again in the extremely near future and would select a destination that coming week. Roger loved the idea because he had become quite smitten with Sloane.

***

After further conversation, they decided on a movie and then some appetizers and drinks after at the local Cactus Club Restaurant. It seemed interesting to Roger that so many people really wanted the same thing. A family that adores them unconditionally and friends who were true, loyal, and always put their needs first. Tough to find. They talked about Roger's late wife Michelle, and she asked about Rose and Brooke, which made sense to Roger because if they ever did get together, she would need to know some of these realities. He was not ready for Sloane to meet his girls face to face, but she had a warm quality about her that he knew Rose and Brooke would simply adore. It was nice that Roger was never searching for things to talk about with Sloane. She seemed to be in tune with Roger and came across as a bright person. As the pair revealed more facts about themselves, Sloane explained more of her background to Roger. She had grown up in Toronto and moved out to Victoria when she was twenty to attend University of Victoria on a Poetry Scholarship for four years. When she graduated, she went on to achieve her Master's in Creative Writing at UBC and then took full-time employment with Penguin Publishing as a Creative Director. Roger gazed across the table thinking to himself, 'Holy Cow. This is one smart lady.' His decision to try dating his polar opposite might be a stroke of genius, however, from his past experiences he knew he should retain a modicum of caution.

As the evening moved on, Roger volunteered to pay the bill and Sloane approved. When the waiter returned with the electronic machine, he entered his card and then added a tip. When he was done, he handed the machine back to the waiter who was dutifully standing there awaiting the return of the device. He started to smile and began to laugh nervously. "No way Roger. Are you serious? Did you want to double check the bill before I hit enter?" The waiter said.

"No. It's correct. I am feeling blessed today and so I wanted you to feel blessed today. Just give me a copy of the receipt." Roger said.

"Of course, sir." He replied. He used the handheld device to provide Roger with the receipt. "Hey Roger? Is it okay if I give you a hug?"

"You got it." Roger said as he leaned in, and bro hugged the waiter.

"That was awfully generous of you. You seem in really good spirits, or you're incredibly high, and it is really hitting you right now?" Sloane commented.

"Sloane I am having a nice evening with a nice person. That is always the perfect combination." They got up and sauntered their way to the door of the restaurant and Roger escorted her right to her vehicle. She opened the car door, but before she entered, she grabbed a big wad of fabric on the front of Roger's shirt, and she pulled him all the way into her body and pressed her lips onto his firmly. Roger was delighted to feel a woman in his arms, if only for a moment, but realized she had not stopped or pulled back, so he continued to kiss her deeply and enjoy one of life's little pleasures. A minute passed and she ceased her hold on his lips. He said goodnight, closed her door, and she drove away.

***

Roger felt it was time to head to his father's cabin in Penticton for a weekend away with Sloane and see how compatible they were while hanging out alone for a few days. Penticton was no hick town in the Okanagan Valley, rather it was a sun-drenched city of 33,000 people with a burgeoning economy in Canada's only desert. Clyde had purchased lakefront property back in the mid-sixties to build a cabin for the family in the summer months and slowly started to add-on over time, but when Roger and Mitch became old enough to build things properly, they took over and revamped it into a seven thousand square foot house and then added some smaller outbuildings for guests and storage. The original cabin remained but it had also been modernized to the point of "unrecognizable." There in frame, but not in spirit. The great part about the property was other family members could be there at the same time as you and not feel like you were in everybody's personal space. Each one of the three houses had a different décor theme and could sleep at least four people. It was an amazing set-up. And to be expected with three lots in a row. There was also a long waterfront section, which allowed them to have two docks out on the water in the summertime. Clyde had ended up winning a sales contest at work many years before and he decided to buy family plots for the entire family, however, the family all wanted to be cremated, so rather than buying plots, he bought some building lots. Three waterfront gems for thirty thousand dollars each and they were all serviced lots ready to build something on, and they did. Year by year things evolved, but the original log cabin feel was still present. It felt homey and comfortable and had the smell of a burning fireplace most of the time, which added to its ambience. It was a unique piece of property, and the Miller's were glad to have it in the family. Clyde was always able to make enough for his family to get by, always.

The cabin was also a wonderful place to bring women. There was a huge deck for sun tanning. There was a lake for swimming.

There was a boat for going motoring or water skiing. It was definitely a beautiful place to take anyone because it was on Okanagan Lake. Hot and sunny for the entire summer. Maxine had made many trips to different boutiques all over the world, finding just the right knick-knacks to add to the summer houses. It took time and diligence. But, once Maxine and Clyde retired, they had nothing but time, so they redecorated the summer houses year after year and one day… they should be perfect.

***

Spring is a wonderful time to visit the Okanagan, right after all of the snow has finished falling on the mountain roads, making them good and treacherous. Once the last of the snow has passed, it makes getting back and forth to Penticton much less stressful for your driving skills. In the winter months you never can tell what type of weather you are going to get, but by the end of April the "Crow's Nest" highway gets cleared and stays that way until the end of October, virtually every year. Over the years, the highway has undergone many upgrades but the snow and the plowing each year wears down the pavement and so every year the highway has to be resurfaced continuously and the vicious cycle continues, and the road is kept quite nicely for excursions to the Okanagan every summer. Another major attraction is the vineyards that produce wine every year. The Okanagan Valley has over two hundred vineyards that are open to the public for tours, tastings, and many of them serve lunch and dinner, so it has become another venue to experience when you visit. Water sports galore on every inch of the lakes, with every water sport being represented. The valley has a plethora of water activities and with the vineyards and all of the charming restaurants all around the city of Penticton, it makes tourists come back year after year to enjoy the ambience. Being Canada's only desert has its advantages as well. Deserts only get ten inches per year of precipitation so the important thing is you always know what the weather will be like every summer in the Okanagan Valley. Absolutely gorgeous. It does actually snow in the winters, but it is the light-as-a-feather drifting snow that seldom comes down and starts to pile up in a hurry. It is a fabulous part of British Columbia, that once you have been, it is hard to not go back. It has warm summer weather you can count on, which is rare for BC.

On the drive to and from the Okanagan Valley, you pass through countless fruit and vegetable stands along the sides of the road each year and it is the perfect place to stop and pick up some snacks for back at the summer cabin. So many fruit and veggie varieties to select from makes it difficult to decide what sumptuous treats you are going to create once you arrive at your destination. Just getting to your vacation spot can be hazardous with all the choices that are made available to you along the way. It is a sight to behold. The pilgrimage is well known to Roger because he had made the trek so many times in the past that he knew every corner, passing zone, public restroom, gas station and snack shop all the way from Vancouver to Penticton. He had travelled this road countless times and still loved the drive every year. You would travel to the end of the Fraser Valley in Hope, BC and then start uphill at an alarming rate, until you hit the first summit in Princeton. As you climb up the mountains and go through Manning Park, you'd be surrounded by evergreens and other non-leaf-shedding (conifer) trees for many hours. Then, just past Princeton, you'd get into the wide-open ranges where the trees become sporadic in comparison to the Hope/Princeton area. Long stretches of open, tall grass and rock and cactus. It changes to desert and the temperatures climb and the precipitation lessens. It really is a unique and special place to visit in Canada.

Roger had arranged to pick Sloane up from her home in Port Moody the day they were leaving for the cabin. He had stopped and collected all the food and drink supplies they would need and also was going to treat himself by using Clyde's sister's 1965 Mustang that was willed to him when she passed away in the 90s. It was the factory-green colour with the leatherette seats and automatic transmission, with a mere forty thousand miles on the odometer. The car was in mint condition and should be on display in a museum, however, Clyde always believed that a car was made to do a job and if it wasn't doing it…it was useless. Hence all of the vehicles that

Clyde owned had to be working cars and not stored in a garage somewhere decaying away. Machines were made to run. Roger stopped by his father's house to collect the car and to move his provisions into the Mustang for him and Sloane and their weekend away. Roger was super excited and even more so after he picked up the Mustang. It wasn't Roger's favorite old type of car, but he loved driving it because so many people marveled at the look of the 60s Mustangs, and it garnered so much positive attention. It definitely boosted his ego whenever he would take it out for a spin. Even more so if he drove it to Penticton on a weekend in the summer.

Roger pulled up in front of Sloane's house and jumped out to go fetch her grips. He scooped up her bags and stowed them in the trunk of the car and then walked around the car to open Sloane's door. She eased into the car, but it was clear that this old Mustang meant nothing to her. To Sloane, it was an old beater car worth nothing. She had no idea of its value or its allure to the public. It didn't matter. He liked the car, and he was driving it up to the cabin, which were all things Roger loved to do. Sloane slid into the passenger seat and strapped herself in, and they were off for the weekend. To the freeway they drove, ready to begin their weekend adventure. Sloane was singing along to many of the songs on Roger's playlist, which delighted him. He loved to watch when people relaxed and let their guard down and accidentally acted like themselves once and while. It's rare, but it is fascinating to watch. He just leaned back into his seat and took it all in as they zipped along down the open road. When they made it to Hope, they did stop for a mutual bathroom break and a coffee to keep them alert. Once they pulled out of Hope, they would be climbing in elevation for the next two full hours, so they made sure they were prepared for the next leg of the journey. Roger always stopped at the gas station on the West end of town in Princeton to fuel up, check the vehicle and, of course, get some penny candy from the store. It had been a tradition to stop and get candy for his wife and girls whenever they would make the trip, and this was the first time Roger had ever made the trip without his late wife Michelle, and the two girls. He was heading out over some new untraveled territory with Sloane, but he also felt in his heart that he had to move on from all of these memories and try to create new memories with different people. He smiled to himself because he really felt like he was growing as a person and finding ways to move ahead with his life with Rose and Brooke and possibly some new friends along the way.

Roger topped off the gas tank, got his candy bag, and paid. They jumped back into the car, and they were off to the big city of Penticton. They clipped along and enjoyed the warm winds rushing through the car windows as they headed to the family cabin. After a considerable amount of time, they were within minutes of the downtown section of Penticton when Roger spotted a familiar looking man standing beside his car on the side of the road. He knew this man and felt awful about the idea of just driving right on by, but he couldn't. He had a conscience. Upon closer inspection, it turned out to be Tony Tanti from Vancouver. His Corvette Stingray had overheated, and he had to stop and let it cool down and get some water. Roger couldn't help himself from being who he always was and immediately volunteered to help and provide transportation to the nearest gas station where he could acquire some water for the radiator. Tony said yes and jumped into the back seat, and they were off. As they drove, Roger could see the big question mark on Tony's face, "Who is this lady?" So, he decided to answer that question before it was asked. "This is my girlfriend Sloane, Tony. She and I are heading up to my parent's cabin in Penticton. How about you? What brings you up to this neck of the woods?" Roger asked.

"Took the Vette out to drive irresponsibly for the day and when I got here, the bloody thing overheated on me. Total downer but no big deal. I'll get it fixed and get under way. Oh, just up ahead there is a Shell gas station, if you don't mind." Tony said.

"How do you boys know each other?" Sloane enquired.

"We used to play hockey together." Roger beaming the death stare at Tony to be sure there was no further conversation about that topic. Tony caught the look and acquiesced.

"Yeah, Roger was my defense partner for years." Tony confirmed.

"Do you both still play together? I would love to come and watch a game one day." Sloane added.

"No, those days are over for me," Tony said, "I am now just a cheerleader. My playing days are done."

"How about you Roger? Do you still strap on the blades anymore?" Sloane asked.

"No Sloane, I gave it up a while back. I do not have the spare time and, any extra time I do have available, I spend with my girls." Roger said.

They pulled into the Shell Station parking lot and waited for Tony to fill up a large jug of water to top up the thirsty car. He came out of the building smiling and carrying the needed water jug and they headed back to the abandoned car to add the water. Within minutes, they had emptied the contents of the jug into the radiator and were revving Tony's engine making sure it was going to stay running. He seemed to be back in control of his situation and so they started saying their goodbyes and climbed back into their vehicles and got back under way. "He seemed like a nice man," Sloane said.

"Yeah, Tony is great. Nice guy." Roger replied.

"He has an amazing body. He had to spend some serious time in the gym to look like that I'll bet." Sloane commented.

"Absolutely. That is a committed gym goer. You can't get that type of physique unless you put in the hours and clearly, he has. Should I be getting jealous here? You seem to have a certain fascination with Mr. Tanti." Roger giggled.

"No, he's not my type. I am always worried about how I would look naked but when you have a muscle-bound he-man, I would feel embarrassed to get naked in front of him. I mean it Roger. It would be intimidating to have him around as a constant reminder that you need to go to the gym today, tomorrow, everyday…you know what I mean. He is just a chunk of muscle, and I am a chunk of…" Sloane tapered off.

"Let's not start getting too down on ourselves here. He made a choice many years ago of how he wanted to look, and he has been committed to that for many years, as you can see. The one thing about a bodybuilder is that, unlike most sports, you see the results. It is hard to spot a volleyball player in a group of people, but it is typically easy to spot the iron-pumping crowd." Roger added.

Roger of course didn't have the heart to tell Sloane that he did in fact have a past with Tony. What could be gained by telling his new girlfriend all about his old girlfriend? It was something that he was not interested in finding out. He decided to leave the Tony and Lori mess swept under the rug.

They got to his parents' cabin in the late afternoon, and he walked Sloane into the house so she could start looking around and getting her bearings as to where everything was located. Roger showed her the bedroom because he wanted to ask her directly if she wanted her own room or not. She was intrigued with the notion of sharing a room together for the weekend. To his good luck, she confirmed that she wanted to sleep in the same bed this weekend. Roger was thrilled. The possibility of intimacy was erotic to him because of the large gap between sexual encounters, but this could work out nicely. He promised himself he would let Sloane take the reins and determine the pace of how things would go. He was a patient man and he wanted Sloane to be completely at ease with him and the environment. He continued to trek back and forth from the car to carry in all the supplies to the house, while Sloane found her way onto the furniture covered sun deck that was ready to entertain. Roger opened up a couple of umbrellas on the deck to create a bit of shade and he also opened the electric awnings that extended from the eaves of the house, to protect the interior of the house from getting cooked in the sun. They extended the full width of the 50'-0" sun deck, so when they were fully opened and pushed out, it created a lot of shade down the front of the deck and kept the mid-day sun off of the sundeck users. There were a couple round tables with chairs and a large sectional sofa with soft seat and back cushions and scores of soft, smaller toss pillows to stuff around your body when trying to get a suntan or get cozy. The outside temperature was currently thirty-four degrees Celsius. They had added outdoor material rugs that had been spread about so you could walk on the rugs and not the piping hot floor, to give some relief from the extreme heat. Roger made his way over to the thermostat and turned on the air conditioning unit to begin bringing down the interior temperature of the cabin. Within a few hours from starting the refrigeration unit, the house would be twenty degrees and simply perfect for sleeping indoors overnight. He kept to task and got everything unloaded from the car and into the house and put all of the perishables away. He was now ready to relax. He walked onto the deck and Sloane was in a micro bikini stretched out on a chaise lounge soaking up the sun. "Sloane, you want a beer or something?" Roger asked.

"Could you fill a wine glass of white to the top please?" Sloane replied.

"My Pleasure." He said. Roger went back into the house to fetch the drinks. By the time he got back Sloane was sound asleep enjoying her time off. He placed her glass on the table in the shade and found a comfy chair and sat down to stare at the lake for a spell. The water was fairly calm, and the sun sparkled brightly as it hit the tops of the ripples. It was so reflective you had to have sunglasses on, or else you had to squint so hard you could barely see a foot in front of yourself. The weather was cooperating beautifully that day. Roger took in a big breath, slowly let it out and drifted off for a while.

When Roger awoke, he looked around the deck and saw that Sloane had moved on. He stood up and walked over to the balcony railing and surveyed the view and spotted Sloane splashing about in the shallows of the lake, enjoying the lake's cool temperatures directly in front of his cabin. She saw Roger moving about and waved to acknowledge that she had seen him moving around and he had awoken from his nap.

The property had a steep slope that started in the backyard, along the gravel road, which crossed all three lots and went down to the corner onto a bigger, busier road. The three properties had space up top to park vehicles, stairs down both sides of the cabins, an open lawn area under the sundeck, and another set of concrete steps that led down to the water's edge. There was a fixed ramp that led to the water and a long, floating dock that people used for water skiing and jumping off. Many dump trucks full of sand were brought in year after year to keep the beach intact, but basic erosion would scoop away most of the soft sand each year, so the sand loads became a regular occurrence. It was so much nicer to have sand everywhere on the lake's edge because it was much easier on the feet and the children loved to play in the sand all day long. There was a long driveway that went down one side of the property, came across the middle in front of the sundecks of each cabin and then went back up the far side of the property to the gravel road. The slope was steep, so they would put any of the boats into the water at the public boat launch and motor them over by water and tie up to one of their docks. The lake water temperature was warm and refreshing and family and guests would frequently come and spend an entire day in the water. Younger kids that would come up would have to be dragged from the water because they loved it so much. It was a fabulous family oasis that they were privileged to have the use of.

Roger was sitting near the railing gazing out and resting his head on his hands when Sloane decided to emerge from the water like a siren from an old sailor's story. She was attractive. In body and mind. She climbed onto the end of the dock and knew Roger was watching her, so she gave Roger her version of "Canada's Next Top Model" and strutted her stuff down the runway/dock, even a passing boat full of young men all gave a hoot or a holler. She was giggling and having fun with it without feeling like she was being judged in any way and she liked it. Roger had leapt to his feet and had run down to meet her near the dock with a fresh white cotton towel and placed it around her shoulders and got in a quick one-arm almost hug to see her reaction, however; she surprised Roger by stopping, placing her arms around his neck, and kissing him on the lips. She hovered for an instant and then moved away. There was to be no make-out session on the beach that day.

The two made their way back to the kitchen where Sloane insisted on preparing the dinner for them. Her own secret recipe. Wasn't going to stay a secret if he watched her prepare it but if it was tasty, shouldn't more people have the chance to eat some of it and be awakened to a greater depth of flavour she had created? On that, Sloane rushed Roger out to the deck so she could work in peace. He was laughing quietly, also because he really didn't want to make dinner that night, so this was a welcome break. He snagged another beer from the fridge on his way outside and "relax city" here he comes. He leaned back and stared into the sky and remembered why the family liked it so much up here. Peaceful, simple living.

Sloane prepared a special family meal that had been passed down through the generations, which was a battered chicken pieces mixed with fourteen herbs and spices called KFC. She called Skip the Dishes when he was outside relaxing and had them delivered, so dinner was ready. They of course joked about the chicken, fries, salads, and gravy for the entire meal. The two relished the moment. They moved into the family room and took a place together in the corner of the large sectional sofa and decided which movie they would attempt to watch. It was evident they both wanted to take the next step in their relationship. They moved to the main bedroom and called it a night. Roger stayed back so that he could pour two snifters of cognac and then he made his way to the boudoir. He was hoping that the evening was just beginning.

The next morning, Sloane awoke to the sweet aroma of freshly brewed coffee. She loved it when there was someone else to do the trivial things once in a while. Staring at the ceiling, enjoying the bliss, she thought about last night with Roger and, although he was a generous lover, he just hadn't hit all of the high notes for Sloane. She wasn't thinking it was over that day. She was willing to give him another chance just in case he was too wound up the first time. She went to the kitchen and fetched a coffee and a fresh scone. "Holy crap," she thought to herself, "Roger really is a wonderful man. He knows how to bake fresh scones." She thought the only box left to check was to save a baby bird, but the day was young.

"I'm going to pop into town for a few things. Do you want to come along or wait here?" Roger asked.

"Wherever you go, I go mister." Sloane said. She vanished and returned with alternate footwear and a coverup for her swimsuit clad body. "Okay. I'm ready."

Roger was again taken with her charisma. She had a gentle way about her that was really beginning to rub off on Roger.

He stopped at a roadside parking spot in the middle of a busy street and explained to Sloane that he would be about thirty minutes and then they could get some lunch. Sloane happily climbed out of the car and hit the streets. She loved window shopping, and she was on her way.

An hour later, the two met up right outside the Lakefront Casino and went inside for some lunch and a touch of air-conditioning. While the two had their lunch, they could hear a man that was making a big disturbance in the lobby raising his voice and sounding dangerous. The voice became familiar with a couple of words. "Oh my God. It's Tony Tanti." Roger thought to himself. Say nothing. Stay in your seat. Offer zero assistance. The voices began to bellow louder by the second and Roger couldn't help himself, so he jumped up and zipped out to the lobby area and saw a couple of men roughing Tony up for some reason. "Tony managed to piss someone off," he thought, "What a surprise."

"What's going on here gentlemen?" Roger asked the two assailants. "Is my friend bothering you in some way? From where I'm standing it appears that you two are beating up on a drunk guy. Sounds about correct? So hit the bricks fellows and leave this guy alone."

"Not going to be that easy…friend. This guy hit on my girl last night to the point that she had to call me and get me down here to defend her honour, so we owe this mother a beating." He said.

"You'll have to beat me first." Roger took up a defensive karate stance and said, "Bring your best boys," and just as he was saying that the police cruiser showed up outside with the cherries flashing full. In a thrice, the two officers entered the premises and asked everybody to hit the deck until they had sorted everything out. Roger was released off the floor when stories started to corroborate his Innocence and he was merely trying to defend Tony. As the police sorted things out, Roger realized that Sloane was still in the bar alone. He bolted around the corner, found her, and brought her up-to-speed on all of the latest events. She returned to the scene of the crime with Roger and had a chance to meet Tony and understand what all the fuss was about.

Tony stood in the hallway of the hotel and began to cry. He was a behemoth sobbing like a baby. Roger was attempting to make a hasty retreat when Tony informed them that he had been ejected from the hotel and now had no place to stay for the night in Penticton.

"Well, we can't just leave him here to sleep in his car. Roger, it's only for one night and then he will be gone in the morning. I'm not leaving him here to sleep in his car tonight. No WAY." Sloane said.

"Okay. He 's coming with us. Grab your grips Tony and we'll go in my car and come back and get yours tomorrow." Roger instructed. They made their way back to Roger's parked car and entered.

"Is this an original 1965 Ford Mustang? Oh my god Roger, your car is worth 50K easy. If you ever think of selling it, let me know and I could line up buyers for you. Seriously, if you are going to sell, let me know." Tony said.

"It's my father's car and it is a family heirloom so it will never be up for sale, unless one of the grandkids sells it off one day." Roger said. "Then that will get Grandpa pretty grumpy."

The couple with their new third wheel headed back to Roger's place. He could not believe that one of his rivals was now going to stay at his house for the night. What was the world coming to? As the evening wore on, a few more questions came forth about the relationship between Roger and Tony and how close they were. Roger evaded the question artfully, but Tony was an ass, so he said, "I met Roger when he ruined my long-term relationship with Lori. I thought we might get married one day but Roger managed to screw up my entire life in just a few months time, hey buddy." He looked directly at Roger and winked. "I don't know dude. Do you think we are even now? You messed with mine and I messed with yours. You're welcome." Tony said.

"Roger? Is this true? Did you ruin this man's life somehow?" Sloane quired.

"No. Yes. Sort of. My sister got involved because Lori said she was afraid of Tony possibly harming her, however, he never did as far as we know. He actually seemed like an okay guy and hence the reason I brought him back here tonight, because he is a good guy. Needs a couple classes in anger management, but he still is a nice man." Roger replied.

"So where is Lori now?" Sloane asked.

"She took her dream teaching job in Tokyo, Japan and won't return for at least two years, unless she breaks the law or kills someone. That kind of stuff. It's her life's dream to teach there, so I do not think she will ever come back. What do you think, Tony?" Roger said.

It was all too much for Tony again and he went back to sobbing and holding his hand over his face so no one could see him. The odd group went out onto the sundeck to breathe the evening air. They all chatted about trivial things from each person's childhood and then the next person would relay their story or fable. They all looked up and chatted away until Sloane announced, "I'm going to bed gentlemen. I'll see you both in the morning. Please Tony, don't leave without having coffee and saying goodbye, okay."

"I won't Sloane, I promise." Tony said.

"Okay there is one more housekeeping thing you both have to remember. This is of critical importance. If you use any of the bathrooms, be sure the tank has stopped running before you leave the bathroom. We had some issues, so please stand, and wait and rattle the flushing handle. This seems to be the most effective method to date. If it keeps running, it will fill the entire house with water. The toilet downstairs is the worst so again, make sure you rattle that thing. Do you both understand? This is critical." Roger finished.

"Copy that, Roger. See you in the morning." Tony said.

"Got it Roger," Sloane replied.

Roger followed Sloane to the main bedroom and closed the door behind them. He knew that she would have some questions about the events of the day once they met up with Tony. He offered nothing and waited to see if she would leave it or want to talk about it. He was really hoping to have some grown-up fun, but he wasn't going to do or say anything. He was simply going to be the world's best listener. "So, dare I ask, who is Lori?" Sloane asked.

"She used to teach one of my daughters, Brooke, that I met while volunteering for the school. Oh, and on parent teacher night. That's it. Never dated her, went out with her, nothing. I had a few dinners with her when she stayed with Anne for a few months, while she waited to get her affairs in order so she could go to Japan and live out her dream. It's actually really cool because my family helped her achieve a life-changing goal in search of her perfect life." Roger said.

"Oh, okay. That all makes perfect sense. Well, I'm good so…do you want to screw?" She asked.

"So glad you asked." Moments later they were having fun. But there's always tomorrow.

***

In the morning, an apologetic Tony arose first to make the coffee and to attempt a peace offering breakfast with whatever he could scrounge up. Roger came into the kitchen and gave a head nod to Tony, and he sent one back. "Coffee?" Roger said.

"Got one thanks." He replied.

The two sat silently at the table just taking in the day and sipping. Minutes later, Sloane appeared and suggested they all go out onto the deck for the morning coffee, which the boys quickly agreed to and followed her outside. The three were standing out in the fresh morning air, watching an aggressive water skier slalom across the smooth morning water and they all heard a snap sound. "What was that?" Sloane said.

"I couldn't tell you. I've never heard that noise before. Let's see if it happens again." Roger said.

Instantly after he said that they all heard a louder cracking sound. What the heck could it be? Roger was standing erect looking off into the distance trying his hardest to tune into the world of sounds when it happened. The sliding glass doors downstairs gave way to the weight of the water building up against the glass all night because someone used the toilet and forgot to make sure the tank was shut off. But over the course of many hours, the water had an opportunity to start amassing some copious quantities and the basement door had hit its weight limit and the water began gushing forth through the basement doors like a dam opening and releasing all of the reserves and heading for the Mustang. The water in the basement gushed forth like a tidal wave and was powerful enough to do some damage before ceding into the lake. The water wall pressed firmly against the side of the Mustang, which was not a match for the volume of liquid weight to be stopped by a mere two-thousand-pound automobile. Well, it wasn't. The water swooped around both sides of the car sitting alone in the middle of the driveway with no impediments to slow down or divert the rushing mass of H2O. The little car tried to keep its tires glued to one spot, but the pounds per square inch were not in the car's favour and slowly, the water washed away all of the light sand and gravel until the Mustang was just hanging on the edge of the driveway. It dropped down to the lakeside, water level, and the three of them could hear the sound of something heavy being dragged across the ground. Without having the opportunity to do anything about it, the car slid closer and closer to the fall-off edge of the lake. The Mustang kept inching along at a snail's pace, but it was too late to run downstairs and try and catch it before it rolled off the last part of the driveway turn around. The car hung by an invisible thread for a few more seconds and then gravity took over and dragged the Mustang down over the edge into the lake's shallow edge water and the car ended up upside down in the water. "Great. Now the car is completely buggered up." Roger thought to himself. The three spectators stood at the railing and simultaneously said, "Holy cow!"

They all were surveying the damage and looking at each other in a complete state of shock. Silence for a few more minutes until, "Roger, I've got to work tomorrow so how am I going to get home?" Sloane asked.

"Hey Tony? I'm going to need a favour from you. I'm going to need you to drive Sloane back to the city. I think I'm going to have to stay here for a couple of days to try and sort all of this out." Roger said.

"Absolutely Roger. I'll go get my car, head back here to collect Sloane and her things. I shouldn't be long Roger." Tony responded.

And now for the really fun part, explaining this one to dad. First the boat, now the car and the cabin. He wasn't sure if he should ever go home.

A couple of days later Roger got a message from Sloane. Their time was so precious, and it meant so much to her, but she had done some heavy thinking about her life and future, and she wanted to say thank you for being such a gentleman and thank you for introducing her to Tony. It seemed they hit it off nicely on the drive back from Penticton and were going to start dating. Roger laughed out loud when he got this information. Tony Tanti told Roger he would get him back and he wasn't kidding. Tony had got him back.

Chapter Sixteen

After a short hiatus from dating, Roger was finding it harder and harder to go through the motions of seeking a new mate. He realized that he had been out with nineteen different women and didn't seem any closer to finding that special someone to spend eternity with. He couldn't believe the next date was twenty dates and nothing to show for it but a seriously reduced bank account. He was so lucky that insurance covered the boat, the cabin, and the car, but people always say that terrible things happen in threes, and that meant he was done with the bad breaks. Only straight up from here on in, he hoped.

He revisited the dating site with hopes of finding another potential match. He wasn't desperate, but he was a bit concerned that he hadn't found somebody that he felt would go somewhere. Roger also knew that he had not been out with one woman on a number of dates. So far it has been one date here and two dates with another girl, but he had not ended up in a committed relationship. He kept asking himself, all the time, if he needed to find a new and novel approach to addressing this dilemma. He felt he had tried many diverse types of activities to keep things fresh, but he also was sick and tired of keeping things fresh. He wanted a woman that wanted to settle down with him and his two girls and maybe even have a couple more kids. He wanted a person that loved children and wanted to raise them together, rather than some nanny everyday except weekends. Having an impact on your kids means that you have to be with your kids, not with somebody else. This was Roger's true happy place. To find a loving woman that loves Rose, Brooke, Roger and wants to grow old with them. Roger's own version of Utopia. He knew it existed and he was willing to keep searching for it, for his girls' sake.

Roger was intrigued to meet Tania. She was attractive and seemed quite nice in the initial correspondences with her, but he was a sucker for an English accent. She had the type that you could understand and many words she would say, you would go in your head, "Awe." She practically boasted about her outdoorsman skills, to the point that Roger made a mental note to never go mountaineering with her because she would be too good at it and end up making Roger feel like a loser if she really could turn water to wine and light a fire using spit, hair, and a match. He wasn't really up for being outshone again. Through their communications, they had decided to go for a leisurely hike together at Golden Ears Mountain and do a large, open looping hike that brings visitors around in a 10 km circular walk back to the main parking lot, which most people use as their starting point. They both had some food, lots of water, dry socks, and a plastic tarp along in their backpacks. The day was cool and dry in the morning but promised to be warmer by midday because of the clear blue skies suspended overhead. Roger had not been walking through this area since he and his siblings were in their early teens, when they came to the park with their father and played in the lake or tried to make it to the top of the Golden Ears Peak, which could be done but would require all day to get across the flats and straight up the mountain to the glacier. Once you cross over the ice, it takes another hour of vertical climbing to get to the small mesa at the top of the 5,600-foot-high rock. Tania had suggested that they stick to the low ground around the base of the mountain and just enjoy the large open trails without all of the ups and downs and climbing over things. At one spot, there is a fairly fast running river that you have to traverse, using the two high cables to hold on to with your hands and one low cable to walk across, which can be tricky. When the water is running high and hard, it is an intimidating thing to ease yourself over the river on wiggly wires and to get over the fear of falling into the water at any given time. They headed off down the main pathway and tried to find a comfortable speed for the two of them to walk, that wouldn't tire them out too quickly. They found their stride and they were off. They trekked along down the trails and had the opportunity to talk and get to know one another. It was a wonderful pace, as it was slow enough that you could continue to chat without running quickly out of breath. After a couple of hours, they stopped to nosh on some food and sat down to rest their legs. While they sat, Tania shot up and said in a whisper voice, "Roger. I thought I heard the low growl of a bear coming from down the path." She turned her body completely around to see as far as possible down the path and there it was. A four-hundred-plus pound bear out for a daily walk and could smell their food and wanted a closer inspection. She looked at Roger and said, "Let's get walking in the opposite direction. Is that okay with you?" The two immediately began walking slowly down the path in the opposite direction and as they created a larger distance, they continued to pick up the pace until the two were doing a slow jog down the trail. They remained silent to not draw any attention to themselves and to keep putting distance between them and the bear. "There does really seem to be a lot of bears in Vancouver. It's hard to feel safe when you are out-and-about like a tourist and always looking over your shoulder to make sure you're not blindsided by a predator." Tania said.

"I'm from here and I still never get used to it. They are big and they can harm you really badly, so I'm with you Tania, we should always keep a respectful distance away at all times." Roger added.

They zipped along at a good clip and when they started to feel that their four-legged friend was no longer stalking them, they started to take stock of the surrounding area and tried to figure out the best way back to the parking lot and the entrance to the walking paths, where they started from. Without paying close attention, the two had removed themselves from the mainstream trails and were now on a path that seemed to have tree branches stretching across them. Something was wrong. They had confidently marched through the forest having a lovely time but forgetting to pay attention to their surroundings and now they had virtually no idea where they were. They needed to double back and find the larger open trails they were on earlier and then find their way back from a bigger trail or even easier, hopefully run into another hiker that could point them in the right direction. They followed each other down a trail that hooked onto a larger, wider trail, but they didn't know which direction they should be walking in on this path. They stood there trying to analyze which direction would lead to their salvation. Tania then commented on the sun in the sky and how it was slowly moving across the horizon and getting ready to disappear for the night. Roger did not want to spend a night outside, especially with a black bear roaming around in the vicinity. He did not want to test his survival skills but as the two walked another path, it seemed to dwindle out into a wide-open field of tall grass. "Now which way?" Roger thought to himself. The open field had what looked like walking trails leaving the undeveloped area, but which path should they take? They realized that the forest area they were in was going to be dark within a couple of hours because it was on the north side of the mountain, so it was in the dark and the warm day temperature was rapidly falling. They decided to get back onto a large trail, which would mean more foot traffic to find a way out of the bush. They were on a main path when Roger noticed a little carved out chunk at the base of a dead tree, but clearly it had been used at one time to have a small fire and hide from the outdoor elements. He suggested that they make camp and try to save energy and take another exit attempt the following day when the sun was back in the sky. Quickly the pair prepared the tree stump for the night. They brought out the two tarps and put one on the ground to keep their bodies dry and fashioned the other tarp over top of them, so as to keep moisture off their heads. The two worked effectively together and soon they had made their base camp for the night. They laid down on the tarp and spooned each other to try and stay warm with the second tarp acting as a blanket. It worked perfectly and the two huddled up and attempted to get some rest. What many people do not know is that the forest is very noisy at night and at every moment, you are listening intently, trying to hear if anything is coming to get you. The other tough part about the forest at night is that the temperature drops down and makes for an uncomfortable sleep. They spooned and held each other tightly all night, fighting off the chill of night. They were both going in and out of consciousness and shivered madly throughout the ordeal. Roger was having a real bout of the shivers when he had an epiphany with his arm draped over Tania, trying to keep her warm. Enough. I'm not doing this anymore. What if something happened to me tonight? Who would look after my daughters? Who is going to raise my kids? He stared into the dark, star-filled sky and realized he needed to set his priorities and put his girls first and himself second. Here he was, in the forest at night, sleeping on the ground. He needed to be at home for his girls and his family, always. He had tried twenty times through the dating site to find a partner and each ended up not going well and Roger not finding love as the end result. When he walked out of the bush in the morning, he was determined to delete his Lava Love account for good. This site was only causing Roger heartache. He was no closer to finding a new love and his heart, mind, and ego just couldn't take it anymore. When Tania finally woke up, she came to and instantly began to look around her surroundings for any creatures that shouldn't be there. He couldn't believe that the pair had just spent a night in the forest. They ate the food they had left and began walking down a large, open path in hopes of seeing people or finding a sign to point them in the right direction. After two hours of walking, they could hear the roar of the river where they had crossed the day before. They made their way to the opening in the forest where you could see the cable bridge cross the river. Once they had made their way over the raging water, they were back on the main path and recognized it from the previous day. This of course began to bring tremendous relief to the two of them because they were now starting to see things that looked familiar. Home sweet home was programmed into their heads, and they zipped through the forest at a good clip, trying to complete the laborious journey. As they pushed onward, they now started to see other people appearing on the trails and making them feel like their odyssey was coming to an end. The final half mile went quickly. They set their sights on the opening ahead that marked the edge of the parking lot and a sense of civilization. Once they got to the opening, they had officially made it. They burst through the trees and walked into the large, open parking lot and now they were no longer covered completely by the forest's canopy of leaves and branches. They could see the uninterrupted sky without looking through the trees. They crossed the parking lot and stood beside Tania's car. She opened the trunk and tossed in her backpack. She looked at Roger and said, "That certainly is one way to get to know someone better. Sleep outdoors and freeze your buns off. We'll have to get together again real soon and do that again. NOT!" Tania said.

"It was a unique experience. Can't say I would want to do that again. I had one ear listening all night for our furry friend to make another appearance while we were sleeping. It does prove that the survival blankets actually work. It was surprisingly comfortable. Thank you, Tania, for a one-of-a-kind excursion. I will always remember our special night."

Chapter Seventeen

He stared at the computer screen and pondered the last couple years of his life and how quickly they got away. He was selfishly working on his own needs and desires and knew he needed to pay more attention to Rose and Brooke, rather than having Anne raise his girls. It is tough to see yourself as sexy husband material when you have two girls that keep you in check at all times. Truth is truth, and Rose and Brooke were always ready to give their version of the truth. Even if it hurt daddy's feelings. Roger scanned down the list of women he had met on the dating site and saw that it had actually kept him busy and engaged with different people and different activities and that it had been an interesting experience. It still had, however, netted him zero long-term romantic possibilities. He continued to gaze into the computer screen as it came to life and was ready to take commands. The question still at hand was simple, "Was this a huge waste of time?" Would God know he was a good person and shower him with marriage opportunities if he promised to go to church for a non-specified length of time? His one chubby digit hovered over the delete key…then pressed firmly down. That was it. He had done it. He had broken the cycle of bizarre dating rituals. He had deleted this plague from his life until the computer asked, "Hello Roger. Are sure you want to delete this program? Please confirm." He got up to reconsider and when he came back to his seat the icon was showing that there was a person writing text messages right now! He opened the dialogue box. He waited. "Are you there right now?" The sender said.

"Yes." He answered.

"This is my first time doing this. I saw your picture and it reminded me of someone, so I sent you a message. Have you done this before?" she said.

"A couple of times, for sure." Roger replied.

Two days later he had not deleted the dating program.

Two days later he still had not heard from Mystery Girl.

"Where did she go? I hope she is okay." Roger thought.

Over a week later Roger received some mail. Her name was Paige, and she was willing to text with him. She indeed was the person that sent the message and then disappeared for a week, but she wanted to do her own detective work and make sure that Roger wasn't a crazy guy causing havoc everywhere he went. She suggested using text messaging for a while because, if they couldn't keep each other interested, they would have no future together. Roger agreed to her terms and so began their texting relationship. It really was a promising idea because they opened up about so many things that even Roger held near to his heart. After a month of texting frequently, they agreed to the second round. Speaking on the phone. It felt like a blind date even though they had communicated countless times. The phone rang and Paige froze in her chair, "Hello." She said.

"Hello Paige. I'm Roger Miller. Nice to finally hear you.' He giggled.

"Nice to meet you, Roger. Sorry about all of the smoke and mirrors but I am not in this for the fun of it. I am looking for a responsible man who loves his wife first and his family second. There used to be lots of them out there but ever since my dad and his cronies all grew up, most of them went away. What do you think Roger? Any of those guys out there anymore?"

"You only need one." He said.

"This is true Mr. Miller. Do you think you're the one?" She asked.

"Yes, I do Paige. I do think it's me." He said.

"Why do you believe that so strongly Roger?" she said.

"Because it was you that stopped me from deleting the entire website the night you sent me that message. I had deleted the page, but the computer asked me one more time, and I said no and began texting with you since then. I gave it one more chance when you came up. That is pure karma." Roger said.

"It does make for an interesting meet-cute story. However, we haven't seen each other in person...yet." She added.

"Boy that is a tasty looking carrot you are dangling in front of me Paige. We can cross that bridge when you are ready. Until then, it's nice to hear your voice." He said. The conversation went on in many different directions but the two were definitely getting along alarmingly well. Roger didn't know if he should be hanging up and keeping her interested, or if he should just go ahead and ask her the fifty questions, he had lined up for her. The conversation just flowed so easily, and Roger asked her if she had ever had any other men in her life that she felt safe with. She dismissed the topic quickly and assertively, then he heard a change in her voice. She wasn't telling him something. But what? He asked Paige if she had ever considered having children of her own in the future. She completely shut down. Something was amiss. He had stepped on a land mine of some kind, and he didn't know any of the details.

"You know Roger, I should really call it a night. I have a few things to take care of before bedtime, so I will speak to you soon." And Paige hung up.

Roger couldn't help but feel he was dismissed from that telephone conversation. He knew he had struck a nerve of some kind but just wasn't exactly sure why? Time would hopefully tell.

Paige called back the next day and left a message for Roger telling him, "We gotta talk."

Roger was a bit apprehensive because he was still at the phase where you assume that every time your girlfriend speaks with you, she is going to break it off. He finished off some odd jobs at a customer's office and then he went to his truck to make a phone call to Paige. He truly anticipated that this was going to be the golden handshake, the see-you-later-dude, but it wasn't. She wanted to get together face to face to discuss some personal matters that she wanted to tell Roger before she felt like they could move ahead. This was frightening because he had never met Paige in the flesh, as of yet, and he was filled with anticipation and his nerves were on high alert. She picked the local Golf Academy on the Westwood Plateau to meet at noon that day. Whatever this was, it was going to happen quickly. This pleased Roger because he hated long goodbyes, taking forever to get to the point, you know, all of that kind of crap. Roger, of course, arrived early and waited in line to get a suitable table on the outdoor patio with an umbrella. He was all set up and positioned strategically so that he could see everybody come and go in the parking lot, so he would know when she had arrived. He felt like a schoolboy for a moment because he was so nervous to meet Paige in person. It seemed so silly, but none of his previous dates had given him this sensation. "Hurry up and get here." He thought to himself. Roger noticed the time was ticking by when he checked his clock and realized that Paige was forty minutes late and probably wasn't coming. He could no longer be shocked or surprised by any developments after twenty dates because you have to be ready for anything. Someone not showing up on time or not showing up at all was the norm. You have to keep your expectations low. That way if they do anything good you will be delighted and amazed. He asked for his bill and was waiting for the card machine when Paige pulled into the parking lot. She was driving a 1965 red Mustang in mint condition with all of the chrome accessories gleaming. It almost felt like she was mocking Roger with this car but how could she possibly know that Roger had just recently destroyed his father's 1965 green Mustang. She got out of the car wearing a headscarf to keep her shiny, cropped, bright blue hair out of her eyes as she drove. She was six feet tall and thin, with small hips and breasts. She was wearing one of Roger's favorite pieces with a short skirt and sleeveless turtleneck top that loosely followed the shape of her body. She sported high heel open toe slingback pumps and she could stop a clock with her beauty. When she sauntered over to the reception area, she walked right past it as if it were there for others but not her. Roger had leapt to his feet in a show of respect, but he also wanted to get a good look at Paige and what she brought to the table. She seemed so confident; Roger was having a tough time believing that she was five years younger than him. She walked over to Roger and said, "So I finally meet the infamous Roger Miller." She leaned in close to him and allowed a light peck on her cheek from Roger.

"It is a pleasure to meet you, Paige. I honestly didn't know how long it was going to be before we met face-to-face. I am delighted to be here with you." Roger said as he sat back down in his chair. He looked across the table and was stunned by how attractive Paige was in person. She had a noticeably short hairstyle that looked perfect for her petite face and strong jawline. Her skin was tanned and smooth in appearance and she had no jewelry but for a string of pearls around her neck. The two started getting to know each other better but Roger could tell that Paige was not at ease like she had been in previous conversations, and he immediately fell into panic mode. He was convinced that he had this one chance to make a connection with Paige and so his number one criterion was to keep the dialogue going, no matter what he was sputtering out. He put out the topic of children to see how into children she seemed, and she was receptive to the concept of having kids. Then Roger asked the million-dollar question, "Have you had children before?"

She visibly paused, and then took in a deep breath and began to tell Roger, "I was married to a man named Kent and we had a four-year-old son named John. One night we were driving home from his parents' house out by the dikes in Port Coquitlam and the car skidded across some black ice and we flew off the road into the dike water, upside down, with our seatbelts on. Within seconds, the car submerged in the cloudy darkness, and everything went black. I fought my fears, found the door handle, and got it open. I was sucked upward to the surface of the water while the car kept going down. The headlights appeared to be off because the water was so murky and dark, there was no way anyone could see that car. I took a deep breath and went back down to try and find the vehicle, but I couldn't. I couldn't find the car, my son, or my husband. They were gone. They were now trapped in a car at the bottom of the dike, and they were about to be that evening's "Top News Story." I made my way to the edge of the water and dragged myself up the bank to safety, but I was too late to save anybody. They were taken from me that night and ever since, my life has been a series of motions without feeling anything. I have been moving through life and not stopping to smell the flowers or anything else for that matter. I will tell you the truth, when I saw your profile picture my heart stopped for a couple of beats because you look so similar to my late husband. I thought God had reincarnated him and brought him back to me. Such is not the case, but I have been desperate on a few evenings when I have had too much to drink, and I start having any of those feminine urges, I think about Kent and how much I loved him. I never dreamt that I would be a single woman with two passed loved ones at this stage of my life. When I saw your picture, I got weak in the knees and a whole bunch of IQ points dumber because I thought I should chase you down and hopefully you would just instantly fall in love with me, and we could live happily ever after. Right?" She said.

"It is a good plan. I am surprised that you are bringing this topic up today because it was one of the things that I want to speak to you about. Many years ago, my wife was fatally injured in a car accident, and I have been a single dad ever since. I moved into my sisters' home with her and her two girls to help keep my daughters' minds off the accident and our new reality. I understand your pain and your thoughts. My heart is breaking right now as I speak to you. Losing your husband is bad, but losing your child too is even worse. I can't imagine what you go through on a day-to-day basis. I hope you have been lucky enough to have professional help to get you over this horrific tragedy. We need to be with supportive people that want the best for us moving forward." Roger said.

"I am so sorry Roger. I had no idea. How old are your girls?" She queried.

"Rose is almost ten and Brooke is eight." He replied.

"How long ago did you become widowed?" She asked.

"It's been several years now. It's one of the reasons I continue to try and find a partner that can help me raise responsible children. I can't even imagine what the world will look like when the girls start to go through female changes and want to meet some boys one day. I have always had an idea of keeping them locked in the basement until they're twenty. Then bring out and let them find their way as grownups." Roger said.

She giggled and said, "I think your plan will work providing you never leave your house again. Sooner or later all kids find a way out."

"Didn't think it was a really good plan. More of a work in progress," he joked back at Paige.

Paige and Roger sat at their outdoor metal top table for the next four hours. The two were having a fun time and she found herself denying the impulse to touch Roger non-stop. He still reminded her of her late husband from specific angles and by some mannerisms. She too was interested in meeting someone, but did she want to get involved with a man that had two kids? If she goes any further with this guy, she knew it was with Rose and Brooke as well, and she hadn't even met them yet. So many new emotions rolling around in her body and mind and Roger so desperately wanting a mother figure in his daughters' lives. The next step for both of them was huge. Were either of them ready for a committed relationship? "Hey,

I've got to get moving along. I have to be at one of my kids' things. Sorry." He stood up, put down a handful of cash, and made a hasty retreat to his truck. In a panic he was gone. Clearly Roger had forgotten that he was to be at something important that night.

He made it to his pickup truck and climbed into the driver's seat. He could feel his heart pounding and he was becoming completely overwhelmed with emotion. It was such a crucial time, not just his life but Rose and Brookes' lives too. He could afford to mess his life up, but not theirs. He needed to accomplish that task for his widow, Michelle. He needed to do something right. So far, he knew that he was doing a respectable job. The girls loved him, and they both got to spend lots of time with their family. The foundation was sturdy and ready for extra activities that may include extra people. Now was the time for Roger to be brave and take chances on love.

The following weekend Paige had agreed to go over to Maxine and Clyde's house for a backyard BBQ and a swim in their large inground pool. The children never needed to be coaxed to go to Grandma and Grandpa's house for a pool party. Mom always had lots of treats for the kids, things for the grown-ups to eat and drink, and a heated swimming pool just begging to coax a whole bunch of children into the water. Paige showed up and came inside to meet the family and hopefully not become completely overwhelmed by the upcoming events of the day. Mitch and Chanel were there with

James and William. Anne was there with Hope and Joy, and Roger had arrived with Rose and Brooke. The kids met the Grandparents on the way by, as they headed quickly to the backyard and the beckoning swimming pool. Grandma was filled with happiness and went about distributing soft fresh cotton towels to the group and began to chat with Paige to get her involved with the activities. Maxine asked Paige if she had any children of her own and for some reason Paige decided to come clean with Maxine and Clyde and told them about the car accident that claimed her husband and her son. Maxine embraced Paige like a family member and hugged her to show her love and sympathy for her loss. Clyde leaned towards her and whispered into her ear, "Only gone, but not forgotten." Clyde patted her on the back and said, "How about a high ball?"

"That sounds marvelous. I'll have whatever you are pouring." Paige said.

The group migrated to the covered outdoor area where Clyde had set up a secondary pool bar to save having to traipse back into the house over and over. As drinks were being concocted, the kids were splashing in the pool in high-gear giggling, calling out, and having good old-fashioned fun. Paige took a couple quick sips of her gin and tonic and padded over to the edge of the pool, disrobed in the blink of an eye, and slipped under the surface of the water without creating a ripple. The mistake she made of course, was resurfacing around all the kids because they each wanted their turn to hang off her and make sure that she included each and every one of them, the way children always want you to. Roger was pleased to see how comfortable Paige was, clad in just a swimsuit, in front of the entire family. He kept feeling like that trepidation was over and she looked fit in her swimsuit, which was extra bonus points. As the day went on, the group lounged and talked, in and out of the sun and took in the day. Roger heard the girls teasing Brooke because she still couldn't do the backstroke, in spite of her lessons. She always ended up sinking under and would have to change her stroke pattern. Paige walked down the pool steps into the water like a Victoria's Secret Model and slid up close to Brooke. She stopped a few feet away and said, "May I help you learn the backstroke, Brooke? Would that be okay?"

"I guess. But I'm never going to learn it because my bum keeps sinking down." Brooke pouted.

It turned out that Paige was a Lifeguard in her youth and for years had instructed kids of all ages to swim. She swam up beside Brooke and slipped her flat palm under her back and began to swim beside her in the water. Down to the end of the pool. Took a break. Down to the other end of the pool. Took a break. Paige just quietly whispered her directions to Brooke and continued to put her hand under her back and they kept going back and forth in the pool. After about ten minutes, Paige was still swimming directly beside Brooke when Brooke finally noticed, "You're not holding onto me. I'm swimming on my own, I'm backstroking alone!" Brooke exclaimed. She doggie paddled at full tilt over to Paige and squeezed her with enthusiasm as she thanked her again and again. "I can do the backstroke Daddy. Do you want to watch me?" she chattered.

"Of course I do. We all want to see you swim down the pool Brooke." Roger replied.

The entire family crowded the pool deck on one side and made a big fuss over Brooke's accomplishment. She was delighted but she also now had a reason to really like Paige. She caught Paige's attention and said, "Thank you Paige. Like daddy says "teach a person to fish..." She beamed. Brooke was a swimmer now and nobody could change that. Paige merely winked at her, slipped under the water, and pushed off to the other end of the pool. Brooke had a crush on Paige that very first day. The group continued with some swimming and pool games and then Maxine started setting out some food for the group inside on the kitchen island and asked everybody to serve themselves. All of the kids grabbed food and went back outside to hangout in the covered pool shed while the adults stayed back under the cover of the upper deck and awnings. The wind blew gently through the house creating a soothing and warm ambience. They all ate and drank and hung out, like families are supposed to, with no drama that day. Paige was giggling a bit when she realized she had a shadow now that she had assisted Brooke with her swimming. She was lurking around the edges like kids do and kept getting a bit closer until Paige turned to Brooke and said, "Sweetie, would you like to sit here so you can put your drink down for a moment? If you want to?"

"Okay." She answered. She walked over and sat down on Paige's lap. Laid her head back onto her chest and curled up her feet.

"Are you comfortable Brooke?" She asked. She didn't answer. Too much excitement for the day. Brooke had nodded off for a power nap on Paige's lap at that exact moment. Kids do the darndest things. Her head fell backward onto Paige's chest, and she was in dream land. The group gathered together and chatted some more until the evening started winding down. They sat outside for another twenty minutes and then brought the kids back into the house and began to make bedtime preparations. Mitch and Chanel grabbed their boys, said their goodbyes and they were out of there. Anne fetched Hope and Joy and they headed for the car. After much hugging and goodbyes, the family all left for home. Roger asked his parents if they wanted any help with the dishes or putting things away, but Maxine would have no part in it. Rose and Brooke stayed in the living room while Roger helped Clyde put everything in the pool area away and then closed the protective pool top for the night.

Roger took the time to speak with his father about the latest and greatest girlfriend. "You will catch no fish if you don't have a line in the water." Clyde said. They talked about the dating scene and how all of that was going. Clyde was concerned because in the last year he had lost his antique boat, his heirloom Mustang and one of the summer cottages. "I'm running out of things for you to destroy, son." he said mockingly. He did inquire how Roger was doing for money and if everything was okay. While they were speaking, Rose had snuck over to the door and could hear Roger and Grandpa talking about money. The way Rose understood things is that Roger needed lots of dollars for the dates he was going on and he still needed a lot more dollars. She had the perfect idea; in the morning she would enlist Brooke and the two of them could gather all their precious valuables and give them to Roger, so he wouldn't have any money worries at all. It would work out perfectly. Clyde went back outside to turn off the yard lights and came back in through the kitchen. Maxine offered to keep the girls at their house for the night and Roger could pick them up in the morning. She looked at Roger and winked. "Is that okay with you darling?"

"Yeah, sure Mom. Sounds great. I should be rolling out of here now also. I'll be by in the morning to collect the girls. Love you guys, see you all in the morning." He said and left the house.

Standing on the front driveway, Roger stopped with Paige so they could say their goodnights. She was still wearing a tiny bikini underneath her swim cover-up, so Roger's brain reminded him that she was almost in her birthday suit under that robe. He fought it off as much as he could, but the attraction towards Paige was making his heart pound faster. He knew he had to go right now. He tried the "okay, I'll see you later" routine, but Paige wasn't having any of that. She walked over to Roger and stood directly in front of him and said, "I want a real hug and kiss goodnight tonight, Roger Miller. I don't want some half-assed attempt either. Bring me the good stuff." She practically leapt into Roger's arms, and she pressed hard and kissed harder. She was telling Roger tonight that she thinks he is a catch. He was a keeper. Roger was ready to share more with Paige than drinks and pleasantries. The next big question was, when would he get this chance again to try and connect with Paige, intimately. He knew he had to be patient, but all good things come to those who wait. And Roger had waited long enough. The two hugged and kissed goodnight on the driveway that night and Paige could feel Rogers' desires as they kissed. She was also extremely interested in taking the next step, whenever that could be arranged. Roger continued to maintain his eunuch abilities and kissed Paige gently on the lips and called it a night. He was thinking so many impure thoughts right now but he just wanted to make it to the truck so he could escape before he got into any trouble. He closed the door, started the truck, and headed back to Anne's house.

Chapter Eighteen

The next morning Roger got to Clyde's house first thing and surprisingly, Rose and Brooke were already up sitting in the backyard by the pool, washing off the unbroken sand dollar shells. "Hey girls, what are you doing?" Roger asked the girls.

"Me and Brooke are helping you, Daddy. You said it costs lots and lots of dollars to have girlfriends in your life so we are trying to come up with as many dollars as we can so you can keep seeing Paige and then she can be our new mommy and you won't have to spend all of your sand dollars on other things." Rose said.

"I like her Daddy. She helps me be a good swimmer." Brooke said.

Roger was not expecting this at all. He was caught off guard right in front of his father. He realized he was leaking fluid from his eyes and needed composure, but he couldn't get it. The emotions started to seep out of him and, to make matters even more intense, Maxine came out onto the driveway to find out what was going on. "Oh, my goodness," Maxine bellowed, "Roger is crying."

"Mom, please, the girls are here." Roger said.

"There is nothing wrong with a grown-up man crying, right girls?" She asked the children.

"It is perfectly alright. Our daddy told that to a boy at school that was being picked on and he told him, 'You go right ahead and cry.'" Rose said.

"Of course, it's okay to cry. Everybody cries. Even grown-up men." Roger said. He walked over and picked up one of the perfectly shaped and cleaned sand dollars and said to the girls, "This one here is worth as much as my truck…I tell yea…" he said in his best pirate voice, "me buckle. You are the best girls in the universe." He knelt down and cradled them both in his arms for a hug and then stood up and said, "I have to buzz out for just a minute dad, can you watch the girls for a second? I will be right back." Roger stated. He hightailed over to his truck cab, got in and started the vehicle. Within seconds he was halfway down the street, but he was finally alone with no one watching him. He pulled over in the open parking lot ahead, shut off the motor and began to cry. He finally had real proof that the girls wanted to find a new woman in their life. He felt foolish but he could not contain the feeling and sensations rising up within him. He sat there in turmoil for about half an hour until he was able to get control of his senses. His daughters were his first priority no matter what, however, they were both endorsing this woman. They both liked her. He suddenly realized that the four of them needed a weekend away together to see how everybody got along. Taking a deep breath, he started the truck, and headed back to Clyde's house to collect the children.

When Roger arrived, Clyde was in the driveway waiting to see Roger but pretending he was doing something really important. "Oh, here is that twist tie." He said to no one in particular. He walked over to Roger, who was just getting out of the truck and said, "No matter what it is, no matter how bad it seems, we are always here for you son. Just because of what happened to Michelle, doesn't mean it will happen to everyone. She was an amazing woman, but she's gone, and you need love for the girls as well as yourself. You are worthy of love, son. You deserve it too. Like I told you, we're ready to support whatever you decide. Maxine and I gotta tell you, we really like Paige. "

"She is a lovely woman." Maxine said. "And the entire family liked her too."

Paige took it upon herself to set up a tea party for the four little girls and a couple of their friends to come over to Anne's house and eat some treats and drink some tea, (or other tastier things), and play some fun games. The ladies all agreed that it would be a subtle way to have everyone get to know each other way better and Chanel adored doing anything girly, because she was blessed with two hulking brutes who were already giant sized, and they definitely were not into drinking tea. To be fair, most of the girl events the boys were not invited to, but they were happy to be dismissed from many of the girly girl events that would spring up over a year. She loved tea parties, and she was wonderful at them. The ladies all put their heads together to make a successful afternoon of it. Mitch, Roger, William, and James all went out on Uncle Mitch's speed boat for some tubing and waterskiing, if they were up for it. One of their favourite things was to go up the Indian Arm a ways and just kill the motor and just float with the tide. It took forever but it always got you to where you needed to be - having fun.

Back at Anne's house, all the girls were getting ready in their best dresses and the grown-ups were helping the girls with their hairstyles. They all had to have their hair in an up-do to look prim and proper. They brought out their best shoes and cleaned them with soap and water, so they were exactly right. Maxine appeared from around the corner holding a bag of presents in pretty packages and the girls fell into a squeak fest. The squeaking and excitement could be heard for miles around and they all loved it. Maxine hadn't bought them all something expensive, but she had bought them all something heartfelt. Maxine had passed out all of the gifts, except for one. She stopped all of the activities and got everyone's attention, pulled out a box, and presented it to Paige. To be expected, she was caught off guard and felt bashful; however, she kept her cool and accepted the present. She opened it and it was a lovely silver locket on a long silver chain. When Maxine put it around her neck and did up the clasps, she stood in front of Paige and opened the locket to show her. She took one look, and on one side was a picture of Roger with his two girls, and on the other side was a picture of Kent and John and her. She gazed at the trinket …and then burst out crying and fell into Maxine's arms. Anne, Chanel, Maxine, and Paige hugged for ten minutes. The kids watched for a moment, but then they got back to being kids and doing other interesting things. Paige's current life story had been shared with the family because Maxine wanted to be sure that Paige was going to be able to handle all of this attention and family love. She was in a unique situation. She had not spent much time with the Millers, but she felt that she and the Millers were attempting to be close, and they were reassuring. They stood in the kitchen for a bit and then got the girls together so they could all eat some treats that the ladies had made and brought along. The women loved the fact that Paige had done some home baking and brought it along. Time would tell if she could actually cook but the children always let you know. Which dish is still intact after a tea party, who is the person that made the wrong dessert? The day pressed on, and the party began to wrap up. Paige stood on the fringe and offered to help but was told they had it under control. Paige was exhausted so she snuck outside to a covered area with some soft comfy furniture and found a cozy spot where she put the brakes on for a minute. She put her head down to close her eyes and quickly fell asleep. Roger's girls were wandering about the house when Brooke had a great idea. How about if they drew a picture of the day on paper and then presented it to Paige when she woke up? Perfect idea. The girls bolted up to Roger's office and needed paper to draw their masterpiece's on and found some scrap paper in his trash can. Rose selected two pieces of paper from the bin, flattened them out and got them ready to receive two separate masterpieces that she would never ever throw away. What Brooke and Rose didn't notice at all is that those two slices of scrap paper were printouts from the computer with all of the girls Roger had ever dated, all listed chronologically on one neat list on the opposite sides of the unveiled artwork. He had only been on twenty dates. He had sex with only one woman on the list because she made him, and he was afraid of Nikita the Russian. The number may seem low, but it proved that Roger kept a list and there are not too many women that would take kindly to finding out that you're just a name on a list, sex or not. Everything was going so well, something had to bring him back to earth.

Paige awoke to something tickling her nose. Her sub-conscience brushed it away, but it came back. She swooped it away with her finger. Her finger hit something firmer, like a child. Rose and Brooke had both drawn a beautiful picture for Paige to take home so she could always remember them but when they came to make the delivery both girls snuggled under the blankets and had become part of her and her surroundings. She regained her conscious thought and re-examined her surroundings. At Anne's house for a tea party. Copy that. She looked at the two pictures created by Rose and

Brooke and chuckled at the rudimentary drawing, but the meaning was there. "We like you, Paige!" She continued to smirk and then noticed some printed material on the back side of each drawing from each girl. The printed material was from Roger's computer and each girl had drawn on the same printout. It was a list. At first Paige didn't even look at what was on the list, but something caught her eye. A name. A particular name. Lava Love. She began to peruse it quickly and then realized what it was. This was a list of all of the women that Roger has had sex with since he became a member of Lava Love. There it was. All the dates were there. It was like a stat sheet for a Professional athlete. He had kept a list of the names, the places he had been to, and how many times he had fucked these women. Her stomach turned, she pushed the two soft, warm bodies aside to create a path of freedom, she was going to throw up. She felt so ashamed. How could this man have duped her? Does his family know? She made her way to the side gate, still undetected and got it opened silently. She quickly walked down the backside of the house to the front driveway. Salvation. Her car was right there. HER PURSE! Forget it. Can't go back now. She had a spare key, and she could never show her face in front of those people again. They all knew. This was one big family joke. It even stung sharper when she thought that Chanel and Anne were getting so buddy-buddy with her. The humiliation was building by the second. She needed to get into her car and at least drive down the street before she completely fell to pieces. Keys in the door, come on, you can do this Paige...

"Everything okay Paige?" Clyde said watering some hanging baskets. "You don't look quite right. Do you need anything?"

"I need to get out of here!" She said and got in and raced away.

Clyde walked over to the piece of paper she cast aside as she motored away and picked it up. He was stunned to see that she had cast aside the drawing created by one of the girls but then he turned it over, he looked at the printed material and knew there was a fly in the ointment.

Clyde entered the kitchen. "Hello Darling, have you seen Paige? She seems to have vaporized." Maxine said.

"It would seem she left in a hurry. She found something that may have spoiled her day." Clyde said. He passed the drawing/history of Roger's dating life, a piece of paper to let Maxine examine it.

"I see. Clyde, could you please get Roger over here right now? There are a couple of pressing issues I would like to discuss with him."

Chapter Nineteen

There was a family meeting planned for the next day. The family quickly gathered in the living room to get to the bottom of the infamous dating list that made its way onto paper. Unfortunately, that list did get printed, and the wrong person found out about it.

"Why for Heaven's sake did you print the list? What was to be gained by having a list of women that you have previously dated?" Maxine asked.

"I was done. I was deleting the website off of my computer for good. After twenty failed attempts at love, I was ending my computer dating life forever. Before I hit the delete key, stupidly, I typed out all of the women that I had been out with and the reasons that things did not go according to plan. I only had sex with Nikita from Russia. That was all. I simply was recapping my disastrous dating history for my own personal reminiscence of the past two years of my life and where they had gone. Nowhere." Roger said.

"How did you end up with a list of women in our office? How did that get onto our computer?" Maxine asked.

"This is insane. I was ready to give up on dating sites when I heard from this woman who said she wanted to chat. I had my finger on the delete key for most of our conversation. We kept talking and she continued to become more interesting as the conversation continued. Next thing I knew, I was asking this girl out on a computer date. The bloody bane of my existence." Roger said.

"And how did it get into our office?" she asked again.

"I sent the list to the printer just to review and get myself worked up again, like now. I never dreamt that my daughters would draw pictures for Paige on the opposite side of the sheet paper. This is an absolute fluke." He said.

"But it did happen. The next step, Roger, is damage control." Mitch said.

"I must tell you, that I really liked Paige. She seemed like a nice woman. It would be a shame to not see where that relationship could have gone." Clyde said.

"So, what do we do now? There is no way she will even speak to me. She is going to think I am the biggest scumbag in the world." Roger said.

"I think the word you are looking for is Playboy, not scumbag." Mitch added laughing.

"Come on boys, let's try to be a bit serious here. This does concern your brother and his future." Clyde added.

"Sorry Dad. I was just attempting to lighten the mood a bit here." Mitch said.

"Do you think it would help if Anne or Chanel spoke to her about what has happened? Would she speak to them and hear their side of the story?" Maxine said.

"I don't think there is a snowball's chance in hell that she will ever believe that the twenty women on that list were the craziest dates I have ever had in my life. I think she will see me as a predator, and I know she is the type of woman that will keep her distance. Let's face it gang, I blew it. I had one chance to get to know her and I buggered it up. I am officially off chasing women." Roger added.

"So that's it Roger? Tossing in the towel. Remaining single until your girls grow up, get married and move out, start their own families, and then you will consider dating again at that time? You should be about seventy years old by then. I like your plan. I guarantee Rose and Brooke will not like this plan at all." Anne spewed out.

"What do you want me to say? She will not believe a single word I say. She saw the list. She has it in her mind. She will never speak to me again. I am taking full responsibility for what happened. I will tell you all, however, I liked Paige. What hurts even more is that the girls liked Paige and now I have to pretend she doesn't like us anymore. I can take it, but it is really going to disappoint them." Roger commented.

"I agree with you Roger. I do not think Paige will be quick to forgive, no matter what the story. Truth or not, she has been hurt like few have ever felt, the death of their child and the love of her life. Now to be burned in the early throws of a new and intriguing relationship, it will be tricky to get past this. But time heals all wounds. The big question is, how much time does she need?" Chanel asked.

The family continued on with the conversation, but they all came to the same conclusion - Paige would need some time to settle down and decide what was best for her.

***

Maxine was a lot of things, but first and foremost she was a mother. She had three adult children that still needed her expert advice and poking her nose into other peoples' business, just like mom's are supposed to do. She knew that Roger and his girls all loved Paige and she just couldn't accept things ending this way when the future had been looking so bright and exciting. She truly felt that this misunderstanding could be smoothed out with the correct motivation. It had been many years, but she dug into the lower desk drawers to retrieve the "good paper" so that she could fashion the perfect letter to explain to Paige what had happened and how the entire thing was all a big misinterpretation of the information presented to her. Maxine took all of the facts and slowly positioned the words into the most prolific apology letter of all time. She read it over several times to be sure she had crafted one of the great literary works to be seen by mere human eyes. She perused the document for the umpteenth time and felt it represented the story from Roger in the best possible light. Maxine wanted Paige to know that she was loved and appreciated for who she was, and that the family would adore seeing her again if she would allow that to happen. Maxine sealed the envelope and applied a stamp to the top corner and walked out the front door of her house to the nearest mailbox to post it. The metal door thudded shut and she knew that everything she could do to help, she had done. It was now going to be up to Paige to see if she believed anything the family had to say and whether or not she actually had real feelings for Roger, Rose, and Brooke. If she were really looking for true love, she would have to take a leap of faith that the Millers could be the right match for her. As she entered the house, she was momentarily smiling and gleeful. She knew she had stuck her nose in Roger's business, but like so many mothers, they just want their children to be happy.

***

Clyde was an easy-going man since retirement. He didn't want to make a fuss or get into any debates with people about issues that meant nothing to him. He was at the point in his life where he didn't care how much a liter of gas cost because he owned a car that ran on gas. No matter how much it cost, he was going to pay for it, because it ran on gas. So many things to worry about on a day-to-day basis, he had narrowed it all down to the love of his life Maxine, and his family. These people he could impact every day and hopefully make their lives better. This gave him a sense of purpose and fulfillment, rather than listening to the world and local news tell him what was wrong with the world. Clyde had tried to shrink his world to just those people around him that he could be useful to and have a positive effect on. He would say yes to looking after the grandchildren, even if that meant missing some other event. He would always say, "Throw the bloody ticket away. I've got big plans tonight." He was there for his family, and he wanted to be there for Roger right now. Clyde knew that Roger was crazy about Paige, so he decided to get out the "good paper," you know from the bottom desk drawer, and write a cleverly worded letter to Paige to let her know what an idiot his son can be at times, but to also let her know that Roger is in love with her. He sat at the dining table for hours selecting each word to create the sublime letter that would have Paige yearning for Roger and his girls again. He read through the copy a couple of times and knew it was ready for press. He folded the paper and slid it into the envelope. He wetted the back of the stamp and pressed it onto the pretty envelope. He marched out the front door of the house and headed to the mailbox. Like all caring fathers, he hoped this would help.

***

As fate would have it, Paige received both letters on the same day, in the same style envelope, on the same type of paper, however, the words were different. At first Paige was fascinated that this family devised a plan to dupe her by having each parent send her a handwritten letter, until she read the letters once, twice, again and again and realized that possibly they could be telling the truth. She could not deny the fact that she too met Roger online on a dating site. That's what you do. You go out on dates. Twenty still seemed like a lot of dates but Roger's parents seemed so honest and appeared to really care about her and her feelings enough that they had both reached out to her. Little did she know that they had done that on their own without knowing the other spouse had sent her a note. Maybe the universe was telling her something? Even if she did believe that Roger was a decent fellow, how could she ever face him or the family again? She would be too embarrassed to see them. To see him. Now that she had read the letters, she felt a tug at her heart. She could not deny that she did like Roger…a bit, well actually, quite a lot more than a bit.

***

It finally arrived. The most coveted event of all time! An invitation to Tony Tanti and his fiancé Sloane's wedding. He chuckled at first and thought about it and considered they could be

350

a really great couple. Sloane was a wonderful person and Tony just needed to be kept in check some of the time (all of the time). He continued to mellow with age and with a calming person like Sloane, Roger could really see the two of them lasting in a long-term relationship. He couldn't believe that he introduced them while on a weekend getaway with her. Kooky. She was Tony's to worry about now. He was having trouble trying to decide how super weird it would be to go to the wedding stag. "Hello there, how do you know the bride?" people would ask. "I was on a weekend retreat trying to score with her but…" the rest is history. On the other hand, maybe he would meet a nice aunt or cousin at the reception. One never knows who they may run into at these things.

***

Over one's life there are a number of duties that we all have to perform, whether for friends or family or work, the "You must attend this event because you were invited. They like you. Try to like them back." He did pass on the church wedding part but did attend the reception at the Sutton Place on Burrard Street in Vancouver later that night. He had told himself that he was going to make an appearance and be noticed so people knew he was there, then split. He entered a magnificent ballroom that was done up like an old forty's movie. All the colours were vibrant, and the feeling was loose and free. The big band spilled out old time hit after hit. It was a jukebox that was stuck in the fifties and sixties and the atmosphere was not a typical wedding. He had assumed ahead of time that he would be seated at the "Weirdo Table" with Uncle Cyclops and cousin Warthog, not a big shock. He was pointed by an usher to his table over in the corner and was ready to meet the Odd-Ball Reunion, but to his surprise, it was an attractive, fun group. They ran through introductions amongst each other quickly right before the wedding couple entered the room. There was a big round of applause as the two lovebirds made their way to the dance floor, as the MC introduced the happy new couple. The music began to play, and the newlyweds hit the floor and began to gracefully spin around, and then other couples rose to their feet and made their way to the edge of the dance floor and waited for the go ahead to join the happy couple. Roger was standing near the dance floor bopping along to the music and smiling to the song when he felt a hand reach into his and begin to squeeze it shyly. He was surprised! Who was that? He glanced upon the face staring back at his and gasped, "Paige. What are you doing here?" Roger uttered. He was in shock. He couldn't believe she was standing right there in front him.

"Okay everybody, onto the dance floor and join the newlyweds in their first dance." The MC announced.

"No time like the present. Let's get dancing." She pulled Roger in the direction of the dance floor and the two began to dance. It was the first time they had embraced in a long time. Roger was not ready for how overwhelmed he was with Paige in his arms at that moment. The two danced and enjoyed the music and the sensation. Roger was still waiting for the other shoe to drop. They continued to dance for several songs, and she told Roger she wanted them to take a quick breather in the lobby. The two went to the lounge in the lobby area and found a pair of comfy chairs to sink into and talk. She told him about the letters she had received. Roger was completely thrown off by the outpouring of love and friendship that had been demonstrated by his parents towards this woman. He could grasp the concept of Maxine and Clyde really liking this woman, but he was still in awe of his own parents coming to his rescue, writing those sappy letters, and sending them to Paige without each other even knowing. Plus, they sent the letters without Roger knowing. This was a clear case of validation for Paige about how this family feels about her. They wanted to right a wrong on their history play-back story by making sure Paige was given every opportunity to continue or break off with Roger. The entire family seemed clear on their intentions for Paige. Get her to stick around a while longer.

Roger made sure that Paige utterly understood what had transpired with the list of girlfriends and exactly what it meant. Once Paige had heard all of the failed dates, she was okay with Roger and what had transpired. She was concerned that she had been misled into thinking that he was an online player of sorts, going out there into the world and sowing his wild oats, but this was not the case. Roger had just happened upon an interesting group of women while he was using the service for what it was designed to do, help you find a mate. He realized he had been on the site for two years and it had done exactly what it was supposed to do. Help get you dates. Whatever they turn into is another thing, but the primary goal of the dating site is to find you dates.

The two talked for a bit more until they were all being summoned back to the ballroom to Cut-The-Cake and pass it out to all of the guests. They sat at the weirdo table waiting for Tony and Sloane to come by and drop off a piece of the wedding confectionary. Sloane seemed pleased to see Roger and Paige together. After she and Roger parted ways, Sloane always thought that Paige would be a good match for Roger. She felt the two of them were the do-the-right-thing kind of people. And the truth was, they were. It was about time for them to do the right thing and make it official, letting people know that Roger and Paige were now a couple. Instantly Roger puffed out his chest farther and felt a surge of Inner confidence rush through him. Paige suddenly felt like a plus one rather than an extra one. She longed to be part of a family again and to be with a man. She was tough but she was getting to her breaking point. She needed a connection...STAT.

Roger and Paige made their goodbyes to the bride and groom and thanked them for the invite. They had actually really helped in getting Paige and Roger back together by inviting them to the wedding and sticking them at the "Special Table."

The two made their way to the parking lot and were saying their goodnights when Roger asked Paige what she was doing on the upcoming Saturday night and if she was interested in the once in life-time backyard screening of "Toy Story." They would hang a white sheet and show the movie on it in the yard to create a Drive-in Theatre sensation. Paige accepted and they made a date to see each other that Saturday. Roger was delighted. He called his mother Maxine immediately to bring her up to speed. He hoped for a better outcome than the first time they all got together.

Time would tell.

Chapter Twenty

That Saturday morning Roger logged into his dating site account so he could make some permanent changes. #1 he was in a committed relationship; #2 he was deleting his dating site profile. At first, Roger had been so perplexed with the dating concept but after a couple years, and a variety of experiences with an assortment of personalities, he continued to marvel at how well this site actually worked. It couldn't find you love, but it sure could put you in front of lots of diversified people seeking love and romance just like he had. His assessment was incredibly positive. It had worked. He had gone online and was able to complete his desired effect. Found potential matches and got the opportunity for an interaction with many of them. One of them being Paige. Roger was ready for the next phase of the relationship with Paige however, he had not really had the chance to become enraptured with her as a woman. He was looking forward to finding a chance rendezvous with her at his parents' outdoor movie night on Saturday. Upon deeper reflection, he was probably going to be disappointed. With all the grandchildren, mom and dad, brothers, and sisters in attendance, that was not going to happen; it was not a big deal. There would be lots of opportunities for that kind of thing at a later date.

On the Saturday movie night, everyone was going to come for dinner and let the kids swim and play and start the movie at about

9:00 pm. That was the plan set out by Maxine. The family began to arrive after lunch and, like normal, all of the kids went to ape-shit when they got into the pool on a sunny day. The afternoon was a blast and the group shared great food with everybody's favourite beverages. Roger was there with Rose and Brooke when Paige entered through the open glass doors leading to the patio and pool deck. She could see that Mitch was holding a Nerf football in his hands and she swiped the see through cover up she was wearing off her shoulders in one move and began to run at the open pool area and yelled to Mitch, "Hit me, I'm open, as she sprinted across patio stones and jumped over outdoor furniture pieces until she leaped with all of her might into the air and barked, "Now!"

Mitch instinctively fired a total spiral strike, and the rest is history. She gathered in the ball and had just enough swagger to make it memorable. Paige had some chops. "She also looked terrific in a two-piece bikini," Roger thought to himself. The group had a family-oriented afternoon in mom and dad's house, and we all know how special that can be. The adults came inside the house and dried off and cleaned up before dinner. Roger took Paige upstairs to a bedroom to change in and show her the bathroom with its fancy shower head. Roger turned around and walked down the hall to another empty room and was about to close the door when Paige was standing right beside him. "Oops. I'm sorry Paige" Roger said.

"Stop being so polite and come over here." Paige said, leading Roger.

"I know this house. There is NO privacy. We need to talk in the bathroom because it has a lock." Roger said.

He scooped her up in his most manly fashion and carried her to the bathroom two doors down. He laughed because he was trying to be romantic in his parent's house's bathroom. Oh well, work with what you got. Roger and Paige finally looked at each other for the first time in weeks. Really looked. Had he seen every line? Every wrinkle? Had she noticed all of his? She was lovely. He was incredibly happy that this gorgeous creature could like him at all. Before they spoke a word they kissed for several minutes and felt each others' bodies with their hands. It was a dream. He was standing here with this girl finally. He let out a sigh and held her tight. She returned the embrace. She grabbed his chin and kissed him while he fondled her hips. He stopped himself. His parents' house and his kids are in the pool. "Hey Roger, could you quickly show me how to use the shower head? I've never seen this type before." Paige said.

"Hold your shit together. Stop hitting on your guests. Get your act together dude." He said to himself. "You just push in this button and the water starts and then you set your temperature. Easy once you get the hang of it." He walked over to the door to exit the room and she walked over to him and pressed into him. "Please stay and shower with me." Paige said.

She closed the bathroom room door and took Roger by the hand and walked into the shower with their swimsuits on and turned on the water. Tap, tap, tap, on the door. "Hello Paige," he whispered. "It's Clyde here. Just wanted to tell you again how happy we are to have you here with all of us and how thankful I am to have you in our family. I know it sounds old fashioned, but we love you, Paige. I hope you're sticking around us for a while. Okay then, sorry to bother you while you are doing your thing, but I wanted you to know how we both feel. I promise I will stop being so meddlesome in the future. See you outside" And he walked away.

Roger and Paige still held each other but the magic spell had been interrupted. Tap, tap, tap. "Hi Paige, it's Maxine. Just wanted to be sure you have enough towels and supplies in that bathroom. I didn't stock it up today."

"I'm okay Maxine. There are plenty of dry clean towels in here." She answered.

"Okay then. Paige, we also want you to know that we are over-the-moon to have you still in Roger's and in our lives. We are grateful. There is a hairdryer in the drawer and plenty of brand-new brushes and combs for you to use. Please help yourself. If you need anything let me know." Maxine said.

"Thank you, Maxine," Paige called out.

Roger could no longer resist Paige's charms and he dropped his swim trunks, walked into the shower, and turned on the hot water. The water came to temperature quickly and he stepped under the waterspout. A second later Paige appeared nude and walked over to Roger. They twisted into human knots. Their soapy skin created a mood of sensuality and they both were enjoying the meeting of two kindred spirits. It was a harmonious experience for both of them. Then they held each other for another five minutes in the beautiful hot water until they heard, Rap, rap, RAP. "Hey Paige honey, we love you and all of that shit but a twenty-minute shower? What are you doing? Trying to put us in the poor house?" Clyde exclaimed loudly through the walls of the house. He could never get his head around a twenty-minute shower.

"Sorry Clyde." She shouted back through the wall. "I'll be right out." Paige said. Roger was hoping that they could do it one more time before movie night, but he heard the girls seeking out his fatherly presence. They looked at each other one more time and then went their own way back to movie night happening in other parts of the house. Roger slipped out and found refuge elsewhere while Paige got herself ready.

When Paige joined the festivities, she was greeted by smiles and positive vibes. She had applied some makeup and changed her hair, and it looked fabulous. She was also feeling good about what had happened with Roger. It was the first time since her husband that another man had touched her in an intimate way, and she felt safe and positive about the encounter.

The parents had created a smorgasbord of many types of food for quick and easy access for the family meal, so the clean up was fast for setting up movie night. Even though it was only blankets and pillows it still took a bit to get it all set up. All of the yard lights were already in place and tied into many of the trees throughout the yard. Many trips to Canadian Tire and many years of perseverance to get everything where it was, but it was certainly a unique space when it was glowing on a warm summer's eve. They scarfed back the food eagerly so they could get to family games. Forty minutes later, they were sitting back and guessing movie names in a rousing game of charades. The young girls all laughed and giggled hysterically if anyone added an accent or some flair to the movie magic. Then came the announcement; it was "Movie Night." Everybody gathered on the small hill in Clyde's backyard and hung a huge sheet secured tightly to project the film onto. It worked perfectly. Everyone moved into their respective groups and Roger made space against his body for Paige to lean on him. The girls cuddled behind them where he kept his arm in the defender mode position. They quickly became hyper-focused on the movie and no longer paid attention to their surroundings. Before long, Rose and Brooke were fast asleep, and

Roger was distracted by the thought of another interlude with Paige, if at all possible. They gave each other the look and Roger slipped away into the house. A minute later Paige slipped out from underneath Rose and Brooke. She made her way undetected to the back bedroom where Roger was waiting. He was eager to get his hands on her and she was ready to receive. He grabbed Paige and began to kiss her and press his manhood against her body. She knew he was certainly ready. Tap, tap, tap. "Daddy, where did you go? We couldn't find you anywhere, Daddy. Grandpa said to check in here and he was right. We want to sleep with you two!" Rose said.

(I'll get him back for that one), Roger thought to himself.

"Of course, girls," she said smiling. She leaned close to Roger's ear and whispered, "I'll give you a handy to get that thing under control once the girls have fallen back to sleep. What do you say about that Roger?" She winked and tossed her head. He nodded yes and they all laid down on Roger's old bed in his childhood room and snuggled in. As to be expected, kids say all kinds of crazy things, however, they usually do not lie. They say how they would like things to be, whether practical or not. They talked about monsters and living under the stairs. They covered the snakes in the walls and the witch in the attic. Then Brooke said, "Will you be my new mommy? Please say yes."

"Oh yes please. That would be fun. Please say yes." Rose said.

"Okay then, Yes." Paige retorted. "When can I start?" Rose and Brooke exploded into laughter and hugged Paige with all their might.

Roger replied, "Effective immediately."

The End